The World Was All Before Them

Carolyn Sanderson

ISBN:

Dedicated to the memory of Mike, who encouraged me in my gardening endeavours, my writing, and so much more...

The world was all before them, where to choose
their place of rest, and providence their guide.

John Milton, Paradise Lost, Book XII

Contents

1

There was once a garden; a Platonic garden, if you like, the type and pattern of all gardens past, present and yet to come. It's still there, sometimes, if you know where to look, stretching as far as the eye can see. At its heart stands an apple tree, a tiny sapling, bending this way and that in the autumn storms; bending, but not breaking. Watch as it fills out, stretches its branches high, explores the sky above it; its roots go deep and wide into the soft earth. In spring the buds open and its blossom is sweet, and when it drops there are the tiniest of tiny apples already beginning to form. Sunlight warms them and rain washes them, feeds them, causes them to swell into ripeness.

A huddle of rough dwellings appears; they grow in number, fall into disrepair. Larger houses replace them. People come and go. Someone gathers the apples to sell in the market. The village grows, and there are good years and bad years, and always there is the apple tree. Perhaps it is not always the same apple tree - one tree looks much like another - but there has always been a tree.

Over the years the village grew into a town. For some years the smoke from the chimneys blackened the leaves of the tree. That was when the long, straight streets were built: the houses all in a row, made of rough, red bricks. One year the town's men disappeared, and only a very few returned, limping, dejected. The garden shrank, but it was never just about its size. It remains a special place, for those who can see it. It holds its own meaning, and different people find different meanings in it. And in the end, Evie discovered that you can find the garden in more places than one.

The map had not told the whole story. Too weary to get out of the car immediately, Evie sat and gazed in horror. A terrace of redbrick houses stood, last remnant of some former Victorian factory-owner's dream of worker housing. All around them lay open land dotted with mounds of bricks, rotting mattresses, twisted skeins of wire. Some of the residents had made spirited attempts at warding off the encroaching scenes of dereliction by painting their front doors in brilliant - and clashing - primary colours, while windows put on a brave face with curtains turned patterned sides outward to hide the poverty within.

Finally Evie dragged herself from her seat and approached number 5, stepping carefully over broken glass and dried-out piles of dog mess. A few remnants of paint still clung to the front door, which was otherwise bare weather-beaten wood, and Evie struggled to open it even after she worked out how to insert and wiggle the key. Putting her shoulder to the door, she fell straight into a dingy living room, and collapsed onto a sofa of indeterminate colour.

'What have I done?' she groaned aloud. 'Whatever have I done?'

Gardens are messy places in their natural state. Evie was to discover this when she had her first garden. People who don't know much about gardening imagine that the manicured lawn and weed-free border are the proper order of things. But gardens, like people, grow and develop over time. They are not always under control. Seedheads burst open and the wind scatters the seed. Plants that were never meant to grow in a particular spot find themselves thriving, while carefully planted specimens unaccountably wither in others. There is usually a reason for the failure, if you know where to look. So it is with people. All of this is what Evie discovered. This is how it happened.

Evie's combative nature carried her through most of the next morning. She had finally slept, after a fashion, in spite of her doubts about the mattress in the larger of the two bedrooms. The plan was for the smaller room to become her study, but it would take a great act of the imagination to transform the musty smelling box room into a place of work.

The house was a disaster; there was no getting away from that. True, the gas was connected, as she had been promised, but she feared death by salmonella if she dared to cook in that kitchen. Her predecessors had clearly been fans of the frying pan and the chip pan, and the greasy accretions of many years of unhealthy cooking coated the walls. Cautiously, she headed up the road on foot, and found a dismal corner shop where she purchased some milk very near its use by date, and a packet of cereal. The only bread on offer was thin, white and plastic wrapped, but she accepted it with the best grace she could, and headed back to her new home.

She was glad that she had brought her own coffee and cups and bowls with her, and contrived to consume some sort of breakfast perched on the sofa while thinking about her situation. What good would it do to go storming down to the estate agent's? She had signed a lease, agreeing to take the property sight unseen, and, looking again at the kitchen, she acknowledged that it wasn't actually entirely unsuitable for human habitation. If she put her energy - and her anger - into scrubbing she might even be able to make the place habitable. As she might have guessed, when she looked under the sink, there were no cleaning materials beyond some filthy old dusters; in a corner, next to the back door, was an almost hairless sweeping brush.

While she stood, gazing hopelessly at the brush, an unexpected ray of sunlight leapt through the grimy panes in the back door, lifting her spirits unaccountably. Suddenly she was Alice in a new Wonderland, game for adventure. The shopping trip for disinfectant and cleaning agents could wait; she would explore the outside. Taking her coffee mug with her, she turned the back door key and stepped out into her own wonderland.

The sheer, unexpected size of the garden was astonishing. Tardis-like, it stretched before her and around her. Was that even possible, given the size of the tiny cottage? How could it seem so wide when the house itself was so narrow? She had a dizzying sense of being somewhere else, outside time and somehow beyond the ordinary everyday world. Then she shook herself. It was her imagination again, of course: being at the end of the row, surrounded by open land, with no adjacent buildings, the eye was drawn outwards. It was an optical illusion. It must be.

It had begun somewhere to the south, in the rolling hills of the Cotswolds, and it had begun with a headache. It was her duty day in the noisy dining hall and the chatter and clatter of 300 adolescent boys - plus a few token girls - and the nauseating smell of watery cabbage, were doing nothing to soothe the stabbing pains at the back of her head. The elegant wooden panelling and downlit portraits of dead white men only made her more than ever aware that she didn't fit in, any more than the incongruous plastic tabletops and the scraping of metal chair legs belonged on decades old parquet. She had tried so hard. Looking up at the curtains as they drooped against the high windows, she grimaced. They looked the way she felt: tired and defeated and entirely in the wrong place.

She had tried really hard to fit in. On first arriving she had quickly realised that her wardrobe was not what was expected, and had purchased, with the help of Matron (a ridiculous title for a skinny woman hardly older than herself) some dark skirt suits and dresses, and even practised twisting her long, slippery hair into a bun that made her look matronly (that word again.) The bun had been the bane of her life for the first term, as it repeatedly untwisted itself, and she found herself teaching through a veil of strands of her own hair that distracted her from her lessons and made her look ridiculous in the eyes of the pupils. By the Christmas of her first year she had abandoned it, and as the year unfolded, so garments reflecting her own personality had also crept into her daily wear to complement the hair that hung, long and sleek, down her back, and made her look like herself again.

'Miss Symmonds, may I have a word?' The smooth tones of her head of department intensified the physical pain in her head and the existential pain in her gut. The words meant: *I want you in my office now, if not sooner*. She rose from her chair, wincing at the noise of metal on wood. Holding herself upright as she carried her tray to the 'used cutlery and crockery' sign, she scraped the largely uneaten remains of her meal into the composting bin and headed off along the dark corridors, with their artificial lavender smell and claustrophobic yellowed ceilings. With no-one to watch, her careful posture was abandoned and her shoulders led the way, her feet following, as in those dreams where however hard you try, you can't walk fast enough and your feet feel bogged down in treacle.

'Take a seat, Evie.' Mr. Head Of Department was always politeness itself, no matter how unpleasant the content of what he wanted to say. He prided himself on never having raised his voice in school, ever, and his thin face wore a glued-on smile, even when he thought no-one was watching.

'How do you feel things are going this year?'

'Well,' she began cautiously, wondering what the correct answer might be. 'I feel I understand the school better now.' Warming to her theme, she added, 'It takes time to get a proper feel for a place like this.' Mr. HOD smiled.

'Quite so.' He moved around the desk and took his own seat, sinking into its leather-cushioned comfort with the sense of entitlement that permeated the school. Then he looked across at her.

'It was always going to be a tough one, wasn't it? Young ladies teaching in a boys' school? Yes, I know - ' he held up a hand to ward off her protests. 'We do have a few girls in the Sixth Form now. But essentially their parents send them here to receive a *boys*' education.'

Evie waited. What was he saying? She felt vulnerable. What was it this time? Too much Carol Ann Duffy and not enough Dickens? Discussing politics in class? Smiling too much? She had been pulled up on all those things over the past three years.

'We are all under scrutiny as teachers. If we expect a great deal from our students they have a right to expect a great deal from us in return, don't you think?'

Evie nodded, uncertainly.

'We must set the standards high. The way we speak, how we conduct ourselves, even in private. For example, we have a certain dress code here, and we expect our students to uphold the highest standards of personal grooming.' He looked down at his expertly manicured fingernails, and brushed a speck of invisible dust from his sleeve. 'For that we require our teaching staff to set an example. I'm sure you understand.'

So it was her style of dress that was at fault. Again. Mr. HOD was speaking once more.

'Since we are now -ahem - *co*-ed, that means that it's more important than ever that female teachers provide a role model.'

And with that Mr. HOD signalled that the interview was over, by escorting her, oh so politely, to the door. There he paused, one hand on the elegant brass handle. In his faux gentle voice he murmured, 'It's not easy, is it? Well, off you go now.'

Evie stalked along the corridor fuming, her shoulders leading the way. A role model! And what about a role model for the boys? Didn't they need to see that the sexes could work together, that women had an equal contribution to make, without pretending to be men? She was still stalking as she entered the classroom for her next lesson, a little more abruptly than she'd intended. The Lower Fourth, all boys, leapt to their feet to acknowledge her presence in the room.

'Oh, sit down. Sit DOWN,' she said, a little more loudly than intended. As she sat in her own chair a look passed between Barlow and Bloomfield that distinctly said: *time of the month?*

As soon as the bell rang for the end of the afternoon, Evie headed over to her rent-free accommodation on the upper floor of a thatched cottage in the school grounds: one of many perks that more than compensated, or so they had assured her when she took the job, for the slightly less than generous salary. The more she thought about it, the more certain she was that Mr. HOD was telling her she was no longer wanted, that she didn't fit in. Acknowledging to herself at last that she was the wrong person in the wrong place left her feeling completely adrift.

Her father's reaction would make it even worse, of course. When she had returned triumphantly from her interview at 'the nice school', boasting of her plum job in an institution with proud traditions and excellent discipline, well-mannered pupils and beautiful, well-kept surroundings, he had scorched her with his comments on meaningless rules and unthinking privilege. How could it be otherwise for a long-serving teacher and union activist, a head credited with turning around several tough comprehensive schools?

'Genevieve,' he had said, using her seldom spoken-aloud full name. 'I am ashamed that my daughter should be prostituting her education - an education provided by the state, by ordinary hard-working tax-payers - in the service of independent privilege and social climbing,' and he had closed down the argument by leaving the room and stamping upstairs to his office. Five minutes later, he had returned, with one thing more to say. 'I wish you'd reconsider, Evie. You'll hate it there. I know you will.'

With her bedroom door slammed shut against the outside world, Evie lay prone on the bed, her angry tears soaking the pillow. Why was she was so enraged and who was she most angry with: the oleaginous Mr. HOD, her father, herself? Or maybe just the system, or indeed the whole wide world? Was it because she had been so determined to prove her father wrong that she had tried too hard? Was it that now he would have the satisfaction of being proved right?

When she reached the dry sobbing stage she sat upright and rummaged under the pillow for the tissues she usually kept there. The sound of running water from the next door flat indicated that Matron was back from a day of tending to sprained ankles and bumped heads, or whatever it was she did when she was in her little cubby hole in the main building. Evie didn't even bother glancing in the mirror, for she knew her swollen eyelids would tell their own story. She slipped out onto the landing and tapped on her friend's door.

'Come in and tell me all about it,' Matron said as she opened the door. 'I've just put the kettle on.'

Finally, fortified by her friend's tea and sympathy, Evie took herself off for a stroll around the village. She walked down the village street as it meandered past the quaint post office and the equally quaint village pub. It was a village that specialised in quaintness. She admired for the hundredth time the striking half-timbered house belonging to the local MP, its rolling lawns sloping gently down to the river, and tried to imagine living in one of the tiny chocolate box cottages further along the lane, with their colourful gardens full of lupins and delphiniums at this time of year, great drifts of verbena and swaying grasses. Swallows winged overhead and she took in great lungfuls of air. A passing car made her jump: you so rarely saw traffic round here. When the car had gone Evie stopped to absorb the stillness, as if committing it to memory.

Perhaps Evie had read too many of the wrong sort of books as a child, most of them her grandmother's; perhaps they had given her an idealised view of boarding school life, but she had been entranced by the groups of jolly chums who had midnight feasts in the dorm and defended each other loyally against the school bully. When the job at Nice School was advertised - and then re-advertised - she found it impossible to resist, and although, strangely, none of the other candidates seemed to be around on the day of the interview, she thought she was incredibly lucky to be appointed against what was surely stiff competition.

If the school hadn't quite lived up to the world of the fictional schools, it must still be better than the alternative, mustn't it? Her mother, who had never reached the dizzy heights of a headship herself, had slithered into early retirement battered and wearied after years of teaching in some very challenging schools. Evie had never cherished any wish to follow her mother's example, but there were days here where she found herself having disloyal thoughts. Her pupils stood as she entered the room: out of duty or habit, or more likely a school rule; she had never taken the trouble to find out. A little spontaneity would be welcome at times. There was never any open disruption in the classrooms, something she knew most teachers would give their eye teeth for, but beneath the surface something less wholesome simmered: the looks of boredom, the resistance to expressing opinions, to exploring, to being alive to the experience of being young and on the world's threshold. They had their futures mapped out: family firms, family traditions in law or medicine. They didn't question, and they didn't enthuse.

Goodness, where had all that come from? Were those really her thoughts, or was this just an expression of her current misery? Or were these even ideas that had been planted a long time ago by her father? She ploughed on for the rest of the week through the fog of her own confusion, and spent a restless weekend unable to settle to anything.

It seemed that the inevitable had happened when, on retiring to the staffroom at break for a cup of super-strong coffee the following Monday morning, there was a little note from Mr HOD. She unfolded it gingerly and was not surprised to find that she was invited, in the neatest of handwriting, to 'have a little chat' at the end of afternoon school. She conducted the afternoon's lessons as models of the Nice School formula, and derived a grim satisfaction from the looks of aggrieved boredom on the faces of her pupils.

'Yes, Evie. Come in, come in. Here, do sit down.' Mr. HOD's manners were as polished as ever, and he sat, smiling - or was that ticking? - like the crocodile in Peter Pan, as she composed herself, or tried to. He allowed several seconds to pass in agonising silence.

'I don't think you're very happy here with us at The Cedars,' he said finally. Evie didn't know what to say, so she said nothing. Mr. HOD leaned forward. 'I've been trying to think how we can best help you.'

Evie supressed a snort; she never appreciated Mr. HOD's hypocrisy.

'Now, as it happens, we've been invited to engage in one of those Government things, social mobility blah, blah. You know the sort of thing.'

Evie wasn't sure that she did, but she nodded and crossed her legs.

'They would like to send a teacher from a state school to teach here for a year so they can get a feel for the way we do things, how we achieve top results, learn from us, best practice and so on... In exchange, one of our staff will be seconded to a large Comprehensive somewhere in the North of England to have a look at what goes on there.' He gave Evie another of his crocodile smiles. 'You, my dear, have been selected to take part in this scheme.' He sat back in his chair with an air of satisfaction at a job well done.

Evie re-crossed her legs the other way while she tried to take this in. Was this simply because of her style of dress? Was she being banished for crimes against tradition? Was she simply not a good enough role model? Her sense of being in the wrong place - despite the fact that it was the one place she really wanted to be - intensified, and she chose her words carefully.

'So you are *offering* me the… *opportunity*… to go to… up North for a year?' She knew that Mr. HOD didn't do irony, but wished desperately at this moment that he did.

'Just so, my dear,' he murmured.

And so - just like that - it was apparently settled.

A garden can be a place of solace. That is what Evie needed now. All around her was beauty, expensively maintained, the trees and shrubs trimmed and pruned and tamed. And yet the garden Evie was soon to leave was an artificial one. Perhaps you think all gardens are artificial? Otherwise, wouldn't they just be wilderness? But there is a difference between a natural garden and a wilderness, and Evie had much to learn. A true garden involves the heart and not just the head. She would need to look elsewhere to find a real garden; she might even need to look inside herself.

One of the skills of gardening is to allow plants to grow where they will flourish. Dogged attempts to make something grow without enough light, or the wrong soil, too much rain or not enough, or one of a dozen other factors, will likely end in tears. Growing and living things cannot be forced.

The summer term finally, agonisingly, drew to its end, the last Friday of term, as always, taken up with the all-important Sports Day. Last year Evie had been allocated to crowd control, preventing high-spirited pitch invasions during the field and track events, checking that no-one was sneaking off for a crafty cigarette (that was mostly the staff) and generally keeping an eye out for any dirty tricks, of which there were surprisingly many. This year, by contrast, she found herself almost weeping with boredom as she stood with her clipboard, recording the heat winners and noting the number of points awarded to each house.

Afterwards, while the pupils showered and changed, she found herself collared by Mrs. Langley-Jones, an over-anxious parent if ever there was one, during the excruciating tea party in the smaller hall, where exhausted staff members were expected to make small talk over the tea and scones as the parents arrived to collect their offspring, glancing surreptitiously at watches and mobile phones, anxious to be on the road before the traffic built up.

'Yes, Mrs Langley-Jones,' she said judiciously, 'James *has* worked harder this term.' This at least was incontrovertible since young James had done no work at all the previous term. James' mother smiled with relief, delicately wiping a crumb from the corner of her mouth.

Evie thought: *if you spent less time in the evenings parading around with the OTC, showing off your uniform to the girls, young James, and just a little more on remembering that you actually need to pass your A Levels to get into University, I would be able to offer your mother slightly more encouragement.* Even so, she couldn't help having a soft spot for James. Like Evie herself, there was something slightly out of place about him.

Of course, Mrs. Langley-Jones expected value for money. If you were paying for an education, even at the frankly second-rate and rather pretentious institution Evie was now beginning to recognise Nice School to be, there was an underlying assumption that results would follow - or heads would roll. Focusing on the notion of thinking for themselves instead of trying to stuff their heads full of Gradgrindian facts did not meet consumer demand.

Finally the students were released into the room to collect up their parents and hurry to the car park. She could see by the strained looks on a number of parental faces that some were clearly dreading the coming seven-and-a-half weeks of actually caring for their own children. More than one had complained to her that afternoon that the terms were far too short, and several had sighed and made the old joke: *it seems the more you pay, the less you get!*

As the last of the cars departed, Evie made her way across the immaculately kept grounds back to the flat. Beyond the school boundaries was rolling countryside, abundant growth, farmland and woodland, but in here it was a different world. All was tamed, controlled, uniform, like the students. Evie went the long way round, skirting the wall of the Principal's private garden. She wished that she too had a private garden, a place where only she was allowed, where no-one could find her, make demands of her, belittle her or make her feel like a failure.

Passing the high, wrought iron gate that fitted snugly into its ancient brick archway, Evie paused to gaze longingly in. She was never quite sure whether this wildly anarchic garden really reflected the Principal's own taste: it seemed unlikely in view of the way he ran the school, where appearances mattered above all else. Perhaps it was his wife, she thought, quietly subverting her husband's regime; or maybe he was after all a free spirit underneath his Oxbridge gown.

Whatever the case, Evie thought the garden beautiful. Roses clambered in wild abundance over the walls of the house, competing with the woody stems of the wisteria as it hung in little purple droplets far above. She could smell the scent of Rose Albertine from where she stood, taking it in in great snatches of breath. The herbaceous borders showed no sign of planning: everything was in flower, colours clashing gloriously, and the grass - you couldn't call it a lawn - was long enough to be richly green and alive.

For Evie it had always been, perhaps a little childishly, the Forbidden Garden, and now it seemed more forbidden to her than ever. She was suddenly reminded of the scene in *Alice in Wonderland* where poor, overgrown Alice stoops to look through the tiny door into a garden forever beyond her reach. Her bookish childhood had provided a mental image for every eventuality.

Back at the flat she reluctantly got on with her packing. The new teacher, the one who would replace her for the whole of the next year, had expressed a strong wish to move in as soon as possible, and since the accommodation was provided rent free, Evie could hardly object, and nor could she blame her. Who wouldn't want to live here? Roses round the dormer window, a thatched roof above, and an outlook over school grounds that mimicked some idealised version of a mini-Versailles. The accommodation, though not large, was comfortable, aesthetically pleasing and five minutes from the day job. Having nowhere else to go, Evie would be spending some time with her parents before her move north.

Should she have contested the 'visiting teacher' plan when it was put to her? Would it have done any good? She sighed and turned round, heading back to where her car stood, ready loaded. She had already said her goodbyes, those that she felt inclined to. Mr HOD would not miss her. Flinging her last bag into the boot she slammed the door shut decisively, climbed into the driving seat, and left Nice School behind in a shower of gravel.

2

Being with her parents was every bit as bad as she had expected. Her father, of course was delighted.

'I knew you'd see sense in the end, Evie,' he said as he opened the door to her.

She found herself leaping to her own defence even before she was fully over the threshold. 'I didn't actually *choose* to leave Nice School you know, Dad. The decision was made for me.'

'Yes, but once you've spent time in the *real* world, you won't want to go back to that place.'

By this time she was struggling up the stairs with two heavy bags. Under her breath she muttered, 'Oh yes I will!'

She noticed that her father didn't offer to help her with her luggage.

Later, as her mother fussed around making a 'nice pot of tea' and opening up the biscuit tin, while her father was busy with some important paperwork or other, Evie remarked that he was home unusually early. His term, unlike hers, still had a few weeks to run.

'Yes, I suppose he has been coming home earlier recently,' her mother said, absently. 'Right, that should be brewed now.'

The tea was strong and hot, and gave her a lift. Her mother had always been the one who sympathised with her difficulties when she was at school, from long before Evie became a teacher. Being the Head's daughter had been only one of her problems. It was the schools themselves: big, noisy, frightening places for the most part, and not very accommodating for a shy, quiet girl unused to other children and preferring the company of books. She travelled in early with her father, her spirits sinking as they neared the tall, forbidding buildings. He was always working, even in school holidays, while her mother recovered from one term and prepared for the next. Greene Park School was the worst, a misnomer if ever there was one, for there was not so much as a blade of grass within miles.

Of course, she knew deep down that he was fond of her, and he did have a gentle side, but she found it disorientating to watch him each day as he put on his teacher persona, terrifying the miscreants sent to him for the school's final sanction. It was even more disturbing, though, to watch the ones who stood up to him, swaggering and mouthing horrible words. She wanted to tell them that he was her daddy, that she loved him, that they should show him some respect.

Even worse were the conversations in the corners of the classroom that stopped suddenly as she approached. She knew what they were saying; all students said horrible things about their teachers, and her mother had told her often enough to take no notice, but it felt too personal to ignore. She always regretted not standing up to them, not putting them right, but she was too timid, too afraid of what they might say to her.

'He's pleased, you know,' her mother said now.

'What?' She'd been lost in the past.

'Pleased you're doing the right thing. Well, as he sees it.'

'I've seen enough of that sort of school. I went to one, remember? More than one. When Dad changed schools, I changed schools.'

Her mother stared into her own mug for a while.

'He thought it would toughen you up. He did it for the best. And because he believes in that sort of education.' She turned to look at Evie directly. 'He really does love you, you know.'

'Yes, I know. And I know how strongly he believes in comprehensive education. As a matter of fact, so do I. It's just that I'm not sure I'm cut out to be the sort of teacher he is. And I've no desire to be a head of anything.'

'I know, sweetheart. I used to think sometimes that you'd have been better off going down the road to St. Cuthbert's, instead of with him.

Evie reflected for a moment. 'In some ways I think that was the worst part, being cut off from my own community. I never really got to know anyone who lived round here because I was always dependent on Dad's timetable: I couldn't come home until Dad was ready, and he always had so many meetings, so much work to do.'

Her mother indicated the teapot. 'Ready for another?'

Evie nodded, absently. The ever-flowing teapot was one of the things she remembered most about home. Perhaps that was why she always drank coffee when she was anywhere else.

'On the other hand, it meant I always got my homework done, and once that was out of the way, I had the freedom of the school library. I reckon I had read my way through most of the fiction section before I left.' She smiled, leaving unspoken the loneliness she had felt, the Saturdays when she had looked out of the window at unknown teenagers passing in groups, laughing and chatting.

'In a way I was quite surprised when you decided you wanted to be a teacher.' Her mother had never said that before.

Evie grimaced. 'Whatever else would I be in this household? I thought it was compulsory!'

The other thing Evie noticed about her father was how irritable he had become. He had always been a bit irritat-*ing* in his passionate belief in what he was doing - although there was no doubt that his commitment and his energy had made a real difference to the schools - and to the young people - who had felt his influence. But this irritability, this sudden lack of patience, even with her, was new.

'This is your chance, Evie,' he said abruptly a few days later, looking up briefly from his laptop. 'Your chance to make a difference. You'll never change the kids at that school where you've been. Too entrenched; and their parents, the sort of people who don't want to take responsibility for their own children.'

He turned back to his spreadsheet before she could get a word out. Her mother breezed into the room.

'Cup of tea, Evie? I've just put the kettle on.'

Unable to sleep that night, Evie found herself thinking about what her mother had said. Why *had* she become a teacher? Was it just to prove herself to her father? To earn his respect as well as his love? She had swallowed down her disappointment at his reaction to Nice School as much as she could, but perhaps he was right, and she had now been given a chance to prove herself. Better get on with it, then!

Next morning, after a quick breakfast and only two cups of tea, she headed off to the local estate agent. It was in fact the only estate agent in the small town, and she had very simple requirements.

'I need to rent somewhere furnished, for one year, somewhere within walking distance of this address.' She placed the details of Other School in front of the rather startled agent, who was disappointed to find that his powers of persuasion were not required. 'Oh, and I want to move in tomorrow.'

Tomorrow wasn't possible, but it was only two days later that Evie said goodbye to her parents. Her mother seemed almost relieved, but sad at the same time, as she waved her off. Her father was busy in his study.

At last, exhausted, not from the long drive from her parents' house, but from the hour and a half of struggling with an insane one-way system and roads choked by pollution-emitting lorries, she finally came to a stop before no. 5 Paradise Row. She had been happy to agree the lease sight unseen; after all, she would only be here for a year, so what did it matter? A quick look at the map had confirmed that it was handy for the shops as well as the school where she was to be the subject of the social mobility experiment.

'What have I done?' she groaned aloud. 'Whatever have I done?'

A garden is a place where mysterious things happen. A seed falls to the ground, or is planted there on purpose. It lies in the cold, dark earth, seemingly inert. But inside, things are happening. It is responding to some ancient, timeless plan. It takes its cue from the outside world, responding to changes in the soil around it. Mysterious things happen to people too, in gardens. They are soothed by the beauty of nature; or they are in awe of the wonder of new life in springtime, or made melancholy by the fall of autumn leaves. Or they may be tempted to sin: but that's a different story.

So here she was; this was to be her home for a whole year. The house was truly horrible, but the garden…! For a moment Evie had to steady herself against the brick wall behind her; it was warm to the touch. Then her heart leapt with an unknown sense of freedom and she took a few tentative steps, the feathery seed heads of the knee-high grasses caressing her legs as she moved. With her eyes half-closed she saw the garden as it had once been, a loved and tended place, and even in its overgrown state the outline of lawn and paths was dimly visible. The whole garden sloped up slightly towards the far end, where a line of trees was already showing signs of early autumnal colouring. Taking a closer look, she saw that they were heavy with miniature ripening fruit, and was able to identify plums, pears, and perhaps damsons. At the centre of this tiny orchard, standing a little forward and apart from the others stood a tree, a very old tree, to judge by its size and the gnarled branches that reached into a sky that had become suddenly blue. The tree was heavy with tiny apples, green now but with a hint of the colour they would turn within weeks. Gardens, of course, are older and wiser than people and can teach us things if we let them; they know more about surviving in this world than most of us. Evie knew instinctively that she would never feel alone in this place.

Afraid of breaking the spell, she moved forward. This would be a place of retreat, a private place to be enjoyed, perhaps with a cooling glass of wine as she leafed through a pile of essays on summer evenings, or lost herself in a good book. She imagined Saturday mornings spent digging the vegetable patch she would create, before soaking away her aches in the bath and heading off into town for a spot of shopping and a trip to the theatre. Not everything in Nice Place was perfect: she acknowledged that now. Out in the beautiful, gently rolling countryside she had nonetheless been deprived of a proper cultural life, and now here she was, within walking distance of an acclaimed regional theatre. Suddenly things didn't seem so bad.

Turning back towards the house, she could see that the garden did indeed extend sideways beyond the house, so that an extra strip of garden lay for the moment in the shade of the side wall of the building. Rammed up against this wall was a new delight: a shed, weather worn but serviceable. Evie had always coveted her father's shed, and now here she was, with a shed of her own - at least for a year. It was unlocked, and she opened it again with that Alice in Wonderland feeling. A jumble of things rattled to the floor as she did so, but she could see spades and hoes and all sorts of useful tools hanging neatly against one wall, and shelves containing who-knew-what along the others. Best of all, right in the middle of the floor space stood a lawn mower. Evie was so excited that she placed her coffee mug on a shelf and had begun to wheel the mower out of the shed before she came to her senses and decided that really, she ought to do one or two things in the house before she began on the garden.

It was a car ride into the retail park, but she found all the things she needed there, and had made significant inroads into the greasy kitchen before her rumbling belly made her aware of the time. She was not yet ready to risk cooking in her new home, and so it was a toss-up between fish and chips and a pizza. The fish and chips won, mainly because she had noticed a chippie just down the road. They were surprisingly good.

There remained one nagging worry: something was going on at home and she wasn't quite sure what. When she phoned to let her parents know she had arrived, hoping for a chance to talk through her situation, her mother had brushed aside her concerns.

'Well, Evie, it's only for a year: three terms, that's all. It might give you some useful experience.'

Evie had fallen silent. This was not quite the soothing balm of sympathy she had been expecting.

'Evie? Evie...are you still there?' There was now an edge of anxiety to her mother's voice. 'Look, I need to go in a minute. I'm sure you'll be all right, whatever happens.'

'Right. Yes... sorry Mum. You go and do whatever...'

But the line had already gone dead. Now Evie had something else to worry about. It was unlike her Mum to be unsympathetic, and it was usually Evie who hung up first.

Towards the end of the first week Evie had achieved a basic level of hygiene and was now able to eat at the kitchen table. Technically, the 'furnished' aspect of the lease correlated exactly with the inventory the agent had emailed her, while still appearing to be very much less than the sum of its parts, and without making the house in any way a home. Late one afternoon, as Evie was sitting over a mug of coffee, brooding on her lack of funds to spend on lamps and cushions, her phone rang.

'Hello - is that Genevieve Symmonds?'

'Ye..es.' Anyone who addressed her as Genevieve was clearly someone she didn't know. 'Who's calling?'

'My name's Rob - Robin Greenwood.' As she paused, the voice added, 'I'm in charge of the English Department.'

'Oh, right.' Reality burst in on Evie. She was steadily overcoming the challenge of the house and was positively looking forward to beginning on the garden, but here was the real challenge: a school she would never have chosen, another place to feel that she didn't belong. In all the frenzy of home-making, she had almost forgotten why she was here in Other Place.

Robin Greenwood continued. 'I'm so sorry - I really should have been in touch with you before now, but I had to go away as soon as the term finished - family issues. Anyway, I'd like to say welcome to our school. Are you free at all to come in for a bit of a chat? I'm sure you must have lots of questions about how we operate here and so on.'

Evie pulled an agonised face; just as well this was a telephone conversation. However, putting the best gloss she could on it, she decided that she was after all an ambassador of sorts for Nice School, and it was important to present herself at her best. Determined to show willing, she said, in a neutral voice: 'I'm free any time, really. Just say when would suit you.'

They arranged a meeting for Monday afternoon, and Evie gave herself a mental shake. The lamps and cushions would just have to wait; she needed to do what her mother always referred to as a 'proper shop'. It was time to stock up the kitchen cupboards and stop pretending that she was merely camping for a few days. After scribbling a hasty list, she checked carefully that the back door was locked, gathered up her bunch of keys and a couple of carrier bags, and slammed the front door behind her, checking that it had shut properly despite its stiffness. Satisfied that her little domain was secure, she set off. She knew that she had passed a large supermarket on her first drive in to the town and set off confidently enough, forgetting about the one way system. Twenty frustrating minutes later she was finally in the car park, and a further twenty minutes later she was at the checkout having walked a considerable distance around an unfamiliar shop with far too much choice for a natural ditherer. By the time she returned to her parking spot outside number 5, dusk was descending.

Looping the carrier bags over her arm, Evie wiggled the key and forced the door open as usual. As she did so, she thought she heard a noise at the back of the house. Telling herself she was being silly she walked quietly into the living room, snapping the light on to reveal nothing at all out of the ordinary. But was she imagining it, or was there something - someone - in her kitchen? Stealthily, in best TV detective fashion, she approached the door that led through to the kitchen, and flung it open while standing back. Again, nothing, apart from a slight breeze that suggested she had left the window open. Careless of her! Then she distinctly heard a noise, a human noise, coming from just outside the back door. In an instant she was through it and unable to do anything for a few moments while her eyes adjusted to the gloom. There was no-one in the garden, and now the sounds seemed to be coming from over by the wall. Perhaps there was someone on the other side, in the wasteland beyond? So that was it. She had seen youngsters playing out there most evenings; not a very pleasant playground, but perhaps all there was. They weren't usually out there this late, though: there was something wrong here, something different. Decisively - perhaps she was no longer a ditherer after all - she returned to the house, closing and locking the back door and heading out the front. As she rounded the side corner of the house she could hear someone groaning; on the ground, up against the outer side of her garden wall, lay a bundle that eventually revealed itself to be a youth.

'Are you OK? Do you need some help?'

'Leave me alone. Go away!'

Evie would have liked to do just that, but he seemed in a bad way. Wearily she asked, 'Where do you live? Would you like me to call your parents?'

The response was a string of obscenities. She really was on the point of walking away when she realised with some surprise that he was sobbing, hard, dry sobs that he was trying to suppress. He must be in serious pain. She stooped and for the first time noticed the dark stain on his tee shirt.

'You're bleeding. Can you stand? Here, let me help.' Awkwardly she got him to his feet despite his resistance; The Boy was much taller than she was, even stooped over his wounded arm, but somehow she managed to get him back round to her front door, which stood open.

'Come on, let's have a proper look in the light.'

They got as far as the sofa before he collapsed, and Evie left him while she got a tea towel from the kitchen - to staunch his wound or protect the sofa, she wasn't sure which. She checked that he wasn't unconscious; she had done a first aid course at Nice School, although she had never been called upon to make use of her training. Looking at The Boy, with his mop of dark hair tumbling forward over his face and his nose running slightly, he seemed much younger than his height suggested. The closed eyes were probably a defence against further questions. He was still doubled up over his arm, and she inspected it as gently as she could, but it was clear that it was badly cut. She didn't have a proper first aid kit, nothing beyond a few sticking plasters and a wholly inadequate bandage; in any case, this was clearly an A & E job. Who knew what other injuries he had besides? Should she call 999? Ambulance or police?

'What happened?'

No reply.

'Did someone do this to you? Who was it?' She was becoming exasperated. 'Look, I'm not going to let you bleed to death on my living room sofa, so if you won't talk to me I'm going to have to call the police.'

'No, don't!' The eyes shot open and he sniffed and wiped his nose on the back of the undamaged hand. 'Please don't... don't do that.'

'So tell me where your parents live and I'll call them, explain what's happened.' The answer this time was more vehement than ever, and he struggled ineffectively to get up. Afraid he would seriously hurt himself, she offered a compromise. 'OK. How about I take you to A & E in my car and we find out what the damage is? Then we can decide what to do.'

The Boy nodded weakly, closing his eyes again, but not before she'd seen the tears squeezing out under the lids.

Just before getting him into the car, Evie went to check that the back door was locked. It was then that she remembered opening it when she heard the noise outside: it had been unlocked. And then she noticed the shards of glass on the draining board, and above it the broken window.

3

The triage system at the hospital was quick and efficient, but then began the long wait for a doctor. Evie and The Boy were seated at the end of a row of plastic chairs next to the entrance, and the automatic doors opened not only each time someone went through them, but each time someone walked past, so that they seemed to open and close more or less continuously for the two hours or so that they sat waiting, letting in an increasingly chilly draught. The Boy's face was the colour of the pale grey flooring, and he squirmed and contorted his long limbs in an effort to find a comfortable position on the angular chair; despite his obvious distress, and the blood that had seeped through Evie's tea towel, it seemed there were far more urgent cases, although for the life of her she couldn't work out what made the young woman talking cheerfully into her mobile phone, or the man in a suit working on his laptop, more urgent than The Boy with his bloodstained clothes.

On the short car journey he had continued to refuse to give his name or that of his parents. No way would he tell her where he lived, and she could just butt out of his life and stop judging him… Evie bit her tongue. She told herself he was in shock from whatever it was that had happened to him: he still refused to tell her what. After one particularly vitriolic outburst she came close to telling him that if he didn't want her help he could just get out and walk to the hospital, but then she reminded herself that she was the grown-up in the situation, and she gritted her teeth and focused on her driving.

It was awkward at Reception.

'Name?'

'Genevieve Symmonds.'

Evie thought she saw the clerk roll her eyes as she glanced in The Boy's direction and then back at Evie.

'*Patient's* name?'

'I'm afraid I don't know.'

'You don't know? Then who is he?'

'I don't know that either.'

'Just a minute.' The clerk, a young woman with hair piled stiffly on her head as though to compensate for her lack of height - she was only just visible above the counter - turned and called to an older woman. 'Mandy, have you got a minute?' Mandy came bustling across with an armful of files and the impatient look of someone who was too important to be bothered with trifles.

Mandy's view, it turned out, was that if the patient didn't want to give his name, then they couldn't make him, but they wouldn't be able to contact his GP, and if he was a minor...She sucked her cheeks in, leaving the apparently dire consequences unspoken.

'So how is it that you brought him here?' Evie was just trying to work out a response, other than the honest one that she heartily wished she hadn't, when to her relief a nurse appeared at her elbow and invited her to bring 'the young man' to cubicle four.

After The Boy had been checked over, lectured by the A&E staff, X-rayed and finally stitched up, during all of which the staff had persuaded her to stay, and The Boy himself had grudgingly admitted that he'd like her to, Evie finally insisted there was nothing more she could do and that she was going to go home and have something to eat.

'Well, just go and say goodbye to him,' said one of the nurses. 'Don't just walk out on him.'

Evie went back to the cubicle. The Boy closed his eyes. 'I know you can hear me,' she said. The eyes remained closed.

'Look at me!' The eyes opened warily. 'I know what you did,' she said calmly. 'What made you think a house like mine was worth burgling?'

He looked at the ceiling. 'What you saying?'

'Oh come on, I know perfectly well that you broke in. You smashed the window to get in, gave yourself a nasty cut, and then presumably when you heard me coming home you left by the back door.'

He shrugged.

Evie finally lost her patience. 'Oh, I've had enough of this game-playing. There are ways of finding out who you are. You're not a man of mystery, not even a proper burglar, just an incompetent one, a silly boy.'

Turning on her heel she headed for the exit, but not before she heard him mutter feebly, 'Yeah. Cheers.'

Next morning Evie decided she needed some gardening therapy to soothe away the irritation of the previous evening. Stepping out into the garden a sense of calm once again descended. She returned to the shed in pursuit of the lawnmower she had been so tempted by on first arriving. It stood where she had left it, but now she realised that it was a heavy, petrol-driven one. At first she thought this was a major setback, but then found a can of petrol next to it, marked ‘lawnmower.’ (At least it didn’t say ‘drink me’ she thought light-heartedly, back in Alice mode.) Deciding to risk it, she wrestled with the petrol cap until it finally turned under her hand, and, shaking with excitement, poured in as much as the tank would take. This turned out to be quite a lot. The grass was going to be a challenge, no doubt about that, but she felt more than equal to it, and, setting the mower to its highest cutting level she tugged at the cord until the motor finally came to life, and she was off. The ground was bumpy and hidden objects - mostly stones and the occasional piece of rusty metal - gave her a nasty jar a few times, but once she had been all the way round she was on a roll, and setting the cut lower she went over it again, and then a third time.

There was an obstinate patch in the middle where the ground dipped and the blades of the mower couldn’t match it. Weary now, she pushed the mower back into the shed and surveyed her work. Not bad, although those strands in the middle were annoying. She wandered thoughtfully into the house and rummaged around in her briefcase, returning to the garden with a large pair of scissors. Crouching in the middle of what might one day be described as a lawn, she lowered her sights to - literally - grass roots level, and began to snip, trying to keep the cuts in line with the rest of the lawn. There was something weirdly therapeutic about the action, and she soon found herself snipping away at all sorts of uneven patches.

After a while she had the uncomfortable sensation that she was being watched. At first she dismissed the feeling as imagination and carried on, but it persisted, and eventually she raised her eyes to the fence that divided her house from Number 4. A head was staring down at her, a head with slicked hair cut short at back and sides, a bristly moustache, and a bemused expression.

'You don't have to do that, you know. I have a lawnmower you can borrow, if you like,' said a deep voice.

That was her first introduction to Mr. Plod. He became Mr Plod in her mind because she discovered that he had been a policeman before retiring from the force, and although he was nothing like the avuncular policeman of Enid Blyton's imagining she had to call him something to herself, and no other name had been proffered. She soon felt that it wasn't so much kindness that had prompted the offer of a loan of his lawnmower, as she balanced on a precarious pile of bricks at the high dividing fence while they talked; it was more a sense of distaste at the state of her garden. Glancing over his shoulder, she could see why: Mr. Plod's garden was mostly 'laid to lawn' as the estate agents' brochures say, a lawn that must have been designed using a setsquare. Along the borders, ramrod straight, stood a parade of dahlias in perfect formation. It looked small and mean, somehow.

'He never could keep it under control,' Mr. Plod said, nodding his head in the direction of Evie's garden. 'Even when he was young and fit.'

Evie looked at him quizzically.

'Old Seth,' said Mr. Plod. 'I don't think he wanted to, really. It was always a bit... out of the ordinary. He had wild ideas. Travelled a lot.'

'Was that the original owner?'

'Yes. Made the garden and neglected the house.' Mr. Plod looked disapproving. 'Then it was let to tenants, and they were no better, none of them.'

'So, what happened to him?' Evie asked, thinking she quite liked the sound of Old Seth.

'The Golden Years. '

Evie looked puzzled.

'Nursing home,' he added, seeing her expression.

Evie thought Mr. Plod would dearly love to get his hands on the curving borders on her side of the fence, still discernible beneath their heavy coating of weeds, and straighten them out. It seemed he didn't much care for her predecessor's choice of shrubs, either.

'Butterfly bush, he called it. Stupid idea. We all know what butterflies mean, don't we?'

Evie shook her head, perplexed.

'Caterpillars!' The word came out as a sort of explosion. Clearly wildlife in a garden was not a good idea in Mr. Plod world. He had already lamented the way the fruit trees attracted birds - and sometimes boys - although he, Mr. Plod, usually saw them off in a hurry. This was the point at which he had revealed his past as a police officer.

Retreating to the back bedroom where she could look down on her garden and do a little planning safe from Mr. Plod's beady eye, Evie could make out more clearly the outline of the curving borders and the gentle mound that had at first puzzled her, until that morning when she stubbed a toe against what turned out to be the edge of a rockery built cleverly into the slope of the garden. Even more excitingly, she had discovered, again the hard way, this time with wet feet, the overgrown pond that lay further up the slope. Reclaiming Eden would be hard work, she mused, and would need time and energy; but then so would preparing for her first term at Other School. With a sigh she turned away from the window to the desk (well, folding card-table bought at a local junk shop) where her books and papers were piled high.

On Monday morning Evie finally crawled from her bed after pressing 'snooze' for the fourth or fifth time. She would have to do better than this when term began. The afternoon's meeting hung over her, and she wandered around house and garden rather aimlessly, unable to settle to anything. Finally, she returned to her bedroom and spent some time searching her wardrobe for what she thought of as 'smart-casual-professional' clothes, and as soon as she had eaten a rather spartan lunch, changed and studied herself in the cracked wardrobe mirror. Would Mr. HOD approve of her appearance? And which HOD was she worried about - the known reptilian one at Nice School, or the unknown one here in Other Place?

Despite all the work she had put into the house, she was still feeling somewhat dispirited by its limitations, and at twenty-five minutes past two, as she approached the school to keep her appointment, she had additional grounds for feeling demoralised. As soon as she caught sight of the school building her heart sank somewhere below ground level. Appearances might not be everything, but how was it going to feel to walk up this road every morning, through those heavy gates, and into this place of solid grey concrete? Not a leaf, not a blade of grass in sight. After she was buzzed through the heavy entrance door, she hesitated in the blue-vinyl floored corridor, wondering if there was any way out.

'Genevieve? Welcome! Sorry I wasn't at the door to greet you - we're having a spot of trouble with the boys' toilets - you don't want to know!' She recognised his voice from earlier, but not the mental image she'd had of him. He was tall, very tall, a bit lanky, like an overgrown schoolboy, and so young-looking that she wondered whether she'd heard aright when he told her he was HOD. His crumpled shirt was rolled up at the sleeves, and his denim jeans had seen better days. For the first time in a long time, Evie felt over-dressed. Belatedly, she took the hand he offered, and was rewarded with a warm, friendly handshake.

'Come on up to my office,' he called over his shoulder, already heading off down the corridor. Evie found herself running every few paces to keep up with him. They turned left, right, right, left, up a flight of stairs, along another corridor - Evie almost spoke her thoughts aloud as they negotiated the warren: *I'm late, I'm late for a very important date.* She really must stop this Alice in Wonderland thing. Finally Rob opened an ordinary-looking door and ushered her in to a square box of a classroom with a glass-walled office off it to the back. It was beyond basic.

She followed him slowly towards the office, looking at the classroom walls to steady herself. It was like being transported into another universe: noticeboards gave prominence to students' work; posters proclaimed things like: *Open a book: grow your mind* and *Mistakes are proof that you are trying.* She was particularly taken with the one that said: *Be awesome! Be amazing! Be you!* and wished she knew enough about who she was to follow its advice.

Rob led the way through to the office and Evie followed, taking the plastic chair he offered.

'Coffee?' he asked.

'Yes please. Just a drop of milk. No sugar.' She realised that she was nervous. Being nervous was her default position for interviews with a Head Of Department. To cover the silence, she added. 'I'm usually called Evie, by the way.'

'Good to meet you, Evie,' he said, sounding as though he meant it. For the next hour he explained how things worked at Other School, laid before her a slightly crumpled copy of her timetable, and ran through with her the content of syllabuses, homework policies, marking protocols. She absorbed as much as she could, and was relieved when he offered her more coffee and asked, 'So what aspects of English Literature fire you up, Evie?'

She was so surprised by this that for a moment or two she couldn't think how to answer. With Nice School HOD she would have had to filter her answers carefully, even supposing he had shown any interest in actual literature. Now she began by naming her favourite authors, sounding like a boring candidate being interviewed for her first job, but when Rob interrupted her to ask: 'Why did you choose English Literature in the first place, though?' she became animated and found herself telling him about her childhood, peopled with more books than living beings, and how she had been thrilled to discover that you can travel to faraway places and open windows on worlds you didn't know existed, find people just like you and people utterly unlike you or anyone you've ever met... She stopped, feeling foolish.

'Brilliant,' he said. 'Just what we need. Someone who believes in the transforming power of literature.'

She trod more lightly on her way out of the building, but still found herself wondering whether literature could ever transform the dismal environment of this town centre school. Despite that, her heart had now risen just a little higher than her boots, and she was especially thrilled to have been given, at Rob's discretion as HOD, an advance on her first month's salary. Now she could buy some of the things she needed to make her nest her own for the year. She had better get cracking, though: term was due to start in only three weeks. She had forgotten that state school terms were so much longer. So what was that, Mrs Langley-Jones? The more you pay... the longer the staff holidays, she concluded.

She was so absorbed in her plans that she found herself at the end of Paradise Row before she knew it. Why was the way back from somewhere always so much shorter than the journey there? The front door presented its usual challenge and she was still having to put her shoulder to it every time she came in, rather dreading what would happen in wet weather if the wood swelled with the rain

Over the next two weeks Evie worked hard at getting her head round syllabuses as she prepared lessons for the classes - larger than she was used to - that she would be facing come September 4th. She might not have chosen to be here, but given that she was, she was determined to make the best of it, just as she had made the best of the horrific house. Besides, she was carrying with her the reputation of Nice School. She had been back into Other School a couple of times since her last visit. Rob seemed to be there a great deal, which surprised her because at Nice School Mr. HOD and most of her Nice School colleagues disappeared after the end of June to their holiday homes in Tuscany or the Auvergne or wherever, and reappeared in mid-September looking refreshed and vaguely self-satisfied. She, by contrast, would have spent the previous summer in the little rent-free flat, wandering the country lanes or lounging in the school grounds reading books she wanted to teach and wondering if she dared.

Here in Other School the classroom she had been allocated looked dingy and neglected; torn posters hung from the walls, and multi-coloured graffiti decorated the plastic-topped desks scattered around the room. It was next door to Rob's bright and orderly room, and she wondered dismally how she would ever make anything of it. He assured her that he would be on hand to show her the ropes, but she doubted that a HOD, however well-meaning, would really have time for her.

The teacher in the room on her other side was Ms Robinson, an older woman with a nice smile, who was busy arranging display boards when Evie popped in for her second visit.

'Good to have you with us,' said Ms Robinson.

'Good to be here,' Evie replied politely.

Another teacher passing along the corridor turned and called over his shoulder,

'You wait until term starts and see if you still think that!'

'Take no notice of Benji,' said Ms Robinson. 'He's our resident doom-monger.' Benji, she later discovered, was the pastoral head of Year 11. She watched his departing back, fascinated by the long braids tied into a rough parcel at the back of his head, and turned back to Ms. Robinson.

'What's the dress code here?' she asked.

'Well, there's a basic uniform: white or grey shirt or polo shirt, grey sweatshirt, that sort of thing.'

Evie realised that she'd been misunderstood - at least she hoped so. She decided to stick with the student uniform for the moment and worry about the staff dress code later.

'And what about uniform infringements?'

The other woman looked at her blankly.

'I mean - what are we meant to do? You know... if they come without a tie or the wrong shoes or ...'

Ms. Robinson turned fully to face her, relinquishing the poster she had been in the act of pinning up. Her voice, still kind, bore an undertone of resigned patience.

'We don't have any of that nonsense here,' she said. 'We have a flexible uniform policy: every item has to be available from a supermarket or market stall; the cheapest possible.'

Evie wondered why they bothered to have a uniform at all, but didn't dare ask. Somewhere in the back of her head she could hear her father's voice,

'Poverty is less noticeable when everyone is dressed the same.'

At the time she had robustly defended the strict uniform regulations at Nice School, but now, for the first time, suspected that he might have a point.

'Look,' Ms Robinson was saying, 'You're going to find this school very different from the one you've come from.'

Of course! Ms Robinson would know about the exchange. She would know all about the school Evie had come from. She already felt herself judged.

'Uniform is a difficult issue at the best of times,' the other teacher continued. Evie looked at her questioningly. At Nice School uniform had always been equated with discipline.

'And non-uniform, come to that. We gave up on non-uniform days ages ago. Naturally.'

Evie looked blank. Naturally? At Nice School they had raised considerable sums for charity by… Oh! Suddenly, she felt pennies dropping in her head with a thud. She didn't trust herself to speak.

'Because of the absenteeism it causes…' Ms Robinson added, breezily. 'Like PE kits, ingredients for Food Tech… And don't get me started on period poverty…'

Evie felt her eyes welling up with shame.

'I'm sorry, I'm really sorry…'

To her surprise Ms Robinson gave her a motherly hug.

'Ssh. Ssh. It's all right. It's not your fault. How could you know, coming from a place like The Cedars?' She stepped back and looked Evie full in the face, a smile of encouragement lighting her own. 'Now come on, you can help me with these display boards, and then I'll come and help you sort out your room, if you'd like me to - and after that I think we'll have earned a cup of coffee, don't you?'

By the end of the afternoon Evie had recovered her equanimity, such as it was, discovered that Ms. Robinson's name was Pat and that she cared passionately about the young people she taught - and that she had a stash of chocolate biscuits in her locker, which she was willing to share.

'By the way,' Evie asked tentatively, over coffee, 'What's the dress code for staff?'

Her colleague smiled. 'What you're wearing is just fine,' she said.

4

Back at the house, as the summer holiday continued, Evie persuaded herself to work, despite the tempting sunshine that streamed in daily through the back window. She promised herself a day in the garden every two days, but only if she worked very hard at preparing her lessons. Apart from the occasional trip to the shops and a nodded 'good morning' to Mr. Plod once or twice, she saw nobody, and so there was nothing to distract her from her goal.

On the days when she did allow herself to work in the garden she began to see some improvement. There was something else too, something she couldn't explain: it seemed the garden itself, or some mysterious presence, approved her efforts. After a day's concentrated weeding, the rockery began to emerge, and she turned her attention to the pond. She heaved out the slimy weeds that were choking it, appalled at the thick black mud that came out with them. She stood panting for a few moments, wondering what on earth to do with them, and then decided to haul them round the corner of the house, past the shed, and up to the fence that separated her from the road at the front. There she found the remains of what had once been a compost heap, and was glad to deposit the stinking pile on top. Turning back, she was dismayed to see that her progress across the garden had left a dark treacly trail across the grass, but decided that there was only so much she could deal with at a time. As she stood gathering her thoughts, there was a rustling from the compost heap; the pile shifted, and after a few moments of involuntary breath-holding, Evie saw something sleek and grey come scurrying out, followed by a long pink tail. She let out a squeal, and a voice from the street side of the fence said,

'Are you all right in there, Luvvie ?'

Edie squeaked a brief answer.

'Come round to number 3, Luvvie, and I'll make you a cup of tea. I'm just on me way home to put the kettle on.'

Loath as she was to stop work, Evie felt obliged to respond to the disembodied voice - and the kindness of its owner - and so duly arrived, ten minutes later, at the scarlet front door, still dishevelled and smelling faintly of black mud despite a quick scrub at the kitchen sink.

The short, roundish woman who opened the door matched her voice perfectly. She looked what Evie's father would have described as 'comfortable,' as well as a little eccentric, in her pink knitted slippers and the straw hat topped with artificial poppies that nodded as she moved.

'Come in, come in! Don't stand on the doorstep. That's right, in here.'

Evie was ushered into a bright clean kitchen, smelling of fresh baking.

'Sit yourself down. Now then, now then...'

She had run out of breath by this time, giving Evie the chance to say, 'This is so kind of you. I'm Evie...' but in the gap where the other should have supplied her name, the kettle gave out a whistle that made Evie jump, and Mrs. Flowerpot, as she became in Evie's mind - a name that stuck for some time - began to bustle about making the tea. While it brewed - and Evie hoped she wouldn't leave it to brew for too long, as she hated strong tea - Mrs. Flowerpot laid out a tray with proper cups and saucers and matching plates, the kind with a blue stripe round the edge. She even had a matching sugar bowl and milk jug. A plate of gingerbread appeared as if by magic, and then she joined Evie at the little scrubbed pine table and they both sat and watched the teapot for some time while Mrs. Flowerpot got her breath back again.

'I saw you move in,' she said, lifting the lid from the teapot and giving the tea a stir. She had made the tea with old-fashioned loose leaves, and now heaved herself up from her chair, which groaned in protest, and over to a set of drawers, from which she fished out a tea strainer. 'It would have been nice to have a family again…Do you take milk?'

Evie nodded, and her neighbour continued to talk as she poured.

'Used to be all families, years ago. Kiddies playing out in the street, mums having a natter…Still, beggars can't be choosers, can they?'

She looked appraisingly at Evie, who was close to apologising for not being a mum with children, but when Mrs. Flowerpot spoke again, her beaming smile held no trace of malice.

'No, beggars can't be choosers - but you're not a student, are you? We've had them in the past. No regard for the neighbourhood, no sense of pride in the place…'

'No, I'm not a student. I'm a teacher… I'm going to be teaching here for a year.'

Mrs. F's eyebrows shot up in the direction of her nodding poppies, but all she said was, 'Are you, now?' There was a short silence, punctuated by slurping and murmurs of appreciation - the gingerbread really was very good - while Evie tried to formulate a relevant comment. Then Mrs. F leaned across towards her.

'So, Dear, what was going on in your garden then?' and Evie explained about the rat.

'Oh yes, terrible rat problem we've got here. Terrible. It's all that... out back.' She waved her hand in the direction of the derelict land. 'It encourages them. 'And then the kids from the school - your school - they don't think, do they? Drop bits of sandwiches and goodness knows what, and there you have it.' Having delivered her wisdom, she sat back.

After the tea with Mrs. Flowerpot, Evie returned to the garden, keeping well away from the compost heap. The black trail was drying in the sun, and she comforted herself with the realisation that it would disappear next time she cut the grass. A little undecided as to what to do next, she wandered around for a while, appreciating the summer air and the few flowers that had risked raising their heads above the parapet in this strange, neglected garden. Idly, she picked up a spade and resumed digging where she had left off a few days previously in the long border that skirted Mr. Plod's fence. Her spade struck something hard, jarring her shoulder, and she bent to see. The something was curved and looked like rusty metal, embedded in the hard soil. She went to fetch a trowel, and patiently, imagining herself an archaeologist of domestic artefacts, she unearthed what turned out to be a horseshoe. It looked old, and she held it reverentially for a while, trying to guess its history. A little further excavation revealed something else, buried deeper, something also made of metal, with two slots at the top and curved sides meeting in a flattened base. It too was rusted with age, and as she turned it over she had an odd feeling that the garden was speaking to her, whispering secrets she could not fathom.

Evie took her finds over to the fence, where she had heard Mr. Plod earlier, engaged in some mysterious activity. The activity turned out to be clipping back a shrub growing over from her side.

'I have a legal right to remove anything intruding into my garden,' he said, defensively.

Evie waved his words aside. 'Yes, fine. Please do. Do you have any idea what this is?'

He took her second find from her, turning it about.

'Aye, I do,' he said. 'It's a stirrup. Pretty old, by the looks of it. Nothing like the ones used in the force these days.'

'The…? Oh, the police force!' she exclaimed, taking it back. 'I wonder what it's doing here?' She handed him the horseshoe. 'I found this in the same place.'

'That's a fair size - carthorse, I'd say.'

'In my garden?'

'Oh aye - this was all farmland at one time. You'll no doubt find all sorts as you dig.'

Mr. Plod went back to his snipping, and she considered herself dismissed. Strange to think of other lives - very different lives - being lived here in the past: different times, different ways. The knowledge gave her a warm feeling. Perhaps that was why she had felt such a strong sense of presence in the garden: the many others who had loved and cared for it had left their imprint in some indefinable way.

For each person who lingers among the things of nature, who feels a strong emotion there, a shadow, a trace remains. Space-time bends and distorts our simple notion of days and months and years and of time that moves only in one direction. The stirrup that had lain hidden for so long was lost by a poor squire at the time of the last Crusade; he had searched for it over many days, for he could not ride away without it.

So it was that, his future unknown at the moment of losing his stirrup, he prospered when so many of his generation failed to return from fighting the infidel. He built a modest house, long since turned to dust, and enclosed a garden, where he wooed a beautiful young woman who became his wife, and tended the garden until she died in childbirth ten years later. Many and different were the emotions the garden witnessed in those years.

Evie returned to her wandering. She was trying to picture the archetypal urban area she was living in as productive farmland. In her mind's eye she saw the ploughboy struggling to keep control as the gentle giant of a horse dipped and swayed ahead of the plough, the furrow running the length of her garden and beyond. She imagined the harvest and the haymaking, and was about to get all *Cider With Rosie* when she felt something hard strike her foot, and realised she had dropped the stirrup. Stooping to pick it up, her mind turned to other times, perhaps earlier times: what kind of place had this been when the land had been worked by simple peasants? And in more recent times, what had the locals thought when the rows of Victorian dwellings were built?

Her mind went beyond the back fence to the open space where many more such houses must once have stood. How had it felt for those who lived in them when they were demolished - all save this final row of five? Come to that, how did her current neighbours feel to be the last ones standing? And how long could they remain? She had walked round the terrace a few days ago and seen how dilapidated No.1 was; in fact it didn't look safe at all, and she had hurried on past it. How much longer could the others survive? And what then of the garden? She found the thought made her sad.

If Evie never takes the stirrup to be examined at the little museum in the town, she will never learn that it is centuries old, never learn the history of this place when the stirrup was lost. The experts might be able to hazard a guess at its likely owner, but they will not be able to tell her the things she feels instinctively. The squire left no record of his life; he never learned to read and write, and the few papers that found their way into his house have long since rotted to a pulp that feeds the plants that grow above them. The lute that he played was passed on to his motherless son, and carried far away to foreign fields. That is another story in its own right.

But Evie knows something, for she has felt it; felt the young man's joy as he creates this garden out of wilderness; his satisfaction as he plants the forerunner of her fruit trees; one day she will also feel his loss as he grieves for his wife in this place. She will feel these things without knowing that they are his, for they will be hers too; they are common to humankind. That is why the story places our ancient forebears in a garden.

The final weeks of the school holiday were busy. The landlord's agent eventually organised a glazier to put right the broken window; Evie finally acquired the cushions and lamps she'd been hankering after ever since her first day in the house; and initial lesson plans were sketched out.

She continued to allow herself some time in the garden, knowing that it would be difficult to organise once term began. On a dull Saturday morning she stepped out of the back door with her second mug of breakfast coffee and narrowly avoided stepping on something grey and squashy, its long pink tail curved around the body. Unlike the previous one, this one didn't get up and run away, but lay there, its eyes wide as if to challenge her. She dropped her mug, cursing as it was a favourite, and ran to the fence without stopping to gather the broken pieces. To her relief Mr. Plod was in his garden, inspecting his grass to see if it had dared to grow in defiance of his instructions. Evie climbed on to the wobbly pile of bricks.

'Can you help me, *please*?' She knew she sounded ridiculously desperate.

Mr. Plod straightened up. 'Whatever's the matter?'

She had been afraid he would tell her not to be silly, or just recommend reporting it to the council, but he offered to come round and remove it, and to report it to the council next time he passed their offices. After he had scooped up the offending corpse into a sturdy plastic bag, he stood looking round at the garden. If she had expected compliments on her efforts at reclamation, she was disappointed.

'Dear, oh dear. It's much worse than I thought, now I see it up close.' he kicked the edge of the rockery with the toe of his polished shoe. 'You want to get rid of that.'

'I've always wanted a rockery,' she said, rebelliously. 'I'm going to plant it with snowdrops and crocuses - it'll be such a welcome sight after the winter.'

'So you're only here for a year and you're going to do all that and leave it for the next tenant? Bulbs aren't cheap, you know. It's a lot of work maintaining a garden. That's what Seth found. You have more than a touch of him about you an' all. That's just the sort of thing he'd've done.'

Evie was feeling so deflated as she let him out through the house that she was barely able to thank him civilly for disposing of the rat, and had completely lost the desire to spend the day in the garden as she had planned. It was true, what he said. She had been so caught up in the idea of the garden that she hadn't given a thought to the fact that she would see hardly any of the fruit of her labours. Old

Seth had created a place he loved, but without him it was forlorn, and even though she had fallen in love with it, had started to think of it as hers, it could never really be that. She found herself unexpectedly tearful. It was true that she was only here for a year, and she had been at Nice School for only three years, and if they didn't want her back where would she go and what should she do? It seemed nothing was permanent and she didn't belong anywhere. On the spur of the moment she decided to visit Mrs. Flowerpot. Surely a visit to that lady would cheer her up.

Despite ringing the doorbell several times, just to be sure, it was clear that the occupant of the house with the red door wasn't at home. As she stood there, the door of number 2 opened a crack. This was the first time that Evie had seen any evidence that the house was occupied, other than the occasional dim light she thought she saw behind the curtains in the evenings.

'She's not in.'

Evie was wondering how to reply to this statement of the obvious, when the thin young woman who had spoken continued, without attempting to step beyond the protection of her front door, 'You're at number 5 aren't you? You OK?'

'Oh, …er, fine, thank you.' There was a bit of an awkward pause. 'Do you know where she's gone?' Evie asked at last.

'She's at the nursing home.' Evie waited for more information. 'Gone to see Old Seth. Goes most weeks.' Then the door was shut, and Evie had added another nickname to her list: Miss Shrinking Violet.

After rather a lot of dissatisfying wallowing the next day, when it rained non-stop, Evie decided it was time to pull herself together and get properly ready for the start of term, now only days away, and so when Monday morning dawned bright and dry, with just the tiniest hint of autumn in the air, she set off up the hill to prepare her classroom. There were a few other teachers around, but she was mostly left to herself, and she spent time arranging tables to her liking, noting that most of the graffiti had been cleaned off since her previous visit. That must have been Pat Robinson's doing. She borrowed a staple gun from Rob, who was busy in his office next door, and set to, arranging books and adding a few posters and headings to the display boards, ready for the students' work she looked forward to placing there before long. In her desk drawer she organised the spare biros, rulers and drawing pins she'd been allocated, and placed her own files on a high shelf.

A little at a loss as to what to do next, and reluctant to return to the house so soon, she went over to the window and stared out at the dismal concrete scene. From here she could see a tall wrought-iron fire escape, painted a fetching royal blue, a seemingly pointless touch which amused her for some reason. She couldn't help comparing it with the view from her teaching room back at Nice School, where her window looked out over rolling lawns and perfectly colour-co-ordinated flowerbeds that reminded her of a visit to a French Chateau she'd once been on. Her group had been shown the view of the gardens from above and their guide had pointed out that this was how they were intended to be appreciated. There was no door leading out into the gardens, and no expectation that anyone would ever walk in them. This had made Evie sad, but the sight of the concrete beyond her classroom made her even sadder. As she turned away from the window she realised that Rob had entered the room and gave a start.

'Sorry, I didn't mean to make you jump.'

'Oh, I was miles away.'

'Back at Nice School?'

Oh dear: had she called it that out loud?

'Well, a bit. But I really want to learn how to be a proper part of this school,' she added, wanting to sound keen.

'Well, young people are young people wherever you meet them, I guess, but there are some differences. Our lot probably lack the social skills you're used to from your pupils, and they don't necessarily show deference to someone just because they're a teacher.' He grimaced. 'A lot of their parents are quite dismissive of authority in any shape or form, or at least wary of it.'

Evie's heart began plummeting downwards, but she thought she'd better make use of the opportunity to ask for advice.

'So, what are the crucial classroom management things I need to know?' She hoped that sounded professional.

'Well, always try and see things from their point of view, and never raise your voice - if you speak quietly they will have to be quiet to listen to you. Don't ever shout over them: they will only talk louder. Besides,' he said with a smile, 'It's not good for your vocal cords.'

'What about the beginning of lessons? Are they expected to stand when a teacher enters?'

He raised his eyebrows. 'Good heavens, is that what they do at Nice School?' He was clearly amused at her chosen epithet. 'I don't think you'd get our kids doing that!'

'OK, got it. Just speak quietly and wait for them to listen. Sounds easy enough.'

It was Wednesday, two days later, and for the first time since her arrival in Other Place, Evie entered a classroom with actual live students in it, and far more of them than the small teaching groups she was used to at Nice School. She wasn't entirely sure what she had expected, but it wasn't this. Everyone had warned her it would be tough, but the thing that took her most by surprise was the way not a single student acknowledged her presence. They were all seated anyhow, some perched on tables, others lounging almost full length on the chairs. There must have been some sort of scuffle prior to her arrival, because several of the chairs had been overturned and her carefully arranged tables were higgledy piggledy. Screwed up balls of paper and sweet wrappers littered the floor, and someone had executed a colourful rude drawing on the blackboard. She took up a central position at the front of the class and waited. This was the signal for them to become respectfully silent and take their places. They didn't. They continued to ignore her.

Several minutes later she was still standing waiting. Panicking slightly and forgetting everything Rob had said, she threw caution to the winds, drew a deep breath and bellowed, 'YEAR NINE! TAKE YOUR SEATS NOW!'

One or two of the students turned their heads.

'Who are you?' asked a girl near the front. She was wearing false eyelashes and spots of blusher giving her the appearance of a china doll, and she was chewing gum aggressively with her mouth open, all of which Evie would have expected to be against the school rules. Her friend, pausing in the act of taking off her trainers - another rule infringement there, surely - replied, without looking at Evie, 'She'll be one of them supply teachers.'

'Oh.'

The other girl returned to the business in hand, which seemed to be retrieving some object from her left trainer.

'Could you please put your gum in the bin?' Evie said to eyelash and blusher girl, as matter-of-factly as she could.

'What?'

This was hopeless! Evie tried shouting again, straining her throat in the process. Rob had been right about that. A few more students noticed her presence. She moved around, speaking more quietly to the small groups that were still engaged in their own loud conversations, but the moment she moved on she was once again ignored.

At that moment Rob put his head round the door. He must have heard her shouting. Evie felt humiliated; she had never had an experience like this at Nice School. One or two of the students caught sight of him, and the atmosphere in the room changed suddenly. They began to move towards their places, righting the fallen chairs, sitting down, straightening the tables. When all were seated, Rob came fully into the room.

'OK, Year Nine,' he said in a quiet voice. 'This is Miss Symmonds. She will be your teacher for this year.'

'This *year?'* said an incredulous voice. 'You mean she's going to stay a whole year?'

There was general laughter and a number of murmurs, all evincing profound scepticism.

'Yes, Tariq. Miss Symmonds will be teaching you English for the whole year. Make sure you deserve her.' Rob spoke in his usual calm voice, and it seemed to have an equally calming effect on the class.

It might have been Evie's imagination, but she thought that Tariq sat up slightly straighter at that. She hoped that she could live up to her HOD's billing.

'Now then,' he said to the whole class, 'I'll leave you in Miss Symmonds' very capable hands.' As he left he added, over his shoulder. 'Remember, I'll be just next door.'

At break Evie almost fell into Rob's classroom. He was back in the glass-fronted office where they'd sat on her first visit to the school, back in the early days of her time in Other Place.

'Hi,' he said warmly. 'Coffee?'

She nodded, too frazzled to speak for a moment. She regained her breath while he spooned the granules into a mug and poured water from the kettle.

'I'm so sorry about this morning. I really didn't mean to disturb your class and I know it was all wrong to yell like that but they were behaving as though I wasn't there and I didn't know what to do…' It all came out in a rush and she felt more foolish than ever.

'Hey, slow down. It's fine. It's their problem, not yours.'

She sipped the coffee gratefully.

'Look,' he said, pausing in the act of pouring milk. 'They've had a whole succession of supply teachers. They come, they go; we've even had some that have left before the end of their first day. You've been very polite about things, but this isn't a school many teachers want to come and work in. This isn't a place many people want to come and live. We're a long way from Westminster here, and people generally feel ignored.'

Evie absorbed this. 'So you think they were just testing me out?'

'Partly that and partly it's just that they don't see any point in getting to know someone who may not be there the next week.'

'So it's hard for them to make relationships with the person at the front of the room, and that has a knock-on effect on their learning?'

'Too right. No continuity. It's been like that for that particular class since pretty well the start of Year 7. That's why we jumped at the chance of taking part in this scheme. We've got you - *they've* got you - for a whole year. But it'll take time for them to really believe it. What you've got to do is just continue to be there, day after day, week after week.'

By Friday afternoon she was glad that her first week had been only three days long, although it felt much longer. She had met most of her classes by then; there was only a Year 11 class still to meet, and only an hour with them stood between her and the weekend. They filed in, fairly subdued, but with an undercurrent of something she couldn't quite identify.

'Please sit'

She scanned the class, taking in the crumpled shirts, grubby fingers, the coats, football boots, lunch boxes, bags, all heaped on the tables in front of them. Rob had already warned her that the students of Other School, in common with many others in the town, were under-equipped with things like lockers and cloakrooms, and that anyway the students preferred to carry their possessions around with them like so many bag ladies for fear of things getting 'nicked.' Evie had winced at this, and so she tried now to be sympathetic as she asked them to put all their clutter on the floor.

It was then that she saw him, slouched almost horizontal in his seat, his long legs sticking out before him, to the annoyance of the girl seated immediately in front who kept turning and poking him. The Boy had one arm in a sling, and his non-uniform leather jacket was slung rakishly around his shoulders.

Before Evie could begin to gather her thoughts the fire alarm sounded. There was the inevitable hubbub as well as squealing from some of the girls, but it was more like excitement than fear. Amid the suspiciously knowing looks of some of the boys, Evie shepherded the class out and down the royal blue fire escape.

5

Of course it hadn't been a real fire, and by the time the whole school had mustered in the car park and weary form tutors had made their way up and down the lines registering them, and the students had dragged their feet on the way back to the classroom, there was very little of Friday afternoon left, and no will on the part of the students, or Evie herself, to attempt to restart the lesson. The Boy had not returned with the others, she noted with mixed feelings, and he had taken his belongings with him.

'Smile, it may never happen,' said an older teacher to Evie as they queued for the stairs with their groups. 'There's always some joker who doesn't fancy last period on a Friday afternoon. Question is,' he said, leaning in closer to speak directly into her ear, 'Whether it's a student or a teacher!'

Evie spent a lot of the weekend on the phone; to her parents - her father wasn't very well and her mother wanted to talk - and to some of her Uni friends who had been wise enough not to enter the teaching profession. She also enjoyed a long conversation with Matron at Nice School, who told her a slightly odd story about Mr. HOD and the Langley-Joneses which left her feeling she was now an outsider in both schools.

She went to bed ridiculously early on Sunday evening, and woke feeling sufficiently refreshed on Monday morning to promise herself that she would do better this week. It could hardly be worse, she thought gloomily, as she swallowed a hasty breakfast in the kitchen while looking longingly out of the window where the sun was glinting on the newly revealed surface of the pond. Suddenly tired again, she dragged herself up the hill to school.

Her first lesson was with the Year 10 group with whom she had already had one fairly chaotic lesson that had produced no written work whatsoever. She was determined to get something out of them this time. She began by introducing a writing task but as soon as she instructed them to begin there was a chorus of 'Ain't got nothing to write with, Miss,' from several of them.

'OK,' said Evie, wearily, aware that her stock of spare pens was already dwindling. 'I will lend you pens and collect them in afterwards. But that's only today. Next lesson, you must bring your own.'

At the end of the lesson there was so much jostling to leave that she managed to collect in only six pieces of scrappily written work and four biros, one of them chewed beyond repair.

And then it was the dreaded Year 11s again. *Not Upper Fifth*, she reminded herself as they arrived in twos and threes. She greeted them in a confident-sounding and moderated voice which belied her feelings. The Boy, despite his height and generally noticeable appearance - he was still wearing the leather jacket, and his hair was now so far over his eyes that she seriously wondered how he could see where he was going - had again seated himself at the back and sunk low as though attempting to make himself invisible.

This class was technically half way through its GCSE syllabus, and she began by asking them about what they had already covered so far. She had seen the pathetically small amount of work in the exercise books Rob had handed her just before term began and was disconcerted to find that they didn't really seem to know what they'd covered. She reverted for a while to Nice School methods by drily explaining what lay ahead of them and what they were going to cover that term, and then told them to write it down in their shiny new exercise books, and then the 'Ain't got nothing to write with' thing started up. She'd already had enough of that with Year the 10s.

'Right. You...' She pointed to a boy sitting grinning near the front. 'What's your name?'

The boy mimed great surprise, pointing to his own chest, shrugging his shoulders, looking around questioningly at his classmates. She had picked on the class clown.

'Well, whoever you are, would you please go to the office and ask for a box of biros,' she barked at him, her annoyance showing.

The boy took his time getting to his feet, this time with a pantomime of being put upon.

'In your own time,' said Evie, exasperated. Her throat was sore already and the lesson hadn't really begun.

Several of the students made an 'Oo' sound, and a couple of them said, 'Sarcasm, Miss. That's not nice.'

'Will you please just hurry up and get those pens,' she said to the boy, biting back her frustration. What was wrong with her? She had never spoken rudely to a student at Nice School. What would her father have said? Always treat the students with respect, was one of his mantras. But how to get them to respect *her*?

When the lesson finally ended, she headed off gratefully to the staffroom, passing the open doorway to the school office as she did so.

'Oh Miss Symmonds,' called the senior school secretary. 'A word, please.'

Evie obliged. What now?

'You sent a student to the office for a box of pens.'

'Yes, thank you so much. Hardly any of them had come to school with anything at all to write with, and I --'

'You're an English teacher, aren't you?'

Evie nodded.

'Then see that the English Department replaces the biros. We're not here to supply the whole school.' The secretary turned back to her computer, dismissing Evie with a last contemptuous look.

After school, when the last of the students had finally quitted the premises, and the sudden silence was still ringing in her ears, Evie approached Rob. He was ensconced in his goldfish bowl office, clearly up to his ears with work, but he looked up readily as she tapped on the door.

'Evie. What can I do for you?' She explained about what had happened earlier.

'Ah, yes. They do get a bit touchy about people taking their supplies. I'll make a note to send some of ours along.'

'I see. I'm really sorry, Rob. I just did what we always did at my previous school. So I need to ask *you* when I need things like biros?'

'Well, you can ask, but I'm afraid I can't do much to help. This year's allocation is almost spent already. I can manage to replace the ones we owe the main office, but the cupboard's pretty much bare beyond that...'

'Oh!' Evie wasn't sure what to say. 'So, how do I get them to write?'

'They know they are supposed to come to lessons equipped. Their form tutors give them a biro at the start of the year, and they are meant to look after them.'

'But they clearly haven't. What am I meant to do? Buy them myself?'

'No, of course not, nobody expects you to do that. Some members of staff do, of course… Hey, come on…' He had noticed the tears forming.

'I'll tell you what we'll do. I'll give you what we've got. You're resourceful: you can find a way of making sure they hang on to them, one way or another.'

Evie sniffed and wiped her eyes on her sleeve. She didn't feel even slightly resourceful at that moment; in fact she felt younger and far less worldly-wise than her students.

Once back at the house she decided to take a bit of time off from worrying about Other School. She didn't, after all, have any marking to speak of, as things stood. Instead she sat at her kitchen table with the door wide open to the garden. The low evening sun blazed through the branches of her little orchard of trees, setting her afire with renewed enthusiasm to show her father that she could be the teacher he wanted her to be.

In the meantime, there were other things she needed to sort out, such as her household accounts. She opened up her laptop and logged on to her bank account. The first month's rent had been taken already, leaving a big hole until payday. The advance Rob had given her was long gone.

Still, paying rent for the first time felt properly grown-up, and she quite liked that sense of responsibility. If only her students would take the same level of responsibility when they borrowed biros!

She continued to run her eye down the statement on the screen. Help! What was that large sum of money paid out just before she took on the rental? What had she spent it on? Then she calmed down and remembered that of course she had paid a deposit, a refundable deposit, assuming she caused no harm to the house. They would owe *her* money. A thought struck her: a refundable deposit. Now there was an idea.

The next time she met the Year 11s she entered the room with a firm step and a determined tilt to her chin. The class seemed to pick up her mood, and were - for them - reasonably receptive.

'How many of you haven't brought a pen to school?' A forest of hands went up. 'Right, here's what we'll do. I will lend you a pen and take a deposit from you, which you will receive back at the end of the lesson, in exchange for the pen you hand in.' She found herself longing for the English Department at Nice School, with its inexhaustible supply of equipment easily covered by raising the termly fees.

There was a hubbub of protest at this.

'What you think we are? Made of money?'

Patiently she explained. 'The point of a deposit is that it is returned when the borrowed article is returned - like an exchange of prisoners. It doesn't have to be money, either. You can give me anything that is of value to you.'

Holding out a pen, she approached a large boy seated at the front, one of the first to declare his lack of writing equipment. He was wearing unblemished trainers of a dazzling white. The school's uniform policy seemed to be relaxed about footwear. 'You - Wayne is it? I'll accept one of your trainers as a deposit.'

After much disgruntlement he leant down, slowly and theatrically undoing his right trainer and handing it to her. She handed over the pen and took the trainer, sniffing it and then holding it well away from her: she had experienced footwear of the teenage male variety before. The class laughed, and the trainer's owner coloured with embarrassment.

Behind him a girl wearing hooped earrings large enough to encircle a pint glass reluctantly detached one of them in exchange for a biro.

'Thank you - Kelly,' said Evie, reading the girl's name upside down on her exercise book.

'How'd she know my name?' Kelly hissed at her friend.

'Now,' Evie said brightly, addressing the rest of the class. 'Who else needs to borrow a pen?' Only a small proportion of the original number raised their hands, and by the time the lesson proper began she had amassed a necklace with a pair of hearts dangling from it, two mobile phones, a packet of tissues, a watch and somebody's front door key. The atmosphere had relaxed, and she even began to feel that she had them on her side. The writing task was accomplished in near silence.

Towards the end Evie introduced a discussion of some classroom rules: hands up if you wish to speak, no put-downs, others have a right to their opinion, and so on.

'What?' came a snarling voice from the back. The speaker had been keeping an extremely low profile so far, once more slouched so low as to be almost invisible. Now he uncurled his length from his seat and stood, one hand raised mockingly. His other arm was bundled inside his jacket, held in place by the grubby sling. He tossed his head in an attempt to shift the tousled dark hair from his eyes.

'What?' he repeated. 'Even if their opinions are shit?'

Evie hesitated, not wanting to betray their previous acquaintance. 'Yes,' she said firmly. 'Even if you think their opinions are "shit." '

She turned to the rest of the class, and said, tersely, 'Pack your things away. Leave your exercise books on my desk on your way out. Class dismissed.'

She was seething: angry with the class and even more angry with herself. Where on earth was her self-control? She had almost scored a victory with that class until she threw it away. Glancing at her watch she realised she had got yet another thing wrong: letting a class out early was a rookie mistake.

It was a whole ten minutes before she heard the school bell ring, and Rob's class next door filed out and clattered down the stairs. He put his head round the door.

'Are you OK?'

'Sorry, I mistimed things,' she mumbled. 'Not quite used to the shape of the school day here yet.'

Rob came over to where she was standing, facing the now empty tables and chairs. 'You've got Danny Desmond in that group,' he said. 'Has he been giving you a hard time?'

'Tall lad, dark hair falling in his eyes?'

'That's the one. You don't need to take it personally. He's a troubled soul. I don't know what happened to him in the holidays, but he arrived back with his arm in a sling and a note from his mum to say he couldn't take part in any games or PE for the next six weeks. It's not broken, apparently, but he has a deep cut and he wrenched his shoulder doing something or other.'

Evie covered her discomfort by nodding.

'His poor mum's at her wits' end. He won't tell her what happened, but apparently he was out all night and turned up the next morning after a few hours in hospital.'

Evie stored the knowledge away. She noticed there was no mention of a father, and it sounded as though the mother was rather ineffectual. No wonder The Boy was running wild, breaking into people's houses…

'Evie… Evie!' She realised that Rob was speaking to her.

'Sorry - I'm a bit tired.'

'Of course you are. The start of term in a new school is always exhausting. You need to get off home and have a good rest this evening.' He smiled encouragingly. 'You're doing fine. Now off you go.'

As he left the room, he called over his shoulder, 'By the way, Danny is left handed!' and he was gone.

The days wore on. Evie felt her second week at Other School was both better and worse than the first; better because she was starting to get the hang of the place and know her way around a bit, but worse because she had lost her curiosity value for the students, and so they felt at liberty to test the boundaries. And test them they did, especially Danny Desmond, although she did score one minor victory when he began the week by claiming to be unable to write because of the injury to his arm.

'And which hand do you write with, Danny?' she asked him, and the slight twitch on one side of his face showed that he knew he'd been rumbled. Evie had been horrified when she'd recognised him in the classroom that first time, and then angry, although whether with him or herself she wasn't entirely sure. She had moments of feeling she'd been made a fool of too, but mixed in with all those feelings was a good pinch of pity for the neglected teenager whose parents allowed him to run wild. He was absent from school from time to time, and she was torn between relief, because the class was much easier to handle when he wasn't there, and exasperation, because it was clear that he was a bright boy who was massively underachieving in his schoolwork.

Evie's emotions constantly see-sawed: one moment she felt she was getting things right and the next she was curled up with embarrassment at the things she was getting wrong. Thursday was a case in point.

It was lunchtime, and Evie had rather hoped that she might get some lunch, but the corridors were full of students, making movement impossible. She was trying to reach the staffroom, but it was like trying to travel on a motorway in a major traffic snarl-up. There seemed to be some sort of specific blockage, just beyond the corner. Looking round for any other members of staff in the vicinity, Evie realised despairingly that she was the only one.

Voices were getting louder, and she was now seriously afraid that someone would get crushed or trampled. Raising her voice here would be useless, and so she began wiggling her way through the crowd; it was a little like wading through neck-high water. She winced as her feet were trodden on and something sharp caught the back of her hand giving her a nasty cut, but she carried on until she was able to see round the corner. Here she met a tidal wave of bodies coming the other way, and in a small space between the opposing forces were two girls. One she recognised as Kelly, the girl with the enormous hooped earrings and the attitude to boot; the other she didn't know, although she looked about the same age. They were grappling with each other, aiming largely ineffectual kicks; the other girl had a clump of Kelly's hair in one hand.

'He never liked you anyway…told me himself. You're just a stuck up cow!'

She gave another vicious tug on Kelly's hair, and this time Kelly succeeded in landing a kick.

'You leave him alone, d'you hear?'

'You're just jealous 'cause he likes me better.'

Were they fighting over a boy? Seriously? Things like this never happened at Nice School. She dithered, unsure of what to do.

Kelly looked over her shoulder. 'We don't need you, Miss.'

Evie ground her teeth in frustration. She sensed real anger rising inside her. How could a stupid, ignorant fifteen-year-old make her feel such a failure? She realised that she was clenching her hands so hard the nails had drawn blood.

Suddenly a whistle blew, and several of the students placed their hands over their ears. Evie became aware of a thinning out of the crowd further along the corridor. A large man in a tracksuit appeared. She had seen him about the place: a PE teacher, she supposed. With admirable lungpower he bellowed,

'Out of here NOW!' and began a countdown that only got as far as three before the corridor was cleared.

'Woah, not so fast! Not you two,' he said to the girls. 'Now, what's this all about?'

They remained glaring at each other, suddenly silenced.

'Miss Symmonds: did you see what started this?'

Feeling useless, she had to admit that she hadn't. The stand-off continued, and Evie was beginning to think that they would still be there when the bell rang for afternoon school, when Kelly finally broke.

'She was looking at me,' she said, with a toss of her shoulders.

'*Looking* at you?'

'She's been doing that all day.'

The PE teacher repeated. '*Looking* at you?'

'Yeah. She's a jealous cow! Can't get it in her thick head that Danny prefers me.'

'Right, my office. Now!'

With that he marched them both off, dismissing Evie with a nod. Once again she was left feeling inadequate, only now it wasn't Mr. HOD pointing it out: the sense of failure was coming from somewhere inside herself. At this rate she would never feel like a proper grown-up.

It was the following evening before she caught up with Rob to talk about the fight. They were in Rob's office, his desk piled with papers and textbooks, used coffee mugs cheek by jowl with a selection of penknives, 'adult' magazines, laser pens and other confiscated items. As Rob searched for clean mugs and spooned coffee into them the atmosphere lightened. She had a sudden mental image of the coffee machine that bubbled away in Mr. HOD's serene office. It was a far cry from Rob's, open to the classroom, in amidst the hustle and bustle of the school day. She found herself rather admiring his willingness to be connected to the life of the department in this way.

She began telling him about the incident at lunch time the previous day.

'I did think I was maybe getting somewhere with Kelly, but some days she is

rude and snappy with everyone, not just me. She doesn't exactly suffer fools gladly; but then yesterday: to get into a fight - an actual physical fight - over a boy!'

'Yes, she can be awkward. I taught her last year.' Rob began to pour boiling water onto the coffee granules. 'I think she's finding home life a bit difficult just now. Having an autistic sibling impacts on the whole family, and I don't think anyone in that house gets much sleep. The father's not much help, mother's worn out... When Kelly draws attention to herself in school I think it's because she gets very little at home.'

Rob handed her the mug. 'And I'm not sure getting entangled with Danny Desmond has been all that good for her, either…'

'Oh.' Evie wasn't sure what to say, and she felt smaller than ever.

Evie had come away from her conversation with Rob feeling chastened; she had a little more understanding of Kelly's situation, which in turn made her feel worse about herself. The next day she got caught for an emergency lunch duty, something she was sure she could handle. She had never liked the dining hall at Nice School, with its faux-Oxbridge College atmosphere, but now she was completely taken aback by the Other School canteen. She gazed in amazement at the compartmentalised plastic trays for the food, the colours bright enough to hurt your eyes, and tables with seats attached as though someone had thought they might be stolen. A ragged queue had formed at the entrance. The noise was deafening: that at least was the same.

It turned out that she was supposed to have a scanner to read the students' ID cards, but no-one had told her.

Failed again! thought Evie, as she went off in search of the scanning device.

6

The one real bright spot was that she had been entrusted with two A Level classes, and they soon became the highlight of her week. The Year 12 students were feeling their way into the greater freedom their new status afforded, and Evie sent them off to the library with a reading list. They were very ill-informed but hungry to know more about the books she described to them in her efforts to whet their appetites. She remembered her own teenage years, haunting the public library and the school library and asking for books as birthday presents; the gulf between her experience and theirs made her sad but more than ever determined to set them on the path of reading.

Year 13 were studying Paradise Lost, and the opening descriptions of Satan and his angels plunging from heaven into the burning lake delighted them like some sort of action movie. They clearly approved Satan's tenacity in the face of his changed situation, and there was some discussion as to whether Satan should be seen as the real hero. She tried to avoid thinking of her own changed situation as any sort of parallel with Lucifer's. No-one could mistake her for the hero in her own story.

The students found it much harder to engage with the text, however, once God had made Adam and Eve.

'No, but really, Miss, they're both a bit wet, aren't they?' commented one of the boys.

'Yeah, especially Adam,' said the girl Evie had already identified as the class feminist. 'Passing the buck. *It wasn't me, God, it was her*. How wet is that!'

'And what about Eve?' The boy wasn't going to let her get away with blaming Adam. 'She doesn't take responsibility either. *It wasn't me, God. It was the snake.*'

'So who was really to blame?' Evie asked.

'God?' suggested a few of them.

'Satan?'

'Human nature?'

Evie enjoyed the discussion, but could see that helping them to analyse the text in detail and see what Milton was saying might be an uphill struggle. They didn't easily relate to the idea of gardens, either, and this set her off thinking about her own. She wondered whether she might be able to invite them to picnic there in the summer.

Then it was back to the Year 10s and the Year 11s, and she was heartily glad when Friday afternoon arrived - no false alarms this time - and Danny wasn't in class. From what she was hearing around the school, the two things might have been related. She planned to stay late and catch up on some marking and preparation, buy a bottle of wine on the way home, and then spend as much of the weekend as possible in the garden.

It rained all day Saturday, putting paid to Evie's hopes of working outdoors, and so after some half-hearted lesson planning, she decided to have another go at visiting Mrs. Flowerpot. This time the door was opened almost before she'd finished knocking.

'Saw you coming, Dearie. Come in quick out of the rain.'

'I hope you don't mind...' Evie began, but Mrs. Flowerpot waved away her words.

'Glad to see you. Come on into the kitchen. I'll just put the kettle on.'

Mrs. F was wearing a different hat today, a woolly one. Evie wondered if she'd been on her way out. 'I hope I'm not disturbing you? You weren't about to go out, were you?'

'No, bless you, no. I've been baking this lot all morning.' She gestured to the worktops where an astonishing array of pies and cakes was cooling on wire trays. 'Harvest supper coming up on Sunday.'

'Oh,' was all Evie could think to say.

'After Evensong. Why don't you come? It's a nice crowd of people.' Evie shuddered. She had sat through the interminable Evensongs in Nice School chapel while the choirmaster scowled at the little boys from the Prep Department and the older ones yawned with boredom. Almost as if she could read Evie's thoughts, Mrs. F said, 'If you don't want to come to Evensong, come afterwards to the church hall.'

Evie had walked past the church a few times. It looked like a distant cousin of the row of houses on Paradise Row, all redbrick and Victorian. 'Oh no, I couldn't. I'm not invited... anyway, the reason I came...' She was interrupted by the whistling of the kettle. Mrs. F bustled around making the tea and from a cupboard produced the remains of a chocolate cake. As they consumed large slices - it was moist and very, very chocolatey - Evie said, 'I called last week, when you were out. The young woman next door said you'd gone to visit Seth, in the nursing home.'

'Oh yes. I try to get there every week if I can. He's not doing too bad, considering.'

'I just wondered,' Evie asked tentatively, 'If you could tell me a bit about what the garden was like when Seth was here. It's such a special place...'

'Ah, well that's because it's all planted with love, isn't it?' She was struck by a sudden thought. 'Just you wait there a minute,' and she bustled off to the other room, from where Evie could hear cupboard doors being opened and closed. When she returned she had a big square biscuit tin in her hands. 'I can do better than tell you,' Mrs. Flowerpot said, opening the lid with a flourish. Inside the box were crammed dozens, perhaps hundreds, of photographs, many in black and white. 'I'll show you.'

The pictures tumbled out onto the table in random fashion, so that as Evie began turning them over the trees appeared sometimes mature, sometimes tiny saplings, while the seasons and the years changed the garden back and forth - spring to winter, autumn to summer - until it felt to Evie that she was gazing at dozens of different gardens while tumbling through time and space.

'Seth left these with me when he went off travelling,' said Mrs. F, as she spread them before Evie. 'They could do with a bit of a sort out,' she added, a little unnecessarily.

Despite the limitations of the black and white and the faded pigments of the colour photos, Evie was enthralled. Although hard to recognise in many of the pictures, it was always, unmistakably, her garden, the garden she was coming to know and love. She could almost smell the springtime blossom and hear the drone of the bees in the summer sunshine, and in the autumn pictures she could have sworn she could see the leaves gently twirling to the ground.

'You all right Chuck?'

'It's so ...' Evie couldn't find the words to express the emotion of holding In her hands the years - the history - of the garden. Like the town it had clearly changed over time; that was how nature was, she supposed, never static, always unfolding and changing, and she tried to apply the thought to her own life. There was one particularly good picture where the colour had not faded as much as some of the others. In it Evie could recognise the sweep of the borders, filled with shrubs and flowers that left no space for weeds. The pond glinted in the sunlight of some long ago summer afternoon, the stones in the rockery were cleaner than now and unbroken. She had the Alice in Wonderland feeling again, and a strong yearning to magically enter the photograph and pass through it to be part of that time and place. Although perhaps that was more Alice through the Looking Glass?

Then Mrs. F picked up another photograph, this time showing a smiling figure in the foreground. 'There he is!' she said triumphantly. 'That's Seth.'

Evie saw a small, round man; his shoulder length grey hair floating around his head like a halo while his exuberant beard completely hid the place where his neck should be. Below the beard he sported a waistcoat in deepest maroon, and he stood, feet apart, looking supremely contented with life.

'He looks just like a Hobbit!' she exclaimed, but it was clear that Mrs. F. didn't know what that was.

Does he, Dear?' she said vaguely. 'Well, that's nice, I'm sure.'

For some reason the visit to Mrs. F cheered Evie up and she was able to complete some marking that evening. The following day was fine, and she was able to potter about in the garden, trying to reconcile in her mind's eye its present state with the glimpse she had been given of how it once looked. At moments she almost felt as though The Hobbit himself were there watching her, smiling and nodding.

From the beginning, Evie had been drawn to the little group of fruit trees at the far end of the garden. She had taken to sitting there sometimes, perched on a precarious plastic chair, out of range of the surprisingly fierce sunshine. From there she could gaze down the garden's gentle slope to the back of the little terrace. She could make out the back of Mrs. Flowerpot's, one along from Mr. Plod's; in fact it was hard to miss as the window frames were painted the same lurid red as that lady's front door. This brought back into her memory the warm kitchen and scrumptious gingerbread, and rather wistfully, she looked at the apple tree in front of her with fruit pie in mind, but it was dauntingly overgrown with brambles.

The next day, having finally got herself some strong gloves, she began to attack the brambles caught in the branches of the apple tree. As they came down she picked the glistening ripe fruit, and when one particularly hard tug brought down a few apples as well, she remembered her intention to make a fruit pie. Apple and blackberry would be perfect, she thought. The flour and other ingredients had finally made it to the cupboard on one of her shopping expeditions, but since then she had been too busy even to think about it.

After her baking session she wondered what to do with the pie. Should she invite Mr. Plod in for a piece? Would he approve? It looked very uneven, and it certainly wasn't a patch on Mrs. Flowerpot's row of pies, now, she supposed, glancing at the time, being hungrily devoured at the Harvest Supper. What about the thin woman behind the door of No.3? She certainly looked as though she could do with something to fatten her up. She must ask Mrs. Flowerpot about her next time she saw her.

The time was approaching when Evie wouldn't need to cut the grass again until spring, and she felt sad to think of losing that regular routine. She was very aware of the days becoming shorter and the signs of autumn were all over the garden now. Fallen leaves littered the grass and much of the fruit dropped, uneaten. Evie had neither the time not the energy to pick it, and in desperation she asked Mr. Plod and Mrs. Flowerpot if they would like to help themselves. Mrs. F immediately said she would take some to Seth.

'Don't you think it'll make him sad?' asked Evie, doubtfully. Mrs. F looked at her in amazement.

'To eat the fruit from trees he planted himself, all those years ago? I should think it'll make him really happy, Dear, wouldn't you? And I'll make him a pie or two to share with the other residents. What do you think?'

'I think that's really kind,' said Evie, trying to stop staring at the latest hat, with its burden of artificial fruit. It must have made it very heavy to wear, but it didn't seem to trouble Mrs. F at all.

'And what about your next door neighbour?' Evie asked, realising she still didn't know what Miss Shrinking Violet was called. 'Do you think she would like something?'

'Yes...she's a hard one to help,' said Mrs. F thoughtfully. 'Had a bad time in the past... Mmm. Leave that with me, Dearie.'

As Evie became more used to the school timetable the weeks took on a rhythm of their own and she sometimes found that Friday had come round again almost without her noticing. She tried to be strict with herself at weekends, insisting that some schoolwork was done before she allowed herself out into the garden.

Danny Desmond was still making her life difficult. When he wasn't in open rebellion he kept up a constant barrage of low-level disruption that amused and emboldened the others and exasperated Evie. There were days when his resistance to her teaching was so strong - and so disruptive - that she could barely make it to the end of the lesson before rushing to the staff toilets for a good cry. On such days she would crawl miserably back to the little house, put the kettle on, and then forget it as she found herself drawn to open the back door and wander out into the garden. The moment she set foot out there she felt healed, as though she had stepped into another world. As the nights started to draw in, she knew it would soon be too dark to see anything out there in the evenings, and she grieved for the loss to come.

Then it was half term, and although she had a lot of preparation to do, she found herself released to work out of doors again in the hours of daylight. She had bought herself a pair of secateurs, and started to cut back the dying foliage of some plants and shrubs whose names she hadn't yet learnt. As she did so she thought of The Hobbit, patiently planting them, and felt overwhelmed with a sense of how much she owed it to him to care for his garden. If only he could be there to advise her... Then she had a sudden thought, and rushed round to Mrs. Flowerpot's, still wearing her gardening gloves and the green wellies she had bought back in the summer.

The latest hat had daisies tucked into the brim, and Evie felt immediately inspired to plant some, but wasn't sure of the right time to do it. After she had taken off her wellies and been ushered into the warm kitchen she asked Mrs. F:

'Do you know when I should plant things for next year - not just bulbs, but flowers - daisies, poppies and such?'

'No good asking me, me dear,' her friend answered cheerily. 'I only grow weeds in my backyard, and they don't take any looking after: they grow all by themselves!' Evie glanced out of the kitchen window while Mrs. F was filling the teapot, and recognised the truth of her words. The garden had been paved at some time in the past, but nature was reasserting itself very forcibly between every joint and crack.

'Why don't you ask Seth?'

For a moment Evie wondered if some sort of metaphysical activity were being suggested, but then it became clear that she was being invited to join Mrs. F on her weekly visit to the nursing home.

'Do you think that would be all right?' she asked doubtfully.

'Why ever not? He'd be pleased to see you! He was so pleased when I told him about the nice young lady who's looking after his garden for him.'

So it was settled, and the next day, after wrestling all morning with a sheaf of essays on Macbeth, Evie gave Mrs. F a lift across town to the Golden Years nursing home. She had visited her grandmother in a home once, and been appalled by the stench of cabbage and wee and the air of resigned depression that hung over the place like a dark cloud. Golden Years wasn't like that at all. They were met by a smiling woman in a crisp blue uniform, who invited them to sign in and told them that Seth was on top form that day. The corridors were lined with bright pictures of parks and gardens, and the whole place smelt like Mrs. Flowerpot's kitchen after a baking session.

As they entered Seth's room, Evie felt as though she were renewing an acquaintance rather than meeting someone for the first time. He was very much as she had seen him in the photograph, wearing the same dark red waistcoat and still sporting the long hair and whiskers. At first it was hard to see why he was in a nursing home at all, for he was full of life and a twinkling energy as he and Mrs. F laughed and joked with each other.

Finally, Mrs. F said: 'Evie has some things she wants to ask you, Seth, and it's no use asking me.'

A little nervously, Evie said: 'I love your garden so much. It makes me happy. I'm trying to look after it for you…'

He looked at her for a long moment, deep into her eyes, as though seeing something there she had not seen herself. 'Yes,' he said, I can see that you do.'

One of the care workers came in just then, rattling teacups on a tray.

'I'll be back in a jiffy with the teapot,' she said, turning towards the door.

'Don't forget the cake,' Mrs. F called after her. 'The one I brought today!'

'Would I do that? I'll be right back.'

Seth laughed, and some good-natured teasing followed on the subject of Mrs. F's baking. Then he turned back to Evie.

'Yes,' he said. 'A garden knows when it's loved. It responds in kind. Have you discovered that?'

She knew what he meant. 'Yes, whenever I've had a bad day at work, or I'm feeling a bit down, I go out into the garden and suddenly the world feels better.' Seth smiled and nodded. Evie continued: 'But I wanted to ask you if I'm doing things right.'

She told him about cutting back the foliage. It was what she had seen Mr. Plod doing, the moment his flowers started looking untidy.

'Ah, well...' Seth looked thoughtful. 'It all depends what you want. You could leave the seed heads on - for the birds, you know. They can look very pretty, specially in the winter when the frost comes. Seems a shame to cut them back before the spring.' For a moment his eyes seemed to be looking inward, contemplating the garden in some deep part of his memory. 'Take the solidago, for example.' Seeing her look of puzzlement, he added: 'The tall, feathery flowers, yellow ones, over by the outer fence. Now they look good in the winter.'

'Oh, I haven't cut those back, and I won't, now you've told me about them.'

'What about the poppies? Did they come up this year?'

'Oh yes, huge ones, deep red, with black centres. They were there when I first arrived, but the petals have fallen now.'

'Have you looked at the seed heads? Once they dry out you can hear the seeds rattling, and then they spill out when the wind shakes them...'

'Nature is... amazing.' Evie knew her words were inadequate, but didn't know the words to express her sense of wonder.

'Oh yes, Nature is a lot cleverer than we are. But we can always give her a hand, work with her. You can shake the seeds out somewhere else in the garden if you want to... and the primroses - they need dividing before the winter sets in.'

The conversation became more technical, and Mrs. F went off to find out where the tea had got to. When the care assistant returned, she was smiling. Everyone seemed to be smiling in that place, and Evie found that it was infectious.

For the rest of the week Evie could sense Seth looking on approvingly each time she found time to work in the garden; indeed, she seemed to catch a glimpse of him from the corner of her eye from time to time. She told herself it was nonsense, but she found it comforting rather than unnerving. Then it was back to school and life got extra busy. There were reports to write, and a spate of parents' evenings, although some of the 'evenings' took place during the day. The times were staggered throughout the week, to allow, Rob said, for the fact that many of the parents worked shifts, although in reality many would not come at all. She was learning things about the lives of her students all the time, in a way she never had at Nice School. Perhaps it was just the difference between a boarding school and a day school, but she felt that it went deeper. The staff at Other School really cared.

One evening, after school, she bumped into Rob in the supermarket. He was standing in the first aisle talking to a student. It took Evie a moment or two to recognise Kelly out of the school context. At Nice School she never saw the students beyond the school grounds.

Kelly sang out a cheerful 'Hello Miss' when she saw her.

Without looking at Evie, Rob said: 'Have you got your list? Right, go and get the things you need.'

Then he said to Evie: 'You didn't see this.' Evie was completely nonplussed. Rob sighed. 'Look, she keeps missing school on the days she has Food Tech. There's no way that family can manage to provide the ingredients, and the school budget doesn't stretch that far…'

'So you're buying them, out of your own pocket?'

Rob looked a bit sheepish. 'She's a bright girl, despite appearances. She really needs to be in school.'

After a few moments of stilted small talk, she saw Kelly reappearing with the basket, and left them to it, but she took up the conversation with him again a few days later.

'Look, Evie,' he said. 'Of course it's not official, but everyone does it. Basic school equipment, PE bags, items of kit...'

Evie found herself thinking back to the expensive school outfitters at Nice School, and the long lists of sports equipment, summer and winter uniforms, ties in different house colours, indoor and outdoor shoes. Art materials, books, anything used or consumed during the school day - these were all factored into the level at which fees were set each year. What a different world. And if the school uniform, such as it was, was more honoured in the breach than in the observance at Other School, how much did that matter in the great scheme of things? A little shamefacedly she told Rob about her deposit scheme for biros. He laughed and approved it wholeheartedly.

'That's good. It hasn't actually cost them anything, and you're teaching them to take responsibility,' he said. 'It doesn't shame them or take from their dignity. You know what, Evie?' He gave her a friendly pat on the arm. 'You're getting it. You're getting what we're about here!'

7

Autumn was coming. The trees knew it; they could sense the days shortening. Chlorophyll production had been cut. The hidden colours that the green had masked since spring now blazed forth for a short time, but soon they would be let go by the trees, redundant workers no longer needed to pass on water and nutrition. Like careful householders, the trees had already absorbed what they needed and stored it securely away.

Nature can manage very well by itself, of course; and it is arrogance that makes human beings believe they are needed to improve on nature. A garden, however, is a different matter: human beings and nature working together in total harmony to create order, beauty and a reminder that there is more to life than the purely material. While the garden seemed dormant and became invisible to Evie, its life still continued beneath the soil. When it froze the insects and other creatures burrowed deeper.

As term wore on Danny Desmond made fewer and fewer appearances in her classroom, even on days when she was sure she'd seen him around the school building. She found herself metaphorically rolling up her sleeves for a conflictual parents' evening when it was the turn of the Year 11s. He wasn't the only poor attender, either, and there was one name on her class register that belonged to a boy who had never yet been in any of her lessons. When she asked colleagues about the mysterious Oliver Stark, they shuddered and told her she should thank her lucky stars he'd decided to give her a miss.

First it was the Year 10 parents' evening. Evie had no great expectations of it, given all she had heard and was beginning to learn about her students and the lives they led. She was surprised then, and touched, at the number of parents who did manage to turn up, many in work clothes. She recognised several of the mums from the checkouts at the supermarket, still in overalls, straight from their shift. Evie couldn't find it in her heart to hurry parents who had made such an effort to be there, spending more than the allotted ten minutes with most of them. Queues began to build up at her table. Glancing round she could see that it was the same across the hall.

'I want her to have the chances I didn't.' said one mother, a woman painfully thin and with worry lines etched into her face. 'Tell me what she needs to do and I'll see that she does it'.

Evie already knew that the woman was working at two jobs to support her four children, and no partner on the scene, and couldn't help comparing her attitude with that of someone like Mrs. Langley-Jones at Nice School, or the many who thought that by paying the fees they were handing over all responsibility to the school. She was becoming more and more aware of things her father had said about education over the years, things she had listened to but somehow failed to hear. For the first time she fully recognised what a man of principle he was, and looked forward to finding a way to tell him that she understood when she went home for the holidays.

Some of the students came with their parents, and sat, unfamiliar in their cheap fashionable clothes and unaccustomed silence, keeping a low profile, while mums or dads spoke about them as if they weren't present, some blaming, some apologising, depending on the family dynamic. Not all of the parents were prepared just to listen to her, of course, and some of them were quite forthright in their condemnation of various aspects of the school. In those cases the best she could offer was to listen. However much she believed in the power of education, she couldn't bring herself to seem to admonish parents who clearly had so many other things to worry about.

It was late when she finally got away, her jaw aching from all the talking and the determined smile she had maintained over the course of several hours. There would be no lesson planning or marking that night; all she wanted was her bed. As she walked slowly back down the hill towards home her head was reeling with all the conversations and the things she had discovered about her students. So many seemed to have responsibilities at home: a disabled sibling to be cared for when parents were at work, or the parents themselves needing care; accompanying a parent to the doctor's to act as translator; living in a foster home…

Evie became aware of footsteps behind her; several sets of footsteps, and voices; young male voices. She quickened her pace, but they speeded up to match hers. She wasn't usually nervous when out and about at night. This was a busy road and there were plenty of other people about, but as she approached the inappropriately named Cherry Tree Lane that led to Paradise Row she knew she would be more isolated. Perhaps they were just off to the pub, and would carry straight on when she turned off. No such luck: they turned when she turned, and now they were calling out, unpleasant things:

'Where you going?'

'Want some company?'

Evie carried on walking without turning round.

'Go on, show us your face.'

'What colour lipstick you wearing?'

'What colour knickers?'

There was a lot of laughter. They were youngish voices, which reassured her, but they were in a pack, three or four of them, which didn't. Suddenly she heard another voice break in, from over the road.

'Olly Stark! What the fuck d'you think you're doing? She's a teacher. Leave her alone!'

There were murmurs of 'Spoilsport' and 'Want her for yerself, do you?' but they moved off, and she was left face to face with Danny Desmond. She wasn't afraid of him; for goodness sake, he was a sixteen-year old boy, and he had just rescued her. He was, however, a lot taller than her, standing there in his leather jacket and ripped jeans, looking threatening. Why had they taken notice of him? Did he have some sort of standing with the group?

'You all right, Miss?' he was saying. She nodded weakly. She was more scared than she'd thought. 'Fucking idiots!' he said and then apologised. 'Sorry Miss. For the language.'

She opened her mouth to thank him, but only a squeak came out.

'They probably wouldn't have hurt you. They're all talk, that lot. Like to think they're big.'

Evie finally got out the words to thank him, looking warily around to see if the others really had gone.

Danny said, 'It's down here, isn't it, your house? Come on,' and he made to go with her. She felt ridiculous being walked home by a boy for whom she was *in loco parentis* during the school day, but then she had discovered that evening that many children of his age and younger did indeed take care of their own parents.

Unlocking the front door, it became clear that he was expecting to come in. She hesitated, knowing it was unwise, but he was already offering to make her a cup of tea. She let him. His arm was no longer in a sling.

'So,' he said, sitting opposite her in the little living room, with a slightly teasing smile 'You not worried I'm going to rob you?' Their first meeting had never been acknowledged between them.

'Why on earth did you break in that night?'

He shrugged. 'Dunno. Something to do?'

She gave him a hard look.

'OK, truth,' he said. 'It was a dare.'

'A dare? Of all the stupid... You could have severed an artery...'

'Yeah, they said all that at the hospital.' He looked away. 'Thanks for that, by the way, for getting me there and everything...'

She felt that he actually meant it. 'So, who dared you?'

He sighed before he spoke. 'When we moved here, last year, things were really bad. I didn't fit in. So, quickest way: join a gang!' He laughed mirthlessly. 'Lucky for you tonight that I did. See, I got some respect, now.'

'But why the break-in?'

'Well, like initiation sort of thing, innit?' he mumbled.

'So you nearly bled to death just to prove a point?'

'Oh leave it. You don't know nothing.' He was becoming agitated. 'Anyway, I get enough of this at home.'

'Do you want to tell me about home?'

A single, vehement syllable. 'No!'

There was a ringing silence, during which Evie told herself more forcefully than before that inviting a student into her house, late at night, had not been a wise thing to do. How many times had she been warned never to be alone with a student; false allegations happened all the time; teaching careers had been ruined for less. She wondered if he was angry enough to do something like that. At the same time she felt a funny little pang of sympathy.

'I found it hard moving here,' she ventured. He looked at her with mild curiosity. 'It wasn't really my choice, and everything is so different from where I was before.' He nodded as though he understood. She began to describe Nice School, with all its advantages, but despite the warmth of recollection in her voice she found that she was telling him about the things she disliked.

'You weren't happy there, but you still miss it,' he said. He had got it so exactly right that she looked at him sharply.

'Yeah, me too. That's how it was for me.' He paused, and after a few moments, added: 'Still, it sounds a good place. I reckon I could learn in a place like that. I bet all them posh parents want value for money. I bet no-one mucks around in class like they do here. You could learn in half the time...'

'Danny, *you're* the one who mucks round and wastes time in *your* class,' she said, infuriated by the contradictions in his argument. He stood up then, towering over her. She could see how wound up and angry he was.

'Oh, you're just like all the rest. You don't understand a thing, do you?' He moved towards the hallway. 'Don't worry, I'll see myself out!' and he was down the hall and out, slamming the front door behind him before Evie was even out of her seat.

It was no surprise to Evie when Danny's seat at the back of the class was empty next day, but she was disappointed rather than surprised that neither he nor his parents were at the Year 11 parents' consultation. She was so overwhelmed with work by this stage that it took her several days to get around to raising the issue, first with the school office, who suggested that the boy had probably neglected to take home notice of the impending consultation; then with Rob Greenwood, who pointed her in the direction of the Head of Year, after which she lost track of what was happening.

Now, as so often, she turned again to the garden for solace. Here she could be alone and allow the garden itself to soothe her, to connect her to something beyond herself. She began dividing the clumps of primroses, redistributing them around the borders. The few surviving rockery plants were straggly and needed to be cut back; there were bulbs to be planted. Evie moved lightly around the garden, all thoughts of school gone, and always with that feeling of a benign presence somewhere at her back.

From the shadows a young squire watched the woman dressed in workman's clothes as she wielded spade and hoe. He watched as in a dream, for he could not have known what would become of the land 900 years after a lost stirrup prevented his journey to the Holy Land. He did not know - how could he? - that the delay had bought him his life, for he was not at the battle where he would almost certainly have been killed, nor was he there when dysentery broke out in the camp. How is it that he could he see Evie in the twenty-first century? Could she have seen him if she had turned? Almost certainly, but she did not turn.

Gardens run to a different scale of time from the rest of us. They hold within themselves memories, and the memories return to life as the seasons change. Thus the seed holds within itself, as it lies deep below the frost layer, the memory, the blueprint, for a whole new plant; the trees know when the daylight fades in autumn, for it comes round every year. They know what they must do, and that knowledge is passed on from each generation to the next.

The year was hurtling on towards its end, and Evie found fewer and fewer chances to be out in the garden. Some early frosts had blighted much of what remained in bloom, and whenever she worked in her little study in the evenings the view from the window was always in darkness. It was as if the garden had ceased to exist. When her mother phoned to ask about her plans for Christmas, she found she hadn't given it any thought at all, and was too exhausted even to contemplate the long car journey down to where they lived. She wasn't sure she really thought of it as home any more, and knew that she would stay here in her temporary, rented place for the holidays. It was only later that she recalled that her mother seemed distracted and almost relieved when Evie told her she wasn't coming.

She had been in Other Place for nearly six months, and had done none of the things she had intended, such as visiting the art gallery or going to the theatre. One Saturday afternoon she wandered up to The Playhouse. She hardly used her car at all here, and as she shut her front door she almost felt the need to apologise to it for leaving it standing once more in the street. It was the only car parked permanently in the row, although occasional visiting cars were to be seen outside Miss Shrinking Violet's house. Up at the theatre - everywhere she walked was uphill from her house, as though she lived at the bottom of a gigantic bowl - she was delighted to discover that they were doing *Macbeth* and *The Crucible*, but not until the end of January. For many weeks before then the programme was occupied with the annual pantomime, not something she felt any desire to see. She combed the programme again and noticed that a small theatre company that specialised in school performances would be putting on a dramatized version of Paradise Lost just before Easter. That was more like it: a chance to reward her Year 13 class (she had learned not to call them the Upper Sixth) for all their hard work getting to grips with something written at a time and from a perspective so alien to most of them. She had enjoyed a successful trip with students from Nice School to a similar performance, not the same company, but this lot sounded good. She would implement this as soon as the Spring Term started. Spring! Just saying the word to herself gave her a lift, and during the walk home her mind drifted to thoughts of what the garden would be like when that season arrived.

Her car stood where she had left it, but along one side was a glaring line of bare metal; it had been, in school parlance, 'keyed.' It looked exactly as if someone had walked past with a sharp object in their hand and held it against the side as they walked. Every single part of the bodywork was affected - the wing, the door and the rear section. As she stood looking at it, Mr Plod appeared from somewhere, clearly on his way home. He walked around it, inspecting it forensically.

'Dear oh dear,' he said. 'That's a bit of a mess. Pure vandalism. I'd get it fixed as soon as possible if I were you. Before it rusts.'

Evie sighed. 'It'll cost a fortune.'

'Aye,' he said. 'Bodywork's not cheap. Still your insurance should pay.'

All very well, thought Evie, but she had tried to keep down her insurance costs by signing up to a hefty excess, and if she made a claim it would also affect her premiums. Mr. Plod nodded to her and went in through his police box blue front door, and Evie took a last, pitying look at her injured car and opened her own front door. The recent rain had made it stiffer than ever, and she was still rubbing her shoulder from the effort of forcing it as she stepped in and saw the post on the doormat. It was mostly junk mail, stuff some hapless unemployed person no doubt had been paid a pittance to deliver so that she and the other householders could put it straight into the recycling without even reading.

She bent and picked up the sheaf of papers, glancing at them even as she prepared to dispose of them. One of them was a little stiffer and shinier than the rest, a folded A5 leaflet with pictures of candles nestled against the branches of a pine tree. It made her feel warm just to look at it, and turning it over she saw that it was from the local church. She wondered if Mrs. Flowerpot would be baking mountains of mince pies for some special Christmas Evensong, and was about to crumple it up with the rest when some words caught her attention.

Volunteers needed. As usual, we will be hosting a special Christmas dinner in church for all who have nowhere else to go on Christmas Day. Please let us know of anyone you think might like to be invited.

To help us with this, we need volunteers to cook turkeys in their own oven, and also people to help serve the meal on the day. The atmosphere at our Christmas Dinner is always festive and everyone is very welcome.

Evie found herself wondering what her neighbours would be doing on Christmas Day, and whether they had anyone to celebrate with. There was very little coming and going on Paradise Row; even the postman seemed to give it a wide berth, and as a rule they received very little in the way of junk mail. Maybe the leaflet deliverers thought the houses unoccupied. Once or twice she had glimpsed a smartly dressed woman hurrying past her window in the twilight, looking very out of place. Perhaps she was lost. On one occasion Evie vaguely thought she had seen her coming from next door, although that seemed unlikely. She did see a car occasionally parked outside Miss Shrinking Violet's house, but never for long, and once she saw a visitor carrying what looked like a doctor's bag. As for Number 1, there was no evidence of any sort of life form - just as well, given the state of the building.

She looked again at the leaflet. It listed Christmas services, a Christmas Fair (spelt 'Fayre') and the intended destinations for its Christmas collections: one a local homeless charity; one a national charity for abused women; and one an international aid agency. Evie found herself thinking about all the need implied by that little list, her mind moving outwards from the shabby row of houses, across the town, out across the whole country and then beyond it to a world where people suffered persecution and violence and hunger and all sorts of unimaginable conditions of poverty and misery. She crossed to the window to look again at her damaged car and found that she was looking at it through a mist of tears. Before she knew it she was crumpled on the ugly sofa crying for herself and for the state of the world

There was something going on in school. She wasn't sure what, but there seemed to be little knots of students everywhere she looked. A whole bunch of them were hanging around outside the gates, even after the bell had gone, and not all of them came into school. Evie mentioned it to Pat Robinson as they went into morning briefing.

'Yes, you're right: there is something. The Head'll be on to it, though. She's good at spotting signs of trouble.'

The atmosphere persisted throughout the day, and when the afternoon bell finally rang many of the students hurried out without their usual dawdling, while others gathered just down the street.

Evie watched from her classroom window. Senior members of staff were heading out now, and then she caught sight of a dark blue uniform out in the street, and then another and another. The crowd had resolved itself into two groups, facing each other. Standing out because of his height in the middle of one of the groups was Danny Desmond. Evie caught in her breath.

Before she could think clearly she was distracted from the scene by the sound of running feet and the door flew open as Kelly burst in,

'Quick, Miss, you've got to help. We've got to get Danny out of this!'

'We'll never get through the crowd.'

'There's a way round the back. I'll show you…'

Before Evie knew what she was doing she had followed Kelly downstairs and out of an entrance she hadn't known existed, and was working her way round to the back of the crowd. None of the students took any notice of her. Their attention was fully on two boys emerging into the centre of the space between the two groups. She was relieved to see that neither of them was Danny. Something caught the light in the hands of one of the boys: a knife! Evie plunged forward to where Danny was standing, grabbed him hard by one arm while Kelly grabbed the other. Together they pulled him towards the rear entrance. He was so shocked that he didn't resist, and they were able to get him back inside the building without a word being spoken.

'You'd better get home, Kelly, if you can,' she whispered to the girl, and Danny nodded at her.

'Thanks, Kell,' he murmured, before she fled.

Now Evie turned to face him.

'I'm not sure what's going on, Danny, but the police are here.' As she spoke a siren was heard, and then another. 'Come on!' she said, urgently. 'Up to my classroom.' Bemused, he followed her.

'Right: sit down. There!' She pointed to a desk at the front and he sat, meekly. She flung a book down in front of him: *Lord of the Flies.* 'Well, that's appropriate anyway, when you all behave like savages.'

Danny looked from Evie to the book and back again.

'We're here for revision, Danny. Got that?'

He nodded.

'Now, do you want to tell me what was going on out there? And why are you involved?'

He was silent for so long that Evie thought he was refusing to speak, but then she saw that his face was twisting as though different emotions were struggling to get out. Finally he looked her straight in the eye.

'Are you going to tell my mum?'

'That depends, Danny. I can't make any promises.'

He took a breath. 'I haven't done anything.' Evie raised her eyebrows.

'All right. Truth. I owe Olly Stark some money.'

'And?'

'I haven't got it.'

'Because?'

'He wanted me to sell something for him. And I didn't. Didn't sell it...them. I kept them.' He was looking down at the desk as he spoke.

Evie had now heard the notorious Olly Stark's name mentioned several times in connection with drugs, and guessed that was the issue. She wasn't naïve; she knew that sometimes even kids at Nice School used forbidden substances. She also knew that there the policy was one strike and you're out. What was it here?

Danny continued to speak, haltingly.

'He was after me anyway, and then that night, when he and his mates ganged up on you…'

Absently Evie wondered whether that was where the damage to her car had come from.

'So this thing, now: it's him and his mates against your mates?'

He nodded, miserably. 'Olly had a knife.'

At that moment the classroom door opened. It was Rob. He looked at Danny, took in the book on the desk and no doubt Evie's expression, and then spoke.

'Oh, sorry. I'll come back later, Miss Symmonds. Good to see you putting in some extra time at your studies, Danny!'

It became apparent next day that Evie's quick thinking had saved Danny at the very least from guilt by association, and at worst from serious injury. As it was, his friend Matt had spent a night in hospital being stitched up, and Olly Stark had been charged with affray. The police had used the Head's office to question a number of witnesses, but it seemed no-one had mentioned Danny's name. Nor could they fully get to the bottom of who had been the aggressor in the fight.

Rob was unexpectedly upset at the emergency staff meeting at lunchtime the following day.

'I taught that boy when he was in Year 7,' he said. 'He was so keen. Attendance was good, homework always handed in…'

'Who? Olly Stark? That little toe rag? Pull the other one,' said the PE teacher. 'Should have been charged with GBH and locked up.'

'Rob's right,' said Pat Robinson, from the other side of the room. 'He was in my tutor group. He was a helpful lad, too.'

'So what happened?'

At that moment the Head called the meeting to a formal start, and went over in a business-like tone the facts that most knew already: a boy in Year 11 had been hurt in a dispute between two groups of students; another boy had been arrested and charged. Witnesses had given statements. She ended by advising everyone to try to create as normal an atmosphere as possible in school that day, to answer any questions as briefly as possible, and not to speak to the press. She herself had already prepared a statement.

'You're upset about this, aren't you?' Evie asked Rob, as they walked back towards the English department together.

'It's hard when you see someone going downhill like that,' he said. 'And you can't do anything to prevent it. You see what's happening, but there's nothing you can do. Olly's mother died when he was in Year 9. His father had always had a bit of an alcohol problem, but Mrs. Stark always held it in check. Once she'd gone, well, that was how he coped. Or rather, didn't. Olly found his own ways of self-medicating.'

Evie didn't know what to say and remained silent.

'Glad you had the foresight to do some revision with Danny, by the way,' Rob said, meaningfully.

8

The Autumn term was the longest, and it was almost over. As Evie reviewed the events of the term one evening, she realised that not all of them were bad: Rob had been happy to sanction the trip to Paradise Lost; the Year 10s had started to shape up, and Danny Desmond had given her marginally less trouble in class. Other events were more worrying, however: an outbreak of 'egging' in the staff car park; eggs smashed on to the cars bonded to the paintwork and caused serious damage. Evie began to feel she had got off fairly lightly with the damage to her car, despite the excess she'd had to pay; the effect on her premium would be revealed in due course. There had been a spate of petty thefts around school and she found herself looking at some of the students with suspicion, something she hated herself for. Violence had largely taken place off school premises, but still lurked in the background.

On the slightly brighter side, she had spoken to Mrs. F about the church leaflet and they had agreed that they should invite Mr. Plod. He had been resistant at first, not liking the idea of someone else planning his day for him. Evie, seeing how important it was for him to feel in control, had rashly suggested he become one of the Christmas volunteers, and somehow found herself agreeing to assist too. Mrs. Flowerpot, she was unsurprised to learn, was already a regular helper at the Christmas meal. That left Miss Shrinking Violet.

'Oh, dunno about her, me dear. She don't go out much, well not at all, really. She's got that thing, you know, where they're afraid of going out.'

'Agoraphobia?'

'That's the one.'

Despite Mrs. F's doubts, they had eventually persuaded Miss Shrinking Violet that Evie could drive her there on Christmas Day. If she took a dose of her medication before leaving the house, and got straight into Evie's car, Evie would be able to drop her right in front of the Church Hall and Mrs. F would be there to get her safely inside while

Evie parked. Mrs. F said the vicar had promised there would be a quiet little table where Miss Shrinking Violet could sit away from the others if she didn't feel up to talking to anyone.

'I don't know your name,' Evie said to her when she went round to confirm the arrangements. The door was opened a tiny bit wider this time, and Evie had hopes that it might even be opened wide enough for the young woman to walk through it by Christmas Day. She had a new CPN, Miss S.V. had confided - a Community Psychiatric Nurse, she explained, and she was helping her a lot.

'I'm Evie, by the way.'

'Rose.' It came out in a whisper, but it felt like a gift. Not a shrinking violet, then, but a beautiful flower of summer. Evie hoped desperately that the sad little figure behind the door would find a way to blossom like her namesake when the summer came. Now it was high time she discovered her other neighbours' real names.

If she were going to be there as a volunteer, Evie reasoned, she really ought to check out the premises beforehand. The best way would be to attend the Christmas Fayre. Mrs. F - it was unfortunately too late in their acquaintance to ask her what her name was, unlike with Rose - would be there early, helping to set up.

'Come to my stall first,' she told Evie. 'Handicrafts and cakes.' In her more recent forays into Mrs. F's kitchen Evie had noticed that bundles of knitting had now made an appearance.

'What do you think of these,' Mrs. F had asked one day, revealing with a flourish a whole boxful of Christmas tree baubles, every one of them knitted in four-ply wool and garnished with glittery bands around the middle.

'They're…astonishing,' said Evie, truthfully, secretly resolving not to have a Christmas tree so that she would have an excuse not to buy any at the Fayre.

When the day came there were hundreds of people flocking into the redbrick hall that stood glumly alongside the redbrick church. Inside, however, it was much lighter and cheerier than Evie expected, and although it was still early, there were lots of people already crowding round the tables. She decided to wait until it quietened down before attempting to find Mrs. F's stall, and headed over to the tea area. Teas were being served from a counter in front of a serving hatch, and a number of small folding tables had been arranged in front of that. They bore bright check tablecloths and some sprigs of holly, artfully decorated with tinsel and fixed into small spice jars that someone must have been collecting all year. Through the hatch the kitchen was a ferment of activity, with smiling middle-aged ladies falling over each other to wash and dry cups in time for more teas and coffees to be poured into them, while another smiling helper dispensed cakes and accepted money at the far end of the counter space. Evie approached, unsure of the protocols.

'What can I get you?'

The speaker had a mellifluous voice and stood out a little from the others, being slender and much younger, perhaps in her early forties. Her dark, wiry hair was attempting to escape from a pony tail high on her head, but just like all the others she was smiling.

Evie dithered. 'Oh, er…' The woman leaned towards her confidentially. Her earrings - little sets of Christmas bells in green, red and while - jangled merrily.

'To be honest, I'd go for the coffee. The tea's more than a bit stewed - and we're waiting for the water to boil up again. But,' she continued, as Evie nodded, 'What you *must* have is some of Molly's gingerbread. Or a slice of fruit pie…or the chocolate cake - or all three if you can manage it. They are just *so* good!' There was laughter in the woman's voice. Evie found herself smiling back. It was clearly contagious.

'You've got a good crowd here!' Evie said, accepting her cup and adding milk from the flowery jug proffered.

'Yes, we're doing well today - and I think people are enjoying it, which is important, don't you think? Have you had a chance to look round yet? I'm sure you'll find plenty of unusual Christmas presents.' Evie suddenly felt guilty. The few family presents she had bought had been hastily ordered over the internet. She selected her cake and handed over her payment, then found a seat at a table occupied by a woman and a small girl. The child was finding inventive ways to eat chocolate cake, and her face, hands and the front of her jumper were sticky with the stuff. She looked hungrily at Evie's gingerbread, but Evie had no intention of giving it away.

'Molly's amazing, isn't she?' said the child's mother, moving her carrier bags to make more room for Evie. 'I don't know how she manages to bake all the stuff she does. Parish events wouldn't be the same without her, that's for sure. And she does so much behind the scenes, you know, visiting and that. Such a kind lady…'

Evie was just opening her mouth to say, 'I'm afraid I don't know…' when Mrs Flowerpot hove into view rigged out in red and white, a Father Christmas hat swathed in tinsel topping off the outfit.

'Good to see you, Chuck. Glad you made it.' She nodded her head towards Evie's plate. 'I see you're enjoying my gingerbread, then.' A piece of gingerbread appeared to go down the wrong way, and Evie coughed and choked a bit, but managed not to say: *oh, so your name's Molly!*

On the second-hand book stall she bought a book on gardening for beginners, and on Mrs. - *Molly's* - handicrafts stall she found a knitted scarf with pink roses worked into the pattern. She wondered if she might give it to the former Miss Shrinking Violet. She could just imagine her all done up warmly in it when she collected her on Christmas Day. Poor girl, she had so little flesh on her she must feel the cold badly.

There wasn't much left on the cake stall by the time Evie got there, but she was drawn to a tiny Christmas cake, complete with icing and silver stars.

'Did Molly make this?' she asked the lady serving behind the table, and when she nodded, Evie bought it and wondered what she was going to do with it. It was the same with the bric a brac: she had no use in mind for the ribbons and bunch of silk forget-me-nots, but they somehow got bought.

Evie had never been alone on Christmas Eve before, and hadn't expected to feel anything but relief at being freed from all responsibility in order to slump in front of the television and watch rubbish: it was all she had the energy for after her long first term at Other School. As the evening wore on, however, she suddenly felt herself becoming restless. She was beginning to regret her offer of volunteering on Christmas Day, but had seen a peaceful Christmas Eve as recompense for that, yet now that the time had come she found herself quite unable to relax. She wandered round the house picking things up and putting them down. She tried the TV, but there was nothing on any channel that she wanted to watch. The old films she usually watched in solidarity with her parents would be on tomorrow while she was in the church hall with all the other sad people who had no-one to spend Christmas with. She phoned her parents and had a brief conversation with her mother, who was in a tizz about the Brussels sprouts and the fact that Auntie Sheila was on her way. When she put the phone down she felt even more restless, and had to remind herself firmly that it had been her own choice to stay.

Suddenly a thought struck her, and she went upstairs to find the bag she had dumped in the study after the Christmas Fayre. After some further searching in a drawer she unearthed a packet of silver tissue paper and began to wrap the rose-patterned scarf. The little cake was difficult to wrap and she felt sure that Mr. Plod - the only real name she hadn't yet discovered - would tut at the untidiness of the package, but in the end she used some ribbon from her bric a brac purchase and wrapped it to her own satisfaction at least. Then she took the rest of the ribbon and the silk forget-me-nots and wrapped those in the remaining tissue paper. She had presents for her three neighbours. The gardening book, then, was a present to herself, and she would enjoy looking at it on Christmas morning before she went to do her duty in the church hall.

At the bottom of the carrier was a leaflet, like the one that had asked for volunteers, but this one - she must have picked it up at the Fayre - also carried a list of Christmas services. She had never 'done' Christmas in the chapel at Nice School, because neither she nor any of the students had been there over the Christmas holidays, but now she found herself wondering what it would be like here in Other Place Church. She glanced at her watch and made a decision.

So it was that at a little before 11.30 pm Genevieve Symmonds crept into the back row of the church clutching the order of service that had been handed to her as she came in. The church was alight with candles and flowers and the expectant faces of all the people crammed into the pews, and there was a kind of collective anticipation in the air. Then the organ struck up and the choir processed in from somewhere behind her, so that she heard snatches of bass and tenor, alto and soprano as they moved past her in a sort of melodic Doppler effect. When they had taken their places in the stalls at the front a figure in white and gold vestments stepped forward to address the congregation.

'Welcome to our Midnight Mass, our first celebration of the mystery that is Christmas,' she said, and it was her musical speaking voice that Evie recognised first, just before the dark hair and the smile. Even without the jingle-bell earrings the vicar was unmistakable as the Christmas Fayre tea lady, and by the time Evie had got her head round that revelation the first hymn had started, and she rose to her feet with the rest of the congregation. She tried to imagine the Nice School chaplain, Revd. Liddel, doing anything as ordinary as serving tea but couldn't, and so she gave herself up wholeheartedly to singing *Once in Royal David's City*.

Even though it was almost one o'clock in the morning by the time the service ended, no-one seemed in a hurry to leave. People gathered in tight little knots, wishing each other a happy Christmas, passing on news of absent friends, hugging and chatting, so for a time Evie was unable to get through the crowd to the exit. She watched idly as various people went about their appointed tasks, extinguishing candles, clearing things away. The choir and servers disappeared behind a door to the side, reappearing one by one in ordinary clothes. At last there was some movement, and she found herself in the line to shake hands with the vicar, who, she thought, must be exhausted and in need of her bed, but she received a warm handshake and no sign of wanting to rush away.

'So glad you could make it. It's really good to have you here. We'll see you tomorrow, then …?'

Evie was just wondering whether the vicar really recognised her or whether she just said that sort of thing to everyone, when from behind her a tall figure in ripped jeans and leather jacket pushed through and slipped in beside the vicar. One of the servers, changed out of his white robe thing, Evie thought.

'Are you nearly ready, Mum?' he said, giving the vicar a bear hug. 'Can we go home soon? it's really late.'

In shock Evie pulled her hand away and fled. She found herself walking back down the hill very fast, her footsteps ringing on the frosty pavement. She was angry. Furious! So, he's been playing the poor little deprived boy all this time while really he comes from a privileged middle class background. She'd let herself be taken for a fool! So much for peace on earth and goodwill to all, she thought as she let herself in to the cold house, bruising her shoulder as she heaved the door open.

Fortunately for Rose, Molly and Mr. Plod, Evie was so tired that she slept better than she might have expected and woke on Christmas morning in a calmer frame of mind, so that when she and Molly tapped gently on Rose's door they were able to coax her out of the house, reassuring her at every step, and getting her safely into the back seat of Evie's car.

To her immense surprise she enjoyed being one of the ladies in the kitchen, and even accepted with good grace the Father Christmas hat someone set on her head. The banter and good spirits soothed her, and she began to feel a genuine warmth for the guests. Some of them, it was true, smelt less than fragrant, and she wondered where the

Reverend Desmond had found them, but was glad that she had, for it was another very cold day. Danny was nowhere to be seen.

At the end of the meal, which she and the other helpers shared companionably, sitting amongst the guests, one of them, a very old man, rather wobbly on his legs, insisted on making a little speech of thanks, and everybody clapped loudly. Evie felt tears springing, and turned away to where Rose was sitting quietly at the end of a long table. She caught her eye, and they smiled at each other, which made Evie want to cry even more for some reason, but then there was the washing up to do and all was bustle and normality again.

Later in the afternoon Evie slipped round to each of her neighbours to give them their presents. Rose was quite overwhelmed and gave her another of her shy smiles. Mr.

Plod surprised her by unexpectedly producing a gift in return.

'It's a hellebore,' he explained gruffly. 'It's already coming into flower.' She lifted up the pot and examined it: the leaves made her think of hands, the fingers cupped slightly to receive something. It bore a number of tight, creamy flower buds.

'I'd better keep it indoors in this weather,' she said.

'Oh no, it'll be quite all right out in the garden; in fact it'll be better. That's where it belongs. It's much hardier than it looks.'

On impulse she leaned forward and gave him a little kiss on the cheek. He blushed with pleasure.

'And you're softer than you look,' she said, smiling.

Molly wasn't back from the church hall, having stayed on to finish some clearing up, but she appeared on Evie's doorstep at about five o'clock.

'I've brought you these, Dearie - it's not too late to decorate your tree, you know,' and she held up a bag containing a dozen knitted baubles.

'Oh, that's so kind,' Evie said, meaning it, but wondering what on earth she was going to do with them. 'Hang on a minute; I've got something for you,' and she fetched the little parcel of hat trimmings, although as Molly was wearing a furry bonnet it was a bit hard to imagine how she would use them until the weather warmed up a bit.

Boxing Day morning was bright and crisp and Evie wandered out after breakfast to check on the hellebore. Despite the frost it looked happy enough. She had with her the knitted baubles. She might not have a Christmas tree in the house, but she did have trees in her garden, and so they became the recipients of her neighbour's gift. She watched them swinging in the slight breeze, and felt that this wasn't such a bad Christmas after all.

Evie had finally discovered Mr. Plod's name. Two names, as it turned out, and quite a story attached. It had come about entirely by chance, following a brief exchange of greetings as they met in the street one morning, a few days after Christmas.

'Morning!' he said, and then hesitated, as though reluctant to go indoors despite the temperature, which was below freezing.

'Good morning!' Evie sang out heartily, and then wasn't sure what to do next. 'I haven't really seen you since Christmas. How are you?'

To her surprise he invited her in for a cup of tea, a little gruffly, as though completely out of his depth with any kind of socialising. Evie expected the interior of his house to mirror the stiffness of the garden and was taken aback to find herself in a room with flower-patterned wallpaper and chintz sofas. Mr. Plod's thick fingers, anomalous against the tea things, touched the bone china with unsuspected delicacy as he placed cups and saucers on the little table and set out the plates beside them.

While he was in the kitchen attending to the kettle, Evie glanced at the row of framed photographs on the sideboard, which suggested that there had once been women in his life. One of them was a child, her smile showing missing teeth.

He returned with a tray bearing a teapot, clothed in a cover that could only have been knitted by Molly, complete with crocheted flowers - and a plate bearing the remains of a chocolate cake that looked as though it came from the same source.

Conversation was a little stilted. He enquired after her garden, and then she enquired after his.

'Oh, fine, fine.' There was a heavy silence, and Evie wondered desperately how soon she could make an excuse and leave without looking rude.

Eventually he said, 'I'm sorry, Lass. December 29th is always a difficult day for me.' He nodded towards the photographs. 'That's the date when I lost them. 29th December: fifteen years ago.'

'Oh.' Evie was nonplussed at the emotion in Mr. P's voice. She murmured, 'I'm so sorry,' and leaned forward in her chair to show that she was listening if he wanted to talk. 'Your wife?'

'Emily. Yes. She's been gone fifteen years.' He gave a laugh that wasn't a laugh. 'Longer than we were married. And my daughter.' He was silent a moment, looking inward. 'Lily. A beauty she were. Full of life.' He sighed deeply, and Evie felt her heart squeeze with unexpected pity. How little we know of people from the outside, she thought. Unsure what exactly 'gone' meant, she asked, tentatively,

'What happened?'

It was a long story. Mr. P had lost his mother at an early age, remembering her mostly as a softly perfumed presence in a silky dressing gown. He'd been sent away to boarding school, away from all softness and all things feminine, and had spent a lifetime trying to toughen himself up. Joining the police force was part of that. His fellow officers thought he was buying women's clothing for a girlfriend, and that increased his standing as a real man, but in private he was Carmen, posing in front of the mirror, trying to find the mother he had lost. The feel of the soft underwear against his skin soothed him, but the repeated requests from his mates to meet the 'girlfriend' for whom he was seen buying clothes, drove him into marriage.

'So,' breathed Evie. 'Emily. You married Emily.'

'When she found out she was upset. Very upset. She saw me, you see; dressed as Carmen. All she said was: *That's very rude, Colin. Please go and put your own clothes on and don't do that again.* That was it: no discussion. Two weeks later, she left me, taking Lily with her, and I never heard from her again.'

'I'm so sorry. That's really sad. What about Lily? Did you manage to keep in touch with her?'

He smiled then, properly for the first time. 'As soon as she was eighteen she got in touch. She wouldn't come to the house, but we arranged to meet, in town. She didn't know - about the cross-dressing. All her mother had told her was that I had disgusting habits and she couldn't live in the same house as me. I told her right away - didn't demonstrate it that time, mind, but she had no problem with it. I guess youngsters are more open-minded: there are so many things now that my generation would've said weren't normal, but they just take them in their stride.'

When Evie left Mr. Plod's - Colin's - house quite some time later, after more conversation and a second and then a third refilling of the kettle, she wondered whether there might be some awkwardness when they next met, but bumping into him in the corner shop, literally, as she was in a tearing hurry and in need of milk, a few days later, their relationship seemed if anything, much easier. There would be no need to refer again to their talk that day, or to Carmen, but Evie's knowing created a kind of bond, and she felt quite honoured that he had decided to confide in her.

9

Despite appearances, Nature was not in a state of suspended animation. Unknown to Evie, it was already making preparations for the warmer days of spring. The seeds were adjusting to the cold, waiting to be awoken, like Sleeping Beauty, when the first rays of spring sunshine bent to kiss the ground; bulbs were settling down too. They had developed roots to anchor them to the soil, tiny stems ready to rise up into the daylight the moment the spring returned.

But the significance of the garden was much more than that, for it had been formed out of the land that existed long before the people came. They had brought bricks and mortar, iron and steel, and these were strong things, it was true. The people subdued nature, or thought they had, but when the buildings grew old, when the metal was no longer of any use, it was the green and growing things, the life force of the planet that overcame them. When a ploughboy, careless one day of his horse's shoeing, let a shoe fall, it was the land that swallowed it up, closing over it and keeping it until the day Evie found it and claimed it. She would never know his story, for like his whole generation it was engulfed in a war to end all wars – except that it didn't. By the time he was old enough to offer himself for the fighting, the war was almost at an end. He arrived in time for the final stages of that bloodiest of wars; he almost escaped unscathed to return to his fields - for the garden had been pressed into duty for growing food, so great was the need - but in the fatal delay for the signing of the armistice at the symbolic time of the eleventh hour of the eleventh day, his young life was cut short by a sniper's bullet.

On the first day of term Evie slipped out into the garden for a quick look round before school started. A scattering of snowdrops beneath the apple tree was a visual reminder of the light snow that had fallen between Christmas and New Year, keeping her snugly indoors. She checked on her pot of hellebores. Several of the buds had opened out into delicate-looking pale flowers hanging their waxy heads modestly; it was only by bending down and looking up into their faces that she was able to see the crimson splashes of colour near the centre of each. She reflected that the same was true of her neighbours: you had to look closely to see what they were really like. Instinctively, she knew that, although the ground, when she walked on it, was hard and unyielding, down below the soil was warming, tiny roots were flexing, and the hidden life within the bulbs which had lain dormant all winter was beginning to stir. Something was stirring in Evie too, although she would not know it for some time. Plants are like people, in more ways than you might think.

The school building, as she approached it up the hill, slightly out of breath, looked just as it had at the end of term. If anything, the angles and straight lines and harsh concrete looked worse than she'd remembered them. She tried to dispel the dark mood that seemed to be descending, straightening her shoulders and holding her head up. Passing the church, it all came back to her: Christmas Eve, the moment when she realised who Danny was; the moment of feeling she'd been deceived, taken for a ride. The angry cloud enveloped her again.

The day began with a short staff meeting, and then straight into lessons. The Year 9s were half asleep, the Year 10s subdued, and then after break it was time to face Danny's class. She walked in and began the lesson with such anger-fuelled energy that she heard several murmurs along the lines of: *what's got into her?* She had set homework at the end of the previous term, a piece of descriptive writing. Only a third of the class had done it, Danny Desmond surprisingly one of those who had. She barely looked at him as he handed it in triumphantly: it was the first piece of homework he had ever completed for her. Pacing round the room she snatched up the others, berating the whole class into abject silence for their shortcomings, and then set the same task again for them to complete in class, threatening to keep them there until it was finished, however long it took.

'That's not fair, Miss.' It was Kelly, her big earrings quivering; the girl who had got into a fight over Danny, who had rescued him from the knife fight, and been saved from the ignominy of being without her cookery ingredients by Rob. She wasn't just a student anymore, a number in a class; she was a person, someone Evie knew. Rob had told her about Kelly's home circumstances, and Evie realised that she had never known so much about any of the students at Nice School. Was that the fault of the school, or was she herself to blame?

Whatever the case, Evie was still angry with Danny. She ignored Kelly. Eventually the girl raised her hand, quite meekly, for her, and Evie felt obliged to hear her.

'Miss, why are some of us being punished when we did our homework?' There was some general murmuring along the same lines.

'If you've done it once, that's good,' Evie conceded. 'Now you can do it again, but better this time. And you have no business complaining, Wayne,' she snapped at the lumpy boy on the front row, nor you, Sharon, nor you, nor you...' Wayne and the others were serial non-homework doers.

Once they were quiet she simply pointed out that the more practice they had at this type of writing, the better prepared they would be for their exam. She added as an afterthought that it also meant she had extra marking, as though that somehow made it right. How had it come to this? Where had all her early idealism gone? She had always believed that young people responded best to encouragement, that making a positive relationship was the first step in successful teaching - and here she was, making enemies of the very people she was here to help.

There was relative quiet for some time. One or two of the more serious students raised their hands to ask questions, and she went across to their desks to answer them. Then Danny raised his hand.

'Yes?' she said, realising she sounded almost aggressive.

'I was just wondering: is descriptive writing more powerful if it's prose or poetry?'

She couldn't work out what trick he was trying to play. 'Just get on with it, Danny.'

When the bell went for lunch there was the usual stampede for the door. Evie collected in the work, giving each one a cursory glance. Some were brief, but she decided none was so brief as to merit a detention, and besides, she really didn't want to spend her first lunchtime back sitting in the classroom with disgruntled students. She dismissed the class, and they filed out with their bundles of belongings, bags and coats. It felt as if she'd hardly been away, even though the Christmas break was two weeks' long. As she gathered her own things up, she became aware that Danny was still at his desk, not in his usual slouching posture, but sitting upright, scribbling furiously.

'Didn't you hear the bell?'

He looked up and gave her a funny little half smile. 'I wanted to finish this.'

'It's all right. You did hand in a piece of homework,' she said grudgingly. 'You don't have to do any more.'

'I'd still like to finish this.'

'Oh for goodness sake, Danny, stop being perverse! Just go and have your lunch! Go!'

In slow motion he banged down his pen on the desk, stood, kicked his chair back against the wall, picked up the sheet of paper, and, looking directly at her, screwed the sheet of paper into a tight ball. Then he walked to the front of the room and dropped it theatrically into the waste paper basket. It was only after he'd left the room, slamming the door behind him, that she realised he'd left his things beside his desk. She supposed she'd have to look after them now. Sighing as she gathered up his bag and coat in addition to her own bag and laptop, she headed for the staffroom. Danny's things would be safe there, and he'd have to come and find her if he wanted them.

'You look as if you could do with a strong cup of coffee,' said Rob, as she sank into an armchair. He went across to the little kitchen area and returned with a mug. 'Milk, no sugar. Right?'

'Thank you. You're a lifesaver!' She gulped at the hot liquid and then set it down, sighing. 'Do you ever wish you could go back and start the day again?'

'Far too often! What is it you wish you'd done differently?'

'Everything.' Evie realised she didn't have the energy to explain the whole Danny Desmond thing. 'Ignore me; I'm just suffering from beginning-of-term-itis.' A number of other staff members came in at that point, and Evie let the general exchanges about Christmas and holidays and difficult journeys wash over her while she drank her coffee.

'By the way, Rob,' said one of the other teachers, 'I've just seen the Desmond boy heading towards the lane.' The lane was the area adjacent to the school where the smokers went to be undetected, unaware that they brought the smell of tobacco back into school clinging to their clothes and hair. 'Something's upset him. Again.'

'Oh, that's me, I'm afraid,' Evie groaned.

'Oh, he's yours, is he? Lucky you!' The speaker turned away in response to a comment from another colleague, and Evie was left feeling unsure whether she was expected to do something about it.

'So it was Danny who reduced you to a trembling wreck on the first day back at school,' said Rob, jovially enough. 'What happened?'

'That might be putting it a bit strongly, but... oh, this is going to sound ridiculous, but he had done his homework and then wanted to stay after the bell had gone to finish his class work.'

'Dear me! Now that is a problem!'

'Don't tease me, Rob. I handled it really badly.'

'What was the work he was so intent on finishing?'

'I don't know, It's in the bin.'

Evie had a double lesson with her Year 13 class in the afternoon. They were still struggling with a detailed textual analysis of the first book of Paradise Lost, and after a lively discussion on Milton's inverted syntax and the reasons he might have had for it, she sounded them out about the proposed theatre trip. They were warm in their enthusiasm, and touchingly grateful, although there was some concern about the cost of theatre tickets. Evie promised to see what she could do.

'Right, then I'll check the date with Mr. Greenwood and we'll get it booked!' She felt a surge of energy within the room, and a palpable sense of concentration pervaded the rest of the lesson, so that several of them jumped when the bell rang.

As the last of the group left, the crumpled sheet in the waste paper basket caught Evie's eye, and all her good humour evaporated. Should she? She decided that she ought to, and stooped slowly to pick it up. The first thing she noticed as she began smoothing it out was that it was well set out on the page, with punctuation and paragraphs. She had seen so little of his work that this was a surprise. The handwriting was legible, too, and in fact quite pleasant to look at, although it deteriorated as she turned over the page, and realised with a pang that he had been trying desperately to finish whatever it was that he was so keen to get down. It began: *Descriptive Writing: Black is for Funerals.* A strange topic for a teenager to choose, and not quite what Evie had had in mind when she'd set the piece of work and suggested they base their description around a colour. She took a deep breath and decided to read it later.

Back in the staffroom some of her colleagues were settling down to mark piles of exercise books, while others were offloading their frustrations with the teaching profession.

'If I'm asked for one more set of data...'

'Do you know, I spent half my Christmas break on paperwork and no time for actually preparing to teach?'

'It's only going to get worse...'

Evie's first instinct was to flee, but she remembered that Danny's belongings were hanging on her peg, and felt obliged to wait for him to come and reclaim them. Making yet another cup of strong coffee, she found herself a relatively quiet corner and turned her chair away from the general hubbub. Several students came and went, knocking peremptorily on the staffroom door and making her jump each time, but no Danny. She decided to use the waiting time to read his work.

Descriptive Writing: The Colour Black

The day began with sunshine. That was all wrong: it should have been raining. The sky should have been black. At 10.45 precisely the undertakers arrived, all dressed the same, with the same expression on their faces. They ushered my mum and me out of the house and into the long black car. It was polished so that you could see your face in it, but it wasn't like looking in a mirror. Everything it reflected looked dark, and that was right, because that was how we felt.

Evie glanced up. The normal hubbub was going on around her, but she felt totally detached; she had entered a strange world, in which a student's work was powerful enough to send shivers down her back. Where had he got the ideas from? They had discussed using visual imagery based on colour in the lesson before Christmas, but she had not expected anything so macabre. She forced herself to read on.

The men carried the coffin on their shoulders. I thought it looked heavy and I felt sorry for them. It was better than feeling sorry for myself. The walk up the path was the longest I've ever known. Mum was holding herself so straight, but her hand on my arm was trembling.

In the church everyone's voices sounded different, as though they were speaking through a blanket. People coughed and shuffled their feet and looked the other way. Then it started, and I stood up and sat down when everyone else did, and it didn't feel real.

This was amazing. How had Danny of all people managed to express himself with such sensitivity? Perhaps he had been to a funeral at some point? But even so, to imagine himself inside the heads of the mourners…

Another knock on the door, and a voice.

'Danny Desmond here for you, Miss Symmonds. Do you want to see him?'

She hurried over to the door. 'Danny, I've been reading your work -'

'Have you got my bag, Miss?' The tone was aggressive, or perhaps just defensive. 'Have you got it? I left it in the classroom. And my coat.'

No use trying to talk to him in this mood. She went and got his things and he took them with a slight nod of the head and was gone.

At home, after a hastily prepared meal and a glass of wine, which she felt she'd earned, Evie forced herself to sit down at the kitchen table where it was still warm and attack the evening's marking. She picked up and put down again the

Year Twelve essays on Paradise Lost, set aside the grubby Year 9 exercise books, and finally turned to the pile of paper from Year 11. There was a small pile of actual homework, and then a larger pile from that morning. Evie sighed again. What had made her get the term off to such a bad start? She remembered how angry she'd been about Danny and felt a renewed surge of anger: all this time he had been pretending to be what he wasn't, some sort of deprived tough kid, when in fact... Strictly speaking, though, he hadn't hidden his identity, had he? She had just made assumptions. Now she was confused by his writing. It was clearly his own: he had done it in the classroom in front of her, without help, and yet it didn't sound remotely like him. She took another sip of wine and turned to the Year 11 pile. Wayne had written

I like the colour red it is my favrite mybedroom is red and my best football team weres red and I

and that was it, apart from a lot of crossing out and some doodles. Evie wondered what she was doing. What kind of a teacher was she when she had done nothing for Wayne despite her efforts and Danny could write perfectly well without any input from her? And why wasn't the school doing anything about his truanting, she wondered irrelevantly. She wasn't going to take the whole blame herself. Sensing that she was in danger of working herself up into an even greater turmoil, she took a few deep breaths and fished out Danny's Christmas holiday homework. It was set out as a poem.

The Colour of Grief

Dull, like tarnished silver, grey;

Tears on a wet window pane,

Heavy like a rainy day

Muddy puddles down a dismal lane.

Someone you love is there no more

Their pain is gone but yours remains.

Between you a locked and bolted door

While outside it rains and rains and rains.

White, the colour of faces you love

White light in an empty sky

Uncaring clouds drifting high above

The silent neighbours passing by.

Doctors in white, nurses in blue

Red the blood, the pain, the death

Everything hurts, nothing is true

All colour gone with his final breath.

Evie sat for several long minutes, stunned. This was no artifice. The writing was remarkable for a sixteen-year-old boy, and he was without doubt expressing real feelings. Who had he lost? Clearly someone close. Was the piece he had been writing that morning, when she had stopped him so harshly, about an actual funeral, perhaps that of the missing father she had despised?

There was no way she could do any more work that night. She moved instinctively towards the back door and stepped through into the darkened garden. Although the days had begun to lengthen perceptibly, it was far too late for daylight, and she felt rather than saw the trees at the far end, the hellebores, the tiny shoots that held a promise of spring. What shoots of hope did Danny have?

When she spotted Danny in the distance next morning, Evie breathed a sigh of relief. She would find a way to speak to him today if it was the last thing she did, perhaps at the end of the lesson, but when he entered the classroom hunched and avoiding eye contact, she felt herself wavering. Her voice sounded brittle in her own ears as she prattled on about writing to persuade and the various techniques they could use, suggesting a debate as a way of getting into the subject; she could feel his heavy physical presence at the back of the room and his total mental absence. The bell rang at last and the class filed out, with only a few scuffles as they crammed together at the doorway. Danny remained seated, still staring at his desk. He had taken no part at all in the lesson.

Carefully she took out the creased pages of his work, holding them out towards him.

'Danny…' she began.

'You read it?' He looked up at her then, and she wanted to cry at the naked pain in his eyes.

'Yes,' she said quietly. 'And I thought your writing was really good, powerful. You have expressed your real feelings, and I was very moved by them.' She waited, keeping very still. At last, he spoke, in a strange, broken voice that she had never heard from him before.

'When he died - my dad - my uncle Jim said to me I had to be the man of the house now.' He turned towards her and she could see the tears glistening. 'I don't know how to be.' The tears fell, unimpeded, and neither of them spoke for some time. Then he sniffed and wiped his nose on his sleeve. Seeing Evie wince he managed a watery smile. 'My mum tells me off for doing that.'

'I'm not going to tell you off, Danny. Do you want to tell me some more about it?'

Danny had been twelve when his dad was diagnosed with a terminal illness. He'd just started secondary school, and his mum was in her first curacy. They'd moved there for her job, to live in the curate's house. It didn't matter to his dad where they lived. He worked with computers and could work anywhere. All this Danny told her while staring out of the window. Then he faced her again.

'I'm useless at all that IT stuff. Must have been such a disappointment to him.'

'I can't imagine that. IT might not be your best subject, but you are good at writing. Surely he'd have been proud of you for that.'

The boy shook his head. 'I was fourteen when he died, just started my GCSE courses. Then Mum - well, it was hard for her, so, she, well she ended up moving. They wanted a vicar here. So we moved.' His face contorted. 'We moved away from all the places we'd been with Dad. When I'd just about made friends, we moved here, to this place. I didn't know anyone; they all had their friends already - the syllabuses were all different. I looked like a right dumbo.'

'But you're not, Danny, are you? You are intelligent and sensitive and you can write powerful words.' She let that sink in. 'What would you like to do in the Sixth Form?'

At that crucial moment there was a respectful tap on the door and the school secretary entered.

'I'm sorry to interrupt, Miss Symmonds. 'There's a phone call for you.'

'Could you find out who it is and tell them I'll phone back? I'm rather busy at the moment.'

'No, I think you'd better come now. It's your mother.'

10

It seemed to Evie that she hadn't properly drawn a breath between her mother's anxious phone call and the moment she swung into a parking space at the hospital. Rob had been very understanding and told her she must go right away. It would be signed off as compassionate leave and they could sort out the paperwork on her return.

'Just one thing,' he said, as she left his office. 'Drive carefully and make sure you and your mum eat something tonight.'

She pocketed the little yellow token that popped out of the machine at the barrier. The car park was crammed full and she'd been lucky to find a space at all. Her mum would have arrived in the ambulance, some hours ago now, and it was already almost dark. She hadn't stopped on the road to phone, anxious not to lose time. Now she was here, and she had time to wonder what was happening. She wasn't even sure where to go. The main entrance was probably the one, she thought, striding with head and shoulders leading the way.

'Symmonds? Just a moment. I'll check.' The receptionist turned back to her computer screen, clicked the keyboard a bit, whizzed her eyes back and forth, and then turned back to Evie. 'Are you a relative? Yes? OK then, he's in ICU. You need to turn right at the double doors, follow the main corridor as far as the lifts, then when you get to the second floor you'll find it's clearly signposted.'

Evie thanked her and set off at a run. Trollies and wheelchairs passed her, pushed by invisible porters; nurses streamed purposefully past. Other members of the public, like her, looked lost and out of place. Up on the second floor she hesitated, then located the signs directing her to ICU. She broke into a sort of lolloping run, and arrived out of breath at the nurses' station. The search for her father's name on the computer was quicker this time, and she found herself being directed to a door with glass panels in the upper half and a large notice requesting anyone who entered to use the hand sanitizer before doing so. She complied hastily and pushed open the door.

At first she couldn't make out her father. There were four patients altogether, each anonymous in their cat's cradle of wires. Machines bleeped and flashed at each of the beds, and it was only when she saw that her mother was seated beside the bed furthest from the door that she knew her father. His nose and mouth were covered with an oxygen mask, and his thick white hair was spread about his head on the pillow. She had never seen him so pale, and she stopped in her tracks. Her mother lifted her head, and Evie was shocked at how ill she looked.

'Oh Mum!'

'Evie!'

They fell into each other's arms, gripping each other tightly.

'I'm so sorry I didn't come home for Christmas. I should have done, but I was tired...' Evie's voice trailed off as her mother released her slightly from her grip to stand back and look at her.

'It's OK.' Mrs. Symmonds stroked her daughter's face, soothingly. 'It's OK. There wasn't anything you could have done...'

Evie frowned. 'Did you know that he was ill?' She remembered her mother's unwillingness to talk on the phone, the sense that she was distracted.

'He hasn't been properly well for some time, but I couldn't put my finger on what it was.' She looked Evie squarely in the face. 'I certainly had no idea he was heading for a heart attack.'

'So what's happening? What do they say? What's the prognosis?' Evie's voice rose in a crescendo of alarm.

'We can go and talk to the doctor in a bit. They said to go and find someone when you got here.'

Suddenly realising how tired she was, Evie sat heavily in the second of the chairs beside the bed, and her mother resumed her own seat. Both women sat and gazed at the unconscious man for some time without speaking.

A nurse appeared silently from somewhere, bearing a tray. On it were two mugs and a plate of buttered toast. 'Best I can do at this time of night, I'm afraid,' she said in a low voice, offering it to each of them in turn. Evie thanked her with tears in her eyes.

'Yes,' her mother said after the nurse had gone. 'They've been so kind. Really kind.' She too was crying, silently, the tears running down her face unheeded. Evie leaned over awkwardly, balancing her mug, and gave her mum's shoulder a squeeze.

'You know Dad,' she said, with far more certainty than she felt. 'He'll be all right. He's tough as old boots.'

Some time later - Evie had lost all sense of time - they went to the nurses' station and were directed to an office where a weary-looking doctor explained that a myocardial infarction is a serious medical emergency and that Mrs. Symmonds' prompt action in recognising the symptoms and calling an ambulance right away, and then administering aspirin while she waited for its arrival, had probably saved Mr. Symmonds' life.'

'So he's going to be all right?' Evie asked.

'It's a little early to say what the eventual outcome will be. We need to monitor him and run some more tests.' He looked up at their anxious faces. 'But he is in the best possible place,' he added. 'I'd advise you to go on home and get some rest now.' Seeing their reluctance, he promised that they would be contacted if there was the least change.

Afterwards Evie couldn't remember driving back to her parents' house. She must have been in some sort of mild hypnotic trance, she concluded the next morning after a restless night. They had arrived back at the house, shivering, long after the central heating had switched itself off. The house bore all the signs of the morning's hasty departure, and her mother made no effort to straighten the random articles that had been scattered in her panic. Evie went into the kitchen and put on a pan of milk for some cocoa, and they drank it in exhausted silence.

In her childhood bedroom, so familiar and yet so alien, Evie tossed and turned and asked herself all sorts of questions beginning with 'what if...?' Her whole life was being continually turned upside down and she wondered how much more she could take. This room held the secrets of her adolescent fears and fantasies; it reminded her of how much she and her mother had lived in her father's shadow; how much she had wanted to live up to his principles, and how she had felt a failure because she couldn't. His was a forceful personality, and she could see now how he had needed to be like that to achieve all the things that he had. Other people had always been full of praise for him, and it was she, Evie, who had struggled to understand why. All she knew now was that she didn't want him to die.

At the hospital next morning - there had been no telephone call in the night - they were greeted by a smiling doctor, a different one from the night before. The sight that greeted them in the ward was also strikingly different from the previous night: most of the wires and machines had gone, and her father was propped up against the pillows, his eyes open. While her mother wept tears of relief over her husband, who told her, characteristically, not to fuss, Evie went to speak to the doctor.

'He's a strong man, your father,' he said. 'There is every cause for optimism, although we can't rule out complications further down the line. However, he will need to observe some changes to his lifestyle.'

'He won't like that,' Evie laughed.

Both her parents agreed that there was no need for Evie to stay any longer than the time she needed in order to rest before her journey back up North. Reluctantly, she agreed, knowing that there was, strictly speaking, no further justification for compassionate leave, and that the missed lessons and the work as a consequence of that would be piling up back at school. She also caught herself wondering how her garden was faring, even though she knew there was little to do out there at this time of year. Her parents had one of those classic, semi-detached gardens, lawn and shrubs requiring minimum effort. Her father was recovering remarkably quickly, and she felt as cheerful as she looked as she kissed him goodbye before setting off home.

It was late on Friday when Evie drew up outside her house in Other Place. Three front doors opened almost simultaneously. Her neighbours had noticed the missing car and absence of lights in the little house and they had been worried that something had happened to her. Colin asked a few questions and, seemingly satisfied, went back indoors. Rose, seeing that Evie was in one piece, closed her door, and Molly tried very hard to make her a cup of tea, but Evie insisted she just needed to go to bed. Once between the sheets, however, she found she couldn't sleep, and scenes from the hospital replayed themselves over and over, until she finally dozed a little just as daylight was breaking.

She spent the weekend in and out of the garden, not really doing anything but just wandering about, observing nature. As ever she felt soothed just by being there, and in the face of near death, the sight of living things beginning to push up through the hard soil reassured her more than all the words of the doctors had done. Somehow, life would continue. Things would be different from now on. She would prove herself to her father, make him proud. She would become the teacher he had wanted her to be.

On Monday morning Evie plodded up the hill to school, mentally running through the day's lessons, trying to repair in her head the rupture in time between last week and now. As she came to the Year 11 class in her run through she remembered with shame how bad-tempered she'd been with them, and then the surprising conversation with Danny. She was trying to leave aside the frightening events that followed, the phone call in the school office with her mother's panicked voice on the other end of the line, the dash up the motorway... She reached the school gates and headed up to the staffroom, where all was kind questions and murmurs of sympathy.

Somehow the day rolled on as she mechanically taught the use of prepositions and connectives to the Year 9s, stumbled through *Lord of the Flies* with Year 10 and fielded questions about the progress of plans for their theatre trip from year 13. During her free period she sat in her classroom staring out of the window with her marking in front of her. She would have to explain to the Year 11s why she hadn't marked their descriptive writing. The bell rang and the sound of restive teenagers outside her door penetrated her thoughts.

'Can we come in, Miss?' One of the students, a girl, had opened the door and even as she asked the question the surge of bodies behind her swept her into the room. Evie gave what she hoped was an encouraging smile. Spotting Danny looming over the heads of the others she was relieved to think that he would now be able to engage in her lessons and that they finally understood each other.

By the end of the lesson Evie had been disabused of this hope, and felt all the old exasperation rising up until it nearly choked her. The boy sat in his usual place in his usual posture, slouched low in his seat; his head remained stubbornly turned away from her. When another student tried to speak to him Danny muttered angrily, without turning to face the other boy, and Evie's attempts to gain his attention were completely disregarded. She felt as though the whole class was watching her, waiting for some great showdown, which she was determined not to give them. As the lesson ground to a halt Evie walked round the room to collect in the homework set in her absence the previous week. When she reached Danny he remained morosely staring out of the window.

'Danny?' No response. 'Danny! Do you have some work to hand in? Please?' Finally, with some huffing and puffing, he shifted his position until he was half-turned towards her. Only then did she see the closed eye, the cuts and bruises on his face. There was a pause which seemed to last for ever, and then Evie was literally saved by the school bell.

'OK. Off you go,' she said to the rest of the class, who didn't need telling twice. Evie remained where she stood. Danny also remained, slumped in his chair. When they were alone she asked, 'What happened, Danny?' He heaved himself out of his chair and stood looking down on her, and she saw that there were more contusions on his neck.

'*You* happened. You come in here all bright and breezy, you get me to show you...' He hesitated. 'Show you...stuff... how I feel and that...'

'It can be helpful to talk about your feelings, Danny, even if they are painful.' Evie was unsure of her ground. 'Perhaps we can find you someone to talk to, a professional counsellor.' Did Other School have a counsellor? She'd never heard talk of one, but there were counsellors aplenty at Nice School to help the Sixth Form girls with anorexia and the little boys in Year 5 who were away from home for the first time.

'Yeah?' said Danny scathingly. 'And how's that going to stop people doing this to me, eh?' He gestured towards his battered face. 'You want to know what happened? You got me to write stuff down - how I was feeling - you got me thinking maybe I ain't so bad after all, could get in the Sixth Form and stuff - then you go off and answer the phone and you don't come back for days.'

Evie was torn between compassion for the young man who had felt abandoned by her - as he had felt, perhaps, abandoned by the father who had died and the mother who had been absent in a world of her own grief, and a stern voice in her head (Mr. HOD's?) which told her sharply she should not allow a student to speak to her like that. She mentally told Mr. HOD to clear off out of her head and told Danny what really happened.

'It was my mother on the phone. My father had had a heart attack. It looked like it was touch and go. But I'm sorry I let you down, Danny.'

The boy absorbed this information. 'Oh, I see,' he mumbled, and sniffed a bit.

'But who did this to you, Danny?'

'Doesn't matter who. They've had it in for me for ages.' He looked her full in the eyes.

'You left my writing on the desk when you ran off. They saw it - saw that I'd been writing…stuff, about feelings and that.' He raised his voice, making Evie jump. 'You don't *do* that around here. You got to be tough.'

He moved away and began pacing in the space at the back of the classroom. Turning back to her, he shrugged. 'I got jumped on my way home, that's all.'

'Oh Danny, I'm so sorry.' He gave a grim little smile, wincing as he did so. The cuts and bruises were clearly troubling him.

' 'S'all right, Miss. Should've seen the other guys!'

As January gave way to February the weather brightened, but one morning Evie

awoke early, shivering a little. It had turned unexpectedly cold, and looking out of her kitchen window as she made breakfast, she saw that her garden was covered with the little crystalline needles of a heavy frost. Slipping into her wellies she opened the back door and was confronted with a magical scene: every plant, every shrub, every blade of grass was outlined in silver.

Her initial sense of wonder was quickly followed by anxiety: would her plants recover? Already the heads of unsuspected daffodils and crocuses were pushing their way up from beneath the earth, and she was sure she had seen signs of tight little leaf buds on the fruit trees. There was even a bank of primroses along the outer edge of the fence. What if all those things withered and there was no spring in her garden that year - her only year here, her only chance to witness Seth's creation? She had been to visit him a number of times since her initial trip with Molly, and returned each time soothed and inspired by talk of the processes of nature. But what if his legacy were destroyed?

The term rumbled on, with Danny sometimes compliant, sometimes sulky and occasionally absent. Evie spoke to Rob about him and was referred to the Year 11 pastoral head, Benji, the resident doom monger, who offered to talk to him, although Evie was worried that Danny would be angry to be spoken about. She didn't go into all the details, but expressed a strong view that the boy needed counselling. Benji laughed mirthlessly.

'We don't have enough money for text books, let alone counsellors! Only hope is for him to go to his GP and get put on a waiting list... with the emphasis on wait.'

Dashed by his negativity - he would probably have called it 'being realistic' - Evie asked what other processes were in place in the school for students with emotional needs.

'Well, sometimes a kick up the backside helps! It's OK, I'm joking,' he added quickly, seeing Evie's face. 'Although that boy's been nothing but trouble since he arrived in Year 10 with an attitude a mile high.' He leaned towards Evie and asked, in a quieter tone of voice, 'Have you heard of the Grafton Street gang?' When she shook her head, he continued. 'Not a very nice lot, to say the least. Young Danny's got in with the wrong types; he's that desperate to belong.'

Evie sighed helplessly. She understood all too well the need to belong; she had felt it with a passion at Nice School, even though it had eluded her. Now she was in another place where she didn't belong, except... at the edge of her consciousness something stirred, something she couldn't yet identify, and it had something to do with belonging.

As she was preparing to leave the room, Benji said, 'I suppose you've spoken to the mother?'

As the weather warmed, the frosted primroses lay crumpled against the black earth. Evie found herself in tears, and wondered why. Was she really crying over some dead flowers? Or was it only now that she could fully recognise the fear she had felt when her father had sustained his heart attack? She felt horribly guilty that she hadn't made the effort to spend Christmas with them, but even as she thought this, she knew that her Christmas in Other Place had been something special, something she wouldn't have wanted to miss. Scenes of the Christmas Fayre flashed through her mind; Molly's Father Christmas hat and the hideous baubles knitted with love; Rose allowing herself to be coaxed from her house; Colin and his touching gift of hellebores. They, at least, had weathered the winter.

Danny's lack of engagement in class - when he was even there - continued to worry her, and so it was that Evie found herself, unaccountably nervous, heading for the Vicarage after school one afternoon, soon after her unsatisfactory conversation with Benji. She hadn't had a lesson with the Year 11s that day, so didn't know whether Danny had even been in school.

The Vicarage was round the corner from the church, tucked away in a little side road, and as Evie approached the gate she could see that the house - redbrick to match the church - was set a long way back, with a large expanse of garden in front. Even so early in the season it was alive with shrubs and trees falling over each other to reach the light, with whole drifts of daffodils, some past their best, and everywhere new life bursting out of the soil, fresh and green and full of promise. Her spirits lifted, and the feeling was given a further boost when the vicar appeared from around the corner of the house dressed in paint-spattered jeans, a threadbare jumper several sizes too large and heavy duty gloves. She was carrying a trowel and a very business-like pair of secateurs.

'Oh Lord! You've caught me out!' she sang out cheerfully. 'So sorry, Evie. This was the only slot in my week for getting rid of some of the heavy growth around the back.' Evie registered that the vicar had remembered her name, decided she felt pleased, although she supposed an ability to remember names went with the job, a bit like hers, and said, doubtfully,

'I'm so sorry - I should have rung first. I was hoping for a quick word about Danny, but this obviously isn't a good time…'

'Nonsense - come in and I'll put the kettle on to boil while I get out of my gardening clothes.'

'They look as though they're your painting clothes too.' Evie indicated the paint splashes, some of which were a soft salmon pink. 'That's a pretty colour.'

'My pink boudoir? Oh yes. Essential to have somewhere restful at the end of the day.' Any further conversation was drowned out by the sound of water swishing into the kettle.

Evie took a seat over by the window and found herself looking out onto a very overgrown area of the garden which the vicar must have been busy trying to clear. She could hear her clattering up the stairs, taking them two at a time. She wondered idly if Danny ever helped with the gardening.

The kitchen itself was what might be expected in a house of this age. Its appearance was somewhere between shabby and homely, and there was evidence all around of generous hospitality: the mega-sized box of tea-bags (fair trade, of course) and catering size coffee tin. Shelves along the far wall held a staggering number of mugs, while others, still with the dregs of cold coffee from some meeting or other, stood on the worktops. An appetising smell was drifting her way from the oven: Danny could obviously look forward to a good meal when he got home.

The kettle was just reaching boiling point and Evie was wondering whether she should do something with it, when the vicar reappeared, looking trim in a neat pair of clean trousers and black shirt. She had not yet inserted the strip of white plastic in the empty slot at the collar.

'I've a PCC meeting later,' she said, 'So I thought I might as well get into uniform. Tea or coffee?'

They sat at one end of the kitchen table with their mugs: the other end was piled high with the stuff of daily vicarage life. The vicar saw Evie looking at the clutter of books, papers, kitchen implements and plates, and apologised.

'No, I understand. Life's too busy,' Evie smiled.

'So, Evie. You wanted to talk about Danny?'

Evie took a deep breath. 'Yes, Mrs. Desmond…'

'Oh please, call me Barbie!'

A vicar called Barbie? Evie couldn't imagine ever calling her that, but nodded in response.

'He's obviously having a hard time at school, and in general.'

Barbie nodded.

'I'm his English teacher.'

'I know.' Evie looked at her in surprise. She hadn't imagined that Danny ever spoke about school when he was at home.

'You're the only teacher he really talks about.'

'Oh, really?' Evie felt her eyebrows shoot up in surprise. 'Well I happen to think he has some real potential in my subject. I'd like to see him doing A Level English next year.'

Barbie absorbed the information.

'You know, since we moved here my expectations have been lowered where Danny is concerned. I think I'd be happy if he just turned up at school every day, and possibly did his homework occasionally.'

'Oh, so... so you know about the truanting?' Edie asked tentatively. The emotional temperature in the kitchen had dropped a bit, and she wasn't sure why.

Barbie was biting her lip. 'I suppose you're here to tell me what a bad parent I am?'

Horrified, Evie quickly assured her that wasn't the case.

'No, look, I'm fond of Danny.' She was surprised to hear herself say this, but supposed it must be true. Ever since their first meeting there had been a kind of connection there. On the other hand, if she ever had children of her own - which she wasn't sure she even wanted - she would like them to be a little less complicated.

'I'm also concerned. I think he needs help, more help than the school seems able to give him just now.'

'I'm not blind, Evie. I know he's no angel; I know he feels neglected. I'm not there for him as much as I should be -- ' At that moment Barbie's phone rang. It sounded like the theme from Star Wars: a strange ring tone for a vicar, Evie thought.

'Yes? Oh right. Don't worry, that's covered on the agenda. No, look, we'll discuss it this evening...' The tone was firmer than Evie had heard Barbie use before. She stood to leave.

'I'm sorry about that. And I'm sorry I've not been able to be more positive, but if you think Danny is capable of doing A Levels, then I'm grateful to know that.'

'And I'm sorry if you thought I was coming here to criticise. Truly I wasn't.'

The phone rang again and Barbie gave Evie a rueful smile. 'You see how it is?' she murmured, picking it up.

'I'll see myself out', said Evie.

It was unusually cold for much longer than is normal at that time of year. Day after day Evie roused herself from her bed, drew back the curtains, and beheld a world carpeted in crisp, gleaming white. In the freezing mist the trees were ghosts of themselves, and later, after she'd gone downstairs and ventured out to say good morning to her garden, she was shocked each time to see her precious hellebores with heads bent low to the ground, defeated by the frost. As the day wore on, though, she noticed their spines uncurling, and with the sun at its zenith, shining misleadingly from an icy blue sky, little by little they regained their upright stance. Unconsciously, she straightened her own shoulders, raising her chin defiantly to face the day.

Then at half term it snowed. Evie woke early to the eerie light that comes with a heavy snowfall. Looking out she could see that the town had been transformed. In place of redbrick and raw ugliness she saw mysterious outlines, softened by a good few inches of snow. The rows of street houses, ranged up the incline on each side of the road, were strangers now in their white covering. It was too early for it to have been churned up by passing footprints and she wondered what her garden looked like in this perfect state.

Going downstairs she grabbed her wellies from the understairs cupboard, deftly pushing back the ironing board dislodged in the process, and headed on out. There she caught her breath. This was another Alice in Wonderland transformation. She might have been anywhere, even back in the lush Cotswolds countryside, but even as she thought this, she knew it wasn't true. When it snowed in Nice Place the sense of transformation was so much less. The countryside there was beautiful always, affluent and tamed, predictable. Snow in such a place meant inconvenience: isolation, no gritted roads, no buses.... but here she had seen the town looking beautiful for the first time, seeing from her bedroom window features outlined in white that she'd never seen before. It made her think of Danny and his mum. There was so much that wasn't visible until seen in a different light.

The snow was still falling and Evie shivered a little in her dressing gown. She remembered that she was in need of groceries and had been planning to do a supermarket shop this week. That was likely to be out of the question: she was nervous of driving in the snow. The joy of living here, though, was that she could easily walk to the nearest shops, indeed she would enjoy it. She showered and dressed quickly, and went into the kitchen to have a quick breakfast. While the kettle boiled she stood at the window, gazing out into her transformed garden, half mesmerised by the downward drift of the large, fluttering snowflakes.

By the time she was togged up in her warmest coat, with extra socks and warm scarf and gloves, the quality of the snow had changed and a strong wind had got up. Tiny particles of snow were driving into her face like icy needles and making her wince. She pulled her hood tighter round her face and as an afterthought tied her scarf over it and covered her nose and mouth, protecting her from the weather, but making breathing a bit difficult, so that she was even more breathless by the time she reached the top of the hill.

Back from her trip with all the essentials she could carry, Evie warmed up some soup and stood gazing out of the window while she waited for it. In the bare branches of a tree sat a robin, its red breast fluffed up against the cold and reminding her of the baubles she had hung in the trees at Christmas. Being made of wool, they had suffered a bit when it rained, but Molly had cheerfully said not to mind, because she could easily knit her some more next year. Evie didn't say then that she wouldn't be there for another Christmas, but thinking about it now made her sad.

With a pang of conscience she realised that Molly would not find it as easy as she had to trudge up the hill to the shops, and she walked the few paces to the scarlet front door in her wellies to see if the old lady was in need of anything. Colin opened his door a crack when he heard her knocking.

'Gone to help out at the homeless shelter, she has,' he informed her. 'Vicar took her.'

'Goodness, I hope they'll be all right.' Evie felt more ashamed than ever, and a little unsure what to do next. 'I came to see if she needed anything from the shops. What about you? I can walk up there easily if you need anything.'

He looked at her, surprised. 'That's kind of you, Lass, but I reckon I've got all I

need. What about that one, though?' He jabbed a thumb in the direction of the fourth house. She doesn't go out. I reckon she might need something.'

'Good thinking. I'll go round there as soon as I've had my lunch.'

It was much later, after she'd eaten and washed up and put the shopping away and generally pottered around, before Evie got herself organised to go round to Rose's. She hadn't seen her since Christmas Day, and truth to tell hadn't even given her a thought. She was a little ashamed that she'd needed reminding that she might need help, and she was also a little nervous about how to approach the fragile young woman.

There was no response to her repeated knocking, and she was just wondering what to do when Colin came and joined her.

'Can you hear anything?'

Evie shook her head. 'I don't think anyone's been to see her for days, with the weather so bad. There are no tyre marks on the road.'

'Hm.' Colin thought for a moment. 'I'm not sure I've seen any lights on either, now I come to think of it.'

'Should we…do you think we should break in?'

'You're asking an ex-policeman to break into someone's house?

'This door's a bit loose…I reckon it would give with a shove.'

Colin said, 'Hm' again. 'Wait a minute.' He bent down and peered through the letterbox.

'Rose! Rose, Love, are you there? Speak to me, Rose.'

It was very still; the sounds of the street were far away and muffled. From the house they heard nothing, not a single rustle or creak. Colin looked again through the letterbox.

'Ah,' he said. 'I see. Can you go and call 999 Evie?'

11

It was the second half of the spring term and at last the weather showed some signs of spring, and although Rose, now settled in the Forrester Centre, wasn't seeing visitors, Evie had at least been able to take some spring flowers for her. Since the treatment wasn't medical in the physical sense, they didn't seem to worry about infection in the same way they did in the main hospital (she'd made that mistake with her father on her second visit) Rose's front door had been repaired - the police had been quite careful when they arrived, closely followed by an ambulance. Evie wondered what it would take to repair Rose herself.

It seemed ridiculous, now, that she had been so worried about the hellebores when they disappeared beneath a deep covering of snow. She had wondered if they would ever again raise their heads, but, incredibly, they had, and all the other flowers with them were still there, peeping out at her as though they had been tucked up in fluffy white blankets all along - which, come to think of it, they had. She hoped Rose would emerge from her ordeal in the same way, but she knew very little about agoraphobia.

She bumped into Barbie in the post office.

'How was your half term break?' the vicar asked.

'Very quiet,' Evie said, truthfully. 'I gather you were busy, with the homeless shelter and everything?'

'Yes, it was certainly no time to be sleeping rough. We were lucky though - despite the weather we had enough volunteers, and the council did their bit as well. Your neighbour, Molly, is a star. She cooked non-stop all week, and she kept everyone cheerful with her stories about the old days.'

'She does so much for other people,' Evie sighed, feeling inadequate. 'She's involved in everything.'

'Well, it works both ways, of course. She helps others and helping others helps her not to feel lonely.'

'Molly? Lonely?' It had never occurred to Evie.

'And you other neighbour, Rose. She seems to be making progress according to the chaplain at the Forrester Centre.'

'Is she? That's good. They won't let me in to see her.'

'No, well, I think that's standard in these cases.' In answer to Evie's quizzical look, she added: 'Her medical history is quite complicated.' We're all so thankful you found her when you did - she could have died of hypothermia - or starvation.'

'I should have gone round much sooner.' Evie sighed.

'Don't beat yourself up over it. It's very hard to help someone like Rose. And don't forget, you managed to get her to the Christmas dinner - first time she'd been out of the house for nearly two years.'

Now it was back to hard work and the school routine. The Year 13s were still struggling to get their heads round Paradise Lost, and Evie was desperately trying to incentivise them with reminders about the forthcoming theatre trip. She had arranged for Benji to accompany them, since no member of the English Department was free on the afternoon in question.

Thankfully there was no transport to arrange, as the theatre was within walking distance, a fact that was a mixed blessing as they lined up in the cold yard a couple of weeks later, with Evie and Benji at the front of the column and another science teacher, hastily drafted in at Evie's anxious request, bringing up the rear. The students were all excited: this was a rare treat for them. Luke, one of the few boys in the class, was convinced that he wouldn't understand a thing. By contrast, Hannah and Milly had brought their copies of the text with them, and were deep in discussion about the nature of evil.

'So, what's all this about, then?' Benji asked, as they headed off across town. Evie told him to ask Hannah and Milly.

As they entered the auditorium it was clear from the students' expressions that most of them had never been to the theatre before, despite its proximity to their homes. Evie had explained that this wasn't like the cinema and that their behaviour as an audience directly affected what was going on before them on the stage.

She needn't have worried: from the moment the curtain went up they were gripped. This was a far more dramatic production than the one she'd taken the Nice School to. It opened with a matt black set and fallen angels swooping on wires to lie in the pit of hell, from which rose dry ice to represent the sulphurous fumes. Satan himself was mesmerising, but when Adam and Eve made their first appearance she heard Benji let out a loud breath at the very same moment that she felt a kind of rapt tension ripple through the entire school party. She had not expected Adam and Eve to be fully clothed, of course, but in the previous production the actors had worn body suits, discreetly embroidered to suggest nakedness. These actors, however, were actually, physically, really naked. Evie felt a wave for pity for them, exposed in this way to a theatre audience composed mostly of school students, but then was so swept up in their performance that she forgot all about it.

The walk back to school would have been better if Benji and the other teacher had managed to behave more like adults. Their silly giggling and sniggering irritated her almost unbearably. By contrast, the students were either silent, or discussed with great earnestness the interpretation of their text made flesh upon the stage.

There was more laughter the next morning in the staff room as soon as Evie opened the door.

'Yes, as I was saying: it's the quiet ones you have to watch!' This was Benji, who had obviously been holding forth to anyone who cared to listen.

'You can put me down to accompany your next theatre trip,' called a member of the PE Department.

'And me!' came a chorus of other voices.

'Not so fast,' said someone else. 'Should we be allowing our young people to be corrupted by members of the English Department?' Evie held her breath, horrified, then released it as the others laughed aloud.

'You're being teased, Evie,' said Benji.

As soon as she decently could, Evie fled upstairs to find Rob in his classroom

pinning up students' work on the display boards. Would this be yet another black mark against her?

'Ah, Evie,' he said. 'I heard your theatre trip was quite something!'

'Oh, not you too, Rob,' she groaned.

'Don't you worry: I think you've brightened everyone's day. And the students are full of it.'

'Oh no. What have they been saying?'

'Well, Hannah and Milly have been saying all the things you might expect. And Luke came in here specially to say that he gets Milton now. He said they behaved like real people in the play and even the language was easier to understand when he heard them speaking it. Honestly, Evie, that's high praise coming from him. And they'll never forget that experience.'

'That's what I'm afraid of!'

'Don't be. Be glad. You've given them something special. They all thought the theatre was for other people. Now they know it's for them too.'

A thought struck Evie. 'But supposing they tell their parents?' She hadn't forgotten the Founder's Day complaint at Nice School. 'What if you get complaints?'

'Complaints? From *our* parents? I don't think so, Evie. Now go and get a coffee and stop worrying.'

In her own garden that evening Evie noted how much longer the days were getting. After such a long dark winter it was as though spring had been waiting just behind the door and had now jumped out to surprise her. The plum trees were suddenly covered with blossom, and on the apple tree the tiny green-gold leaf buds were beginning to unfurl. Bulbs that hadn't been there last week were suddenly inches high and the forsythia was already fully out. The daffodils swayed in a gentle breeze from the south and Evie felt that time was moving rapidly and that her exile would soon be over, but even as she thought about this she felt a strange longing for something that she couldn't identify. She wanted things to be different, but she wasn't at all sure what that meant. Lines from *Paradise Lost* haunted her:

The mind is its own place, and in itself

Can make a Heaven of Hell, a Hell of Heaven.

Is that what she had been doing, in the Heaven of Nice School and the - as some would have it - Hell of Other School? She recalled the strange warmth she had felt as her colleagues teased her in the staff room after the theatre trip, and wondered if that was what belonging felt like.

The term continued to move on apace and the pressure was on. Even some of the students were beginning to feel a sense of urgency at last. At times Evie felt she was clinging on by her fingertips, and that it was touch and go whether she would get to the Easter holidays in one piece. On the other hand, it was light when she crawled out of bed in the mornings now, and even when she stayed after school for meetings or to do some marking in her empty classroom, it was still not quite dark when she reached home. Home! The little house was starting to feel like home, something she could not have believed possible six months ago.

She had another awkward telephone conversation with her mother, remembering all too clearly the regret she'd felt after not going home at Christmas when her father had had his heart attack. Should she come down at Easter, perhaps, as soon as term ended?

'Well, darling, that's up to you.'

Evie didn't find this helpful. 'Would you like me to come? I mean, how's Dad?'

'Absolutely impossible!'

Evie heard her father saying something in the background, and her mother answering him. She caught the tail end as her mother turned back to the phone.

'...and for heaven's sake stay there this time. He won't rest, Evie. He behaves as though he hasn't been ill at all. It's all right for him: he didn't live through that time while he was lying there unconscious and I was out of my mind with worry, waiting for the ambulance.'

'Oh Mum,' said Evie, resolving to deal somehow with the mountain of marking and preparation that awaited her at the end of term and still find time and energy for a trip home.

'What?' her mother was saying, sounding far away. 'Yes, in a moment. I'm talking to Evie...'

'Sounds as though you need to go, Mum,' Evie said. On the other end of the phone her mother sighed deeply.

'Oh, it's your father. I'd better go…' and she was gone. Evie found herself feeling irritated with both parents, and then irritated with herself for feeling like that.

On a Saturday morning in early March she was strolling round the garden inspecting it for signs of new growth, exclaiming in delight at each newly opened daffodil, each mysterious shoot that had not yet shown its true colours but seemed to hold a promise. It seemed a million miles from the grey concrete of the school playground, and even from the carefully kept gardens of Nice School, which in her memory now took on the appearance of a museum, beautiful but lifeless. That was a paradox, of course. How could something be full of growing things and yet lifeless? Was that what the school itself was like, the reason she had felt alienated there? Or had she just not yet found where its true life lay?

She was walking past the pond when she had the same sense of not being alone that she had experienced when Colin first appeared above the fence and offered the loan of his lawnmower. What a lot had changed since then…

At that moment she thought she heard something. There it was again: a distinct plopping sound. She moved closer to the pond. There was something in there, she was sure of it. As she looked, bubbles rose to the surface; then nothing. With a sigh she went back indoors. The marking wasn't going to do itself. From her little table in the back bedroom she could see the pond quite clearly; the choking weeds were gone and the clear water now lapped over proper green aquatic plants in the gentle breeze. She wrested her attention away and back to the pile of essays on A Midsummer Night's Dream. Fairies at the bottom of the garden? She was clearly getting carried away. She took one more look, and this time she could see a definite disturbance in the water, although she still couldn't make out what was causing it.

With no after-school meeting for once, Evie was home from school early on the Monday. It gave her a chance to wander around the garden again. It had been raining, but the sun had come out, and the last long rays made the wet garden sparkle. She breathed in great gulps of air, sighing with pleasure. Over to the east a faint rainbow was visible, filling her with all sorts of fanciful notions when suddenly, there it was again: a distinct plopping sound.

Puzzled, she returned indoors and began half-heartedly marking a pile of Year 9 essays, seated on the living room sofa, which hadn't improved at all with better acquaintance. The light coming through the window at the front of the house was decidedly overcast, but when she gave herself permission to wander back out into the garden, the sun was shining on that side. It was strange. She had noticed this before; whatever the weather when she returned each evening, at the back of the house the sun was always shining. Or maybe it just felt like that?

She wandered back over in the direction of the pond. The sun had sunk lower in the sky so that it now illuminated the water in such a way that she could see right to the bottom. To her utter delight there was the answer to the puzzle: frogs, dozens of them, fat-bellied ones with mottled skin, smaller, greener ones, crawling about in the water at the bottom, carelessly clambering over each other. She laughed aloud for sheer joy. She would speak to Benji tomorrow. The Year 11 pastoral head was also a biology teacher.

As she turned back towards the house she felt her phone vibrating in her pocket. It was still on silent. If only her students were as disciplined during the school day! Swallowing down her irritation at this abrupt end to a peaceful interlude, she pulled it out and looked at the number. By the time she had worked out that she didn't recognise it, the caller had given up. Tempted as she was to stuff the phone back into her pocket, Evie was sufficiently disquieted to call the number back.

'Hello? This is Evie Symmonds. I think you just called me.'

'Evie. Where are you?' The unmistakable tone of her mother's older sister rang out, causing Evie to move her head away from the phone. She had no recollection of Auntie Sheila ever having called her before.

'I'm at home.'

'Are you sitting down?'

It was an odd question, even for Auntie Sheila.

'No, I'm in the garden.'

'I think you should go straight into the house and sit down, dear.'

Evie's irritation gave way to concern. What was going on? Nonetheless, in the face of her aunt's insistence, she went in through the kitchen door and sat at the table, still piled high with the books she had dumped there on her way in.

'Right, Auntie Sheila. I'm sitting down.' She noticed that the book at the top of the pile was Danny's, and gave a half-smile at the thought of what she might find in there.

'I'm afraid I have some bad news, Evie.'

Evie held her breath as her mind ranged over the possibilities. Her aunt was still speaking

'… and this time, even though the ambulance arrived within five minutes, there was nothing they could do…'

'What?'

'I'm so sorry, Evie.'

'Sorry? Sorry…what? What are you saying?'

'Your father died an hour ago, dear. Your mother was with him.'

It seemed to Evie that the world stood still. The sun had gone in, the birds had stopped singing. Her mind struggled to catch up with the words she heard.

'Dad? He's dead?'

'Yes, Evie. An hour ago. It was very quick. There was nothing anyone could do.'

She noticed a spider dangling from one of the cobwebs she must have missed in her erratic cleaning regime. It swung gently, either by its own efforts or because a faint breeze was blowing in through the open door, she wasn't sure which.

'What? Sorry: what did you say?'

'I said you really mustn't worry about a thing. Your mother is being very brave, and she has everything under control. I'm going to stay with her and help her with all the arrangements. I'll let you know as soon as the date is fixed. For the *funeral*.'

Evie grimaced. Sheila pronounced the word as though she was mouthing it; a word too terrible to speak aloud. Yet she had just told her that her father was dead. What could be more terrible?

'There's no need for you to come rushing up here until then. I'll look after your mother.'

The spider was hauling itself back up its own thread as she finished the conversation. Sheila was right: there was nothing to be gained from setting off immediately. No amount of hurrying would bring her father back. It was too late for the father-daughter conversation she had been looking forward to, too late to tell him he had been right about so many things, too late, too late.... She shrugged her shoulders, feeling numb with a nameless misery. She sat for a long time as the light faded. Then, slowly, she went upstairs and packed a small case.

To her surprise, she slept that night, half-waking only once with a strange feeling that something had happened, if she could only remember what it was. When she telephoned Rob the next morning, he made no objection to her going right away.

'Just for a day or two. I really need to be with my mother. I'll come back, and then once I know when the funeral is perhaps I could have another day off...'

'Evie, just go.' His tone was gentle but firm. 'You need to be there and you need time to grieve. And you need more than just a day for the funeral. You should probably stay with your mother until it's over.'

'But I'll miss so much...'

'Don't worry, Evie. I can cover a lot of your lessons. You really won't be in any fit state to teach anyway.'

'Well, if you're sure. I'm so sorry to let you down...'

Rob was right, of course. She could no more have focused on teaching than fly to the moon. It was all she could do to concentrate on driving, and she missed two motorway junctions before she finally drew up outside her parents' house - her mother's house, she supposed she would have to get used to calling it now. Since no one had stopped her or arrested her she supposed she had driven within the law and without accident. Her mother met her on the doorstep and for several minutes they clung to each other like two drowning women. It was late that night before either of them retired, despite Auntie Sheila's urgent admonition that they needed their sleep, as she headed off to bed herself, her hair in old-fashioned rollers that made them both giggle surreptitiously.

By lunchtime the next day Sheila had made a dozen phone calls, and everything was arranged.

'Mum, are you sure you wouldn't like to do some of this yourself?'

'Oh, she's always taken charge, ever since we were little.'

'Yes, but this is a bit different, isn't it?'

'Sometimes it's easier to just let her get on with it.'

The date was set for the following Monday. Evie would only miss just over a week of school. The arrangements bore all the hallmarks of Auntie Sheila's taste, dour and conservative in the extreme. On the day itself, Evie was too miserable to cry, and her feelings turned inwards. Everything about it seemed cold and didn't represent her father in any way. She found herself wishing Barbie could have done it; she would have brought some common sense and humanity to it. She even found herself smiling at the thought of the cheerful woman with the jingly earrings and her own grief to contend with, and wondered how she did it.

When it was all over she worried about leaving her mother, but again Auntie Sheila insisted her mother would be fine and pointed out that she had some very supportive neighbours. Evie knew that this last was true; her parents had been blessed with good friends in their little community, although how much she would enjoy Auntie Sheila's rather coercive help Evie was less sure.

On the Wednesday following the funeral Evie was back at Other School, still shell-shocked by the death of her father just when she had believed he was getting better. She sleepwalked through the rest of the week at school, not even venturing outside her back door when she got home, as she wrestled with the need to concentrate on her schoolwork. She had still not shed a tear for her father.

12

It was a week later, the day before the end of term, that she came home and felt there was something amiss. She had no idea what, or how she knew, but she knew. Instinctively, she headed for the garden. For what seemed like minutes, she forgot to breathe. The green lawn she had been nurturing since the previous July lay churned up into deep furrows; her rockery was torn apart, the rocks thrown into the pond; others lay smashed and scattered over the trampled borders. She moved forward slowly, barely taking it in. Reaching the end of the garden she stood beneath the ancient apple tree, the tree she had sat beneath last year, gazing up at the blue sky through the canopy of autumn leaves that drifted lazily to earth when the breeze blew. Now it stood, maimed, its branches rudely ripped from its trunk, the budding blossom mangled. For the first time since her aunt had phoned, Evie felt the tears flow. She doubled up on the grass, howling with a pain she could not name. And then she saw him. He was over in the corner near the shed, a pile of twigs and leaves in his arms.

'You!' She was hysterical with rage and grief. 'Get out! Get out of my garden!'

Danny dropped his bundle and came towards her. 'I'm so sorry, Miss. You made it so beautiful. This is just awful…'

'How could you? How could you?'

'No, Miss, No - you've got it all wrong. It wasn't me…'

'I suppose it was the snake?' she snarled.

He stared in puzzlement, which infuriated her even further.

'Get out! Get out! Get out!' she screamed, and he fled.

It was dark in the garden, darker than she'd ever known it. The streetlights had gone out. Every light in her life had gone out. For a long time she remained, crouched on the ground beneath the tree as the darkness fell. All around her, unfamiliar shapes leered out of the darkness; the garden sounds, which she had come to know so well over the past months, now were harsh and menacing in her ears, and everything was changed, everything was spoilt. The trees, which had been her friends, were dangerous, alien. She cried the noisy, hiccupping sobs of the little girl she had once been, when Daddy had been there to comfort her, and for the first time she fully absorbed the fact that he would never be there for her again. Then she remembered the shock of seeing her garden, the desolation - and Danny, The Boy, always bringing trouble, and she wasn't sure if she was crying for her father or for her garden, or even on behalf of Danny and the father he had lost. She stayed there for a long time, and eventually, when the sky began to lighten, she went slowly into the house to bed. She called in sick that day.

This was not the first time that grief like this had been felt in this garden. A young man who had cheated death when his stirrup was lost spent a night there when his wife died, and with her the child she was carrying. Like Evie, he had wept until daybreak; like Evie he was wracked with regrets and what-might-have-beens. If he had taken greater care of her… if he had sent for the physician earlier… if he had simply loved her more.

There were others, too, for a young woman had been walking the fields that the garden had become out of cruel necessity, as she shivered in the cold November wind of 1918, when news reached her of a death on the battlefields of Northern France. It was especially bitter, for it came at the same time as the news that the dreadful war had ended. Later, the dead man's mother joined her, and they wept together, and before long all the girls and women of Europe wept with them.

Another young man too had wept there, long before his beard had grown and whitened. He had recreated the garden and eased the sorrows of his heart by doing so; in his many restless travels he had continued to carry it, with all its unpredictable beauty, in some inward place, and found a kind of peace. And so, although she did not know it, Evie was not alone in her grief. In truth, no-one ever is.

It was almost noon when she dragged herself groggily downstairs. At first she avoided looking out of the window, even when she filled the kettle for a belated breakfast cup of coffee. In the end the pull of the garden was too strong, and eventually she tugged on her wellies and went out. In the raw light of midday it was even worse than she had thought. She wandered aimlessly around, and as she passed the pond she saw that the water had settled and cleared after its churning of the previous night. A sudden shaft of sunlight pierced it to the bottom, and she let out a howl of pure grief: not a single frog remained. Now her tears fell freely, and she blundered back into the kitchen, filled with steam from the kettle she had switched on and ignored. Abandoning the idea of breakfast she kicked off her boots and headed upstairs to the desk piled with papers. Scrabbling about she found what she was looking for: a poem, written by a sixteen year old boy: *The Colour of Grief.* She read on.

Dull, like tarnished silver, grey;

Tears on a wet window pane,

Heavy like a rainy day

Muddy puddles down a dismal lane.

Someone you love is there no more

Their pain is gone but yours remains

Between you a locked and bolted door

While outside it rains and rains and rains.

White, the colour of faces you love

White light in an empty sky

Uncaring clouds drifting high above

The silent neighbours passing by.

Doctors in white, nurses in blue

Red the blood, the pain, the death

Everything hurts, nothing is true

All colour gone with his final breath.

Her tears blurred the words. She ran downstairs without stopping to put her boots back on, and winced as the cold stone of the patio seeped into her feet. Then she saw them. There was something left from the destruction after all: the hellebores smiled shyly at her from their pot, and if she'd had the strength she would have picked it up and kissed them.

Barbie was used to distressed-looking people hammering on her door, but Evie was probably the last person she would have expected on the Thursday before Easter, the last day of term, when she should have been in school. She let her in without a word and Evie collapsed onto a kitchen chair scattering papers without even seeing them.

'You look terrible,' the vicar said. Evie's eyes were still puffy from the night before, and a morning of suppurating under the duvet hadn't helped.

'Where's Danny?'

'In school, as far as I know. I went to morning prayers before he was up, and by the time I got back he'd gone. Why? Has something happened at school?' She was using her calm, professional voice, but the anxious parent was in there too, somewhere.

'Did he tell you what happened? To my garden?'

'I think you had better tell me.'

'I got back, on Wednesday, after school...' Evie felt her face contorting again. She had been determined not to cry any more: surely she had no more tears left? It appeared she had. Between heaving sobs she described what had happened. It was only afterwards that she remembered what Danny had said. *No, you've got it all wrong. It wasn't me.*

'Did you believe him?' Barbie asked.

'I don't think I even heard him, to be honest. I was so distraught. All that time, all that care and love I've put into the garden. And for me there won't be a next year...'

'And you've lost your father,' said Barbie gently. 'You've had no real space to grieve.' She crossed to the worktop where the box of tissues lay, half-buried under a mound of ironing. After a few minutes, when Evie had composed herself, she said: 'I just screamed at him, told him to get out.' She looked Barbie full in the eyes. 'I'm so sorry. It was wrong of me, so wrong.'

In answer, Barbie moved across to give her a comforting hug.

'I'm just worried about the effect it may have had on Danny...' At that moment Barbie's phone rang. As soon as she heard her say: 'Yes, I see. Thank you.' Evie knew. Danny had not appeared at school that day.

'Look, it's probably nothing,' Barbie was saying. 'It's not exactly the first time he's played truant.'

After the inevitable boiling of the vicarage kettle, a ritual that must have taken place many hundreds of times in this kitchen, Evie thought, the conversation turned to Evie's father.

'The funeral was awful, just awful. There was nothing of him in it at all. He was such a passionate man, passionate about what he believed in, about education, about the people he taught, the people he felt were disadvantaged.' She looked at Barbie through the tears that had started up again. 'I wish *you* could have taken his funeral. You'd have made it all right.'

'You know, I'm not sure there's any way of making it all right when someone you love has just died. You just need to acknowledge the ghastliness of it. The reality of grief. That's what we'll be doing tomorrow, in a way.'

Evie looked at her, puzzled.

'Good Friday.'

Suddenly, she didn't know why, Evie was angry. 'And then on Sunday you'll all turn up to sing about new life and hope when really there isn't any? Have you read the newspapers recently? Have you seen the news? What sort of world are we living in? What hope is there?' She knew her voice was becoming shrill with the anger she had been holding back since her father's death but she couldn't stop now.

The vicar remained silent, waiting.

'And what about you? I don't understand you. Your husband died, horribly, but here you are, standing up at the front of your church, spouting about peace and hope and all that stuff. Why aren't you angry? Why aren't you hurting? I don't understand...I just don't...' As Evie ran out of words, they were replaced by sobs, the kind she had wept at her father's knee when she was a little girl, the kind she had wept when her pet cat died. She had never been able to face having another pet after that: she had wanted never again to feel the pain of loss like that.

She reached for a tissue, but the vicar got there before her and handed her one - a man-sized tissue. Evie dabbed her eyes and gave her nose a hefty blow, then scrunched the disintegrating tissue into a ball and in the absence of anywhere else to stow it, tucked it beneath her on the chair.

'I lost count of the boxes of those I went through when my husband died,' the vicar said. 'Of course I knew it was coming, so it wasn't a shock when the end came - not like for you. I was still angry, though - bloody angry! And the diagnosis was a shock. I did a lot of swearing and shouting - the vicarage had thick walls, so I don't think any of the neighbours heard me.'

Evie raised her eyes from the floor, which she had been staring at during this little speech, to look into the other woman's face. She was aware that her own eyes were swollen with crying, so they didn't open wide with the surprise she felt. Were vicars supposed to behave like that? She knew she was being contradictory: she was angry that the vicar didn't seem distraught, and angry that she was now admitting that she did. She was angry with everyone and everything.

'There were some very bad moments: telling people was the worst. Then, what to do with his possessions, how to deal with people's sympathy…and worst of all, how to even begin to help Danny…'

She was looking towards Evie, but not at her, as if reliving some inward scene that she could not escape. Evie felt contrite.

'I'm sorry, she began..' but the vicar stopped her.

'Do you really think it's any different for me? In some ways it was worse, because people expected me to know how to cope, and they didn't know what to do when I didn't. So…I grafted on a bright artificial smile and my best professional clergy manner, and went about my business of telling people that there was goodness and hope in the world.'

'Did that help?'

'Not really. Well, yes, for a bit. Until I broke down in church one day and had to admit I wasn't coping.'

'What happened?'

'The Bishop himself came to see me… I won't bore you with the details, but the upshot was that I had some leave and then we negotiated a change of parish.' Evie felt conscience stricken. She had attacked this woman for not appearing to have natural feelings, when in fact her feelings had been overwhelming.

'I'm so sorry,' she mumbled, 'I really shouldn't have...' Her words petered out as she failed to find the right ones.

'It's all right, Evie. I'm only telling you so that you'll know I have some idea of how you're feeling. Every bereavement is different, so I'm not saying I know exactly how you feel, but I do want you to know that I at least understand.' Evie gulped and accepted another man-sized tissue.

'So how did you... not get over it, but, well, start to get back on your feet?' The vicar took a tissue for herself. Somehow this touched Evie more than anything else, and she felt the tears welling again. They both dabbed their eyes, but when the vicar spoke again there was less distress in her warm voice.

'Well, I had some counselling. That allowed me to acknowledge my feelings. I don't think you can start to deal with feelings like loss and anger until you admit them to yourself.'

Evie winced. She recognised now that the anger she had directed at the vicar didn't belong with her at all, but with herself for not making the effort to visit her father while she had the chance.

'But the thing that helped me most of all,' the vicar was saying, 'Was recognising that Danny needed me more than ever. He was confused and angry and grieving, and not only had he lost his father, but I wasn't really there for him - and then, on top of everything else, I moved him to this place, where he felt he didn't fit in, didn't belong, and I still wasn't really available because of my job.'

And this, Evie thought, was the woman I had down as a feckless parent.

Aloud, she said, 'But you two have a close relationship. I've seen you together. I've heard him speak about you.'

'Yes, I've been so blessed. I feel he's come back to me. But he's still a troubled young man. I expect he's given you a hard time in school?'

'Yes, he has, but he's also surprised me sometimes - in a positive way. You said that knowing how much Danny needed you helped?'

'It made me look beyond myself; gave me a sense of purpose; a reason for going on.'

'And your...' Evie hesitated over the word. 'Your faith?'

'That goes without saying. I was angry with God, of course. I tried turning my back on God, but I couldn't actually bring myself to deny all that I believed. That would have made a lie of my whole life, and I knew that there had been too much goodness in my experience for me to deny it. Andrew, for one thing. We had shared so much, and our child was there, needing my help.' She paused for a moment. 'I wonder what there is in your life, Evie,' that needs your attention right now?'

13

And so Evie headed back to her garden. It was still as she'd left it, maimed and broken, but she walked round it, acknowledging the damage each plant had sustained, greeting it in its new and altered form, reassuring it that she still cared for it. Strangely, she seemed to love it even more, now that it was so damaged. She wandered round, touching the broken stems of the plants, and feeling unexpected gratitude when she came across new, undamaged shoots. She returned several times to marvel that her hellebores had remained unscathed, and it delighted her that they had remained in flower so long. *They're clearly tougher than they* look, she thought. *Maybe I am too.* She still didn't have the heart, though - or the sheer physical energy - to begin the clearing up.

The next morning - Friday - she was sitting in the kitchen drinking a second cup of coffee when she heard the church bell: not the clamorous ringing that accompanied weddings and special occasions, but the slow ringing that she supposed was just to let people know it was time. It sounded like the tolling of a funeral bell, and the loss of her father and the loss of her garden became one and the same. She could even recognise in her own anger the same anger Danny had spat at her when she first knew him, his loss still raw as he grappled with all the changes in his life and left-behind childhood; another kind of loss.

And what of her mother's loss? To her shame Evie recognised that she had been so bound up in her own feelings that she had failed even to consider how it must be for her mother. She made a decision. Schoolwork loomed large over the next couple of weeks and she simply could not spare the whole of the school holiday to be with her, but she must at least go and spend some of the time there. She was doubtful about her ability to be much help in her present state of mind, but forced herself to make the phone call.

'You'll never guess what,' said her mother's voice in an unexpectedly upbeat tone when she answered. 'Sheila's taking me on a cruise!'

'What?'

'Yes. It's true! Isn't that lovely of her? She found a website where you can book things at short notice...'

'Are you sure that's what you want to do?'

'Totally, darling!' Then, more soberly, she added: 'I really need to get away from here, from the house, from everything.'

'I understand,' said Evie, slowly. 'But... I was planning to come and stay for a while...' Her voice faded.

'Oh, Sweetheart, I'm so sorry... I should have thought. Will you be all right?'

'No, Mum...I meant I thought you might like me to come and stay...'

'That's sweet of you, Evie, but I know how busy you are, and the last thing I want is for you to feel you need to look after me.' There was a pause, and then her Mum said: 'I'm fine, Evie, I really am. I have to deal with this in my own way. And don't worry about me,' she added. 'Sheila will be here to make sure I behave myself.'

Gracious! The very idea of her weary, duty-bound mother even thinking of not 'behaving herself' left Evie open-mouthed with amazement.

Colin came round to commiserate. Perhaps he had seen from his window, or heard her shouting at Danny. She showed him the damage, and he whistled through his teeth and clucked his tongue and made all the sympathetic noises he could.

The most disappointing thing was the pond: the frogs seemed to have gone again and no movement disturbed the surface of the water. Evie felt so sad that she avoided looking at it.

'Don't worry, they'll be back next year,' said Colin, kindly.

'But I won't' she wailed.

'No, but you'll know that they're there.'

He must have told Molly, because she came round a little later with that cure for all ills, a whole chocolate cake. Evie was deeply touched by their sympathy, but glad when they'd gone. She needed to be alone with her grief a while longer.

Saturday morning was both bright and chilly, as if hedging its bets between the seasons. Evie got up early to go out and do some shopping, awakened at last to the fact that a Bank Holiday was upon her and her cupboard was bare. As she was trying to decide between her winter coat and a lighter one, the local free paper was slipped through the door. Picking it up, she was surprised to see a photograph of a student in the uniform of Other School, a boy... a boy she knew only too well. The headline jumped about before her eyes. She held the paper with both hands to steady it, or perhaps to steady herself.

LOCAL TEENAGER MISSING

Vicar's son Sixteen-year-old Danny Desmond has been missing since Thursday morning, when he left his home to go to school. He never arrived...

In a daze she climbed into the car, seeing without registering the still faintly visible mark where the scratch along the side had been repaired. As she flung her bags on to the passenger seat and started the engine, she noticed a uniformed police officer knocking at number 1. After a brief pause he moved on to Rose's door, and by the time he had given up on that one Evie was had already driven past the corner and didn't see if Colin was at home to answer the knock.

The supermarket was crowded and Evie allowed herself and her empty trolley to be moved along by the general flow of people and other trolleys. She had no volition of her own. She picked up a large bag of pasta as she passed the dried goods, and then wondered why she had done so. *Bread*, she thought. She must have bread. *And milk*. But how to get from here to the chiller aisle? Somehow she battled through and arrived at the end of a very long queue at the checkout. It moved at a snail's pace, which suited her at that moment. More people joined behind her, and she heard two women talking.

'Policeman come to my door this morning.'

'Oh aye?'

'Yeah. Asking questions about that boy what disappeared.'

'Ooh, I saw that! In the paper.' The speaker sounded excited: a bit of gossipy news to add interest to her day. Evie tensed, but their further conversation gave her nothing she didn't know already, and annoyed her even more with unfounded criticisms of his family background. Just then the conveyor belt lurched forward, and the groceries piled high by the person in front began to topple to the floor, causing a diversion while she helped them pick things up. By the time order was restored the conversation behind her had turned to another topic - something to do with 'women's troubles' - and Evie was able to retreat again into her own chaotic thoughts.

Back at Paradise Row Evie was just putting her shoulder to her front door when she saw Colin's open. Giving up the attempt to open her own door she left her bag on the step and went to where he stood, holding his door open for her. Without a word she went in and sank into one of the chintz sofas. Looking up she saw that he was holding out a glass: not tea, this time, but brandy. She took it gratefully.

'Looks like you needed something to put the colour back into your cheeks, Lass,' he said, sipping from his own glass while Evie gulped and spluttered over hers. 'The police came round while you were out.'

She nodded. 'Yes, I saw the officer knocking at doors,' she said.

'A boy from your school… gone missing.' Seeing her eyes well up, he added quickly, 'Now it's early days, and the door-to-door questioning is just routine. It doesn't mean anything, and I gather the lad in question was a bit…well a bit disgruntled with life.'

Evie found herself suddenly confiding all her fears about Danny, which meant telling Colin the whole story of how she came to know him so well - or thought she did.'

'Aye, these bad lads… there's often a story like that. It's hard, growing up without a father…'

Evie thought of Colin's own daughter, growing up without him. They were both silent for a few moments. 'Do you… do you think I should tell the police all that, what I've just told you?' she asked at last.

'You just need to answer their questions, Lass. They know what they're doing. You may find that something you tell them will help them find this lost lad. Or he may come home on his own, once he's cooled off a bit.'

'Do you think they'll come back here to question me then?'

'The usual thing is to do the door-to-door and make a note of anyone not in - then they'll come back later. But don't worry: just do like I said and answer their questions. You want them to find this boy, don't you?'

Colin's concern for her, and his attempts at reassurance, together with the brandy warming her from within, enabled Evie to return to her house, gathering up her shopping from the front step as she did so. She opened her bag and began mechanically putting stuff away. She must have been more distracted than she realised: instead of the extra milk she thought she'd bought there was only a single pint, and instead of bread there was only the packet of hot cross buns. Still, they'd do. It wasn't as if she was feeling hungry. The idea of food appalled her, and she couldn't imagine that changing until Danny was found.

She wandered out into the garden. It seemed the natural thing to do, but it seemed to hold no answers for her. It was as though it too was waiting. She wandered to the far end, hiding herself among the damaged trees. They no longer held the menace they had on the night when she had wept among them in the dark, and it felt to Evie as though they were holding something back, a secret they weren't ready to tell her. *Must be the brandy* she thought. Eventually she emerged from the gloom and walked slowly back towards the house. She nerved herself to look at the pond. The water had fully settled now, and it was clear that the frogs really had gone. She had thought she had finished crying, but this started her off again.

Half an hour later she was seated at the kitchen table nursing a cup of rapidly cooling coffee. *I need to deal with this in my own way* her mother had said. That part of the conversation had seemed real, and Evie knew that it was an important truth. She too must deal with her loss in her own way. Suddenly energised, she ran upstairs and changed into her old clothes, and grabbing her wellies from the cupboard as she passed, she positively strode across the garden to the shed and pulled out spade, fork, hoe - everything she could think of. She began with the borders, cutting back the things that had been snapped off, pulling out the weeds between them, and in doing so she noticed how many tiny shoots were starting to push through. She walked to the pond and contemplated the rocks that had been dumped in the deep end, but the effort needed to wade in and pull them out seemed too much, so she moved on down to the trees. She began to pile up the branches that had been broken off, but there were some that were only half off, dangling awkwardly. Amputation was required, but she would need a ladder and a saw, and that too felt more than she could manage at the moment. She contented herself with a little further pottering, pulling out weeds and reacquainting herself with the garden. Completely exhausted by so little effort, she was just putting the tools back in the shed when she heard someone knocking at her front door, and kicking off her boots raced through the house to open it before her visitor got tired and gave up.

Why she had allowed herself to think it might be Danny, she couldn't imagine. The police officer who stood there looked for a moment at Evie's dirt-streaked face and old clothes, and then said,

'Sorry to disturb you in the middle of a job. Am I speaking to Miss Genevieve Symmonds?' Evie nodded and opened the door wide enough to allow the young policewoman to enter. Smart in her uniform, she had perfect blond hair swept into a perfect bun beneath her cap, the kind of perfect hair control that had completely eluded Evie when she had tried to conform to the Nice School dress code. She led her visitor into the kitchen and offered to put the kettle on, but the officer - PO Jane Wheeler - declined.

'Nothing to be alarmed about,' she said. 'We're making house to house enquiries about a young person who has gone missing from home.' She brought out a photo of Danny, looking implausibly respectable, with shorter hair and a solemn expression. 'I believe you're a teacher at this young man's school?'

Evie nodded.

'Is he in any of your classes?'

Again Evie just nodded. Her mouth was dry.

'He wasn't in school on Thursday, the last day of term. Had he missed school before?'

Struggling to find her voice, Evie said, 'Yes, his attendance was poor, especially earlier in the year. It was getting better, though.'

'So it was a surprise when he wasn't in school that day?'

'I wasn't in school myself that day. I only heard about it later.'

'Can you tell me why you weren't in school that day please, Miss Symmonds?'

'I was unwell.'

'Unwell?'

Was she being accused of something? Evie felt acutely uncomfortable under the remarkably elegant gaze of PO Jane Wheeler.

'Can you remember the last time you saw Danny?'

Evie explained in as few words as she could that she had found her garden vandalised and that Danny was there. To her relief she wasn't asked whether there had ever been a similar trespass.

'Right,' said the PO, noting something in her notebook. 'That matches what the boy's mother told us. I believe you are a friend of hers?'

'Oh...' Evie felt taken aback, but not displeased. She realised how much she would like to be Barbie's friend. Carefully, she said, 'Well, she's the vicar. I guess a lot of people go to her when they're upset.'

'Were you upset about something?'

'My father died a few weeks ago. Suddenly. From a heart attack.'

'Oh, I'm sorry to hear that, Miss Symmonds. My condolences.'

The woman sounded as though she meant it. Evie had forgotten again to look for the person hidden behind the exterior, and thought of Colin in his Mr. Plod days with his secret life. Who knew anything about other people when it came down to it?

'Can you think of any reason why Danny might have done this?' the PO was saying.

'He said that it wasn't him,' Evie said. 'But whether it was or wasn't he is an adolescent struggling to deal with a whole lot of difficult things in his life. He was angry with the world; it's not unusual for people of his age.'

'You sound as though you care.'

'Of course I do. I'm a teacher.'

PO Jane Wheeler raised an eyebrow. 'Then he's lucky to have you. Not all teachers care.'

'Oh, I think they do, but sometimes the demands are so heavy that there isn't the space for caring. It's wrong, but it happens. But St. Mary's is a good school; a caring school.' As she said it, Evie realised she meant it.

'Well, thank you for your time, Miss Symmonds.' The officer pocketed her notebook. 'You will let us know if you hear anything from Danny, won't you?'

As she opened the door for her, Evie asked, 'How is Danny's mother?'

'Well, she's coping. It's a busy weekend for vicars, isn't it? Probably helps keep her mind off things.'

It was nearly lunchtime, but impulsively, Evie phoned Matron at Nice School.

'Hi Evie,' said the slightly surprised voice at the other end. 'Good to hear from you. How's it going?'

'Oh well, you know...Look, the reason I've called is, well, it's complicated. I'm not going home - bit of a long story - but I need to... well I'd like to get away for a few days. Do you think there's any chance I could stay at the school?'

'Yeah, that'd be great. Come and stay in my flat. We've got some overseas students staying on, so I'm here for the duration. When do you want to come?'

'How about now? Is that OK?'

If Matron was taken aback it didn't show in her voice. 'I'll expect you in about three-four hours then. You can tell me all your news then.'

After a hasty bit of packing Evie loaded her things into the car, all the while telling herself she was a fool to think of driving that distance when the roads would be full of people heading off on holiday. She hadn't gone far when she realised she'd left her phone in the kitchen after speaking to Matron, and swearing softly under her breath, went back into the house. As she entered she thought she heard something at the back. *Oh no* she told herself, *we're not having a repeat of all that.* There was no broken window or unlocked kitchen door, nothing untoward, and if the trees seemed to be swaying on a day with no wind, well, what of that?

The drive down the motorway was every bit as bad as she had anticipated, and Evie was feeling frankly frazzled by the time she arrived at Nice School. For the final half hour of the journey she had been stuck behind a farm vehicle going at less than ten miles an hour; she had stalled the engine twice, and when the driver of the other vehicle had finally swung round into a gate she had been forced to pull over towards the ditch to avoid an oncoming car driven by an idiot with a death wish.

The sign board loomed on her left, bearing the familiar words: *The Cedars. An Education that adds polish…* Evie just had time to change down a gear before turning into the sweeping driveway. She had left this place a mere nine months ago and now, fleetingly, she saw it as a stranger might: a cluster of imposing buildings, some clearly very old, all suggestive of stability and tradition. The immaculately maintained grounds spoke of high standards and careful control, a world away from the careless littering of the streets around St. Mary's and its harsh, urban concrete. Out of habit Evie headed for her usual parking spot, even though there were plenty to choose from. The car park was almost empty and the whole place looked odd without its groups of uniform-clad students heading purposefully towards lessons. She climbed stiffly out of the driving seat and took a good look around.

Ahead of her was the oldest part of the site; despite changes over the years the solid stone walls had been preserved, and without the busyness of the school day going on around it, Evie had for a moment a sense of how it must have looked when it was first built as a fortified manor house. As she gazed, the new blocks surrounding it seemed to fade from her vision; the arts block became again the tithe barn it had once been; the chapel lost its nineteenth century steeple, and the pristine lawns and flower beds softened into a garden of wildflowers and fruit-bearing trees. Then she blinked and the vision was gone. What was wrong with her? She'd become obsessed by gardens. Before she could drown in the inevitable link between gardens - her garden - and Danny, she heard Matron's voice calling.

'Evie! Come on in. You must be shattered.'

Her friend crossed the car park at a trot and gave her a warm hug. Evie clung on, suddenly quite weak, and Matron frowned but refrained from saying anything until they were indoors and she'd put a glass of wine into Evie's hand.

'Oh, I've missed this,' said Evie, taking the glass and smiling gratefully at Matron. 'I'm sorry for landing on you like this, but I really felt the need to get away.'

'Poor you. Has it been really dreadful?'

'It's been an experience!'

Just then there was a knock at the door and Matron opened it to find a small boy standing there.

'Please Miss, I've been sent to ask for a compression bandage.'

'Have you now! And who sent you?'

'Mr. Dawson. We were in the changing room and -'

'Right. Go back and tell Mr. Dawson I'll be right there, as soon as I've picked up my things.' She turned to Evie. 'Sorry, I'd better go and see what's going on. Shouldn't be too long though.' She picked up a bag and a set of keys and as she reached the door she turned back and pointed towards the little table at the centre of the room. 'There's plenty more in the bottle,' and with a reassuring smile she was gone.

Much later, after two more interruptions and a meal that, happily, was not interrupted, Evie finally started telling Matron her story.

'It sounds as though you've made some interesting friends up there. Your Mr. Plod and Mrs. Flowerpot sound a real hoot. And,' Matron said, raising one eyebrow in a way Evie always envied, 'I see you're still doing that names thing… I'll bet you even still call me 'Matron' don't you?'

Evie blushed.

'You know it's not even technically my job title any more, don't you?'

'I'm sorry, *Rosalind*. It's just I always thought of you as Matron when I first came here, and it sort of stuck.'

'Now you're going to the other extreme. 'Ros' will do fine.' Her friend looked steadily at Evie for a few moments, then said, 'Come on, Evie. You rush up here on a whim, arrive looking half dead, spend two hours telling me a lot of funny stories, but I don't think you're telling me the real one.'

Evie started again, carefully explaining about Danny and Barbie and her father's death and her worries about her mother and her experiences at Other School.

'There you go again, Ros interrupted. 'What's the school actually called?'

'St. Mary's. It's next to the church where Barbie is vicar.'

'And what's Barbie's real name?'

'No, she really is called Barbie. I couldn't make that one up, could I?'

Finally, when Evie had run out of words, Ros said, sympathetically, 'Poor you. You really have had a tough time, haven't you?' and when Evie simply nodded, added, encouragingly: 'Only one more term to get through, and you'll be safely back here.'

'Hmm,' Evie said.

Next morning Evie awoke to the sound of church bells, the proper ones this time, great falling chains of sound that swooped and rose in the clear spring sunshine for the whole world to hear. It was Easter Day, and her thoughts flew instantly to Barbie.

After breakfast she went for a wander round on her own. Ros had warned her about the building work going on in the English Department, but it was still quite a shock to see the lawns along one end ripped up and furrowed by the wheels of the contractors' vehicles. The extension stood, half-finished, tarpaulins flapping at unglazed windows. Inside the older part of the building though, nothing had changed at all, and she soon forgot about the work at the far end as she walked tentatively around, her footsteps echoing eerily. She had somehow forgotten the rows of desks arranged precisely, and the imposing teacher's desk set squarely at the front on a little raised platform. What a privileged place to teach; why did the knowledge that she would soon be back here not fill her with greater joy? She thought of the chaotic conditions of her teaching room at St. Mary's, and found she was laughing out loud at some remembered antics on the part of Wayne or Kelly or even some of her Year 13s.

The ordered notice boards contained instructional material but showed nothing at all produced by the students themselves. Why had she never noticed this before? She recalled Mr. HOD - all right, Ros: Mr. Whyttingham-Smythe - explaining to her that it was important that the students only saw what was excellent around them; anything that appeared on the walls must be an example of what they must strive for. If she was honest with herself, even at the time a small voice inside her had questioned this: so how do we show that they are valued? How do we affirm their efforts and offer them encouragement? She found herself recalling how Rob had told her that she was doing that just by being there for a whole year for them. Funny, she now thought, no-one at The Cedars had ever told her that she was valued as a teacher or told her how she as a person could make a difference.

The sun came out and although it was still a little chilly, Evie went outside to greet it. It was the same sun that shone on Paradise Row, and yet it was a different world. The groundsmen had already been out, tearing up the spent bulbs and putting in the bedding plants that would so impress the parents as they arrived to deliver their offspring at the start of term. That led her back to thinking about her own garden, and when the sound of bells drifted over again from the village church, she remembered again that it was Easter Day and that Barbie would somehow be celebrating the idea of new life in the midst of her own desperate anxiety for the son she loved. There were too many paradoxes here to deal with, and shaking her head clear of them she returned to Ros' flat in time for a pleasant lunch and a few reminiscences about old times at Nice School.

After a satisfyingly long walk across the fields on Monday morning - they had taken

that route to avoid being mown down by holiday drivers on the unpavemented roads - Evie resisted her friend's urging to stay longer, thanked her profusely, and set off. The return journey seemed much easier; it always was, she thought, when you were heading home.

14

The weather had been mixed as she travelled, with the clouds clearing progressively as she headed North. Evie's first action on getting back was to go into the house and straight out again into the garden; here the sun was shining strongly, and as she wandered around she could see that it didn't look so bad after all. There weren't quite so many rocks in the pond as she thought she remembered, and she wasn't sure if it was her imagination, but the trees didn't seem so ragged. Was she dreaming, or had some of the snapped boughs actually repaired themselves? Suddenly thirsty, she went back into the kitchen for a drink of water, and stood, looking out of the window while she ran the tap to get it cold enough. She could see from here that the lawn was still in a sorry state, and she thought she needed some advice, unsure whether she could use grass seed or whether she would need to consider returfing. She would ask Colin. The thought struck her then that maybe Colin was responsible for the mysterious improvements. If so she must thank him.

He wasn't in, and as she turned away from his front door she realised that she hadn't yet brought in her bag from the car. As she opened the boot, she heard a front door slam, and looked up to see if it was Molly heading out to greet her. There was no sign of her, however, even after knocking at her door. It seemed Evie was alone in Paradise Row, although she was sure she had heard something.

Later, Molly came round. She had seen the car on her return from visiting Seth. Barbie had given her a lift.

'How is she?' Evie asked.

'Still no news.' Molly shook her head. 'It's not looking good. To be honest, I think she really wanted to come with me this afternoon to keep her mind off it.'

Evie put the kettle on and apologised for her lack of anything to go with it.

'Bless you, Chuck, we had cakes at the care home. I don't need anything else - just a cuppa and your company.'

In the course of their conversation Molly confided that some odd things had been happening: pies left out in her backyard to cool had disappeared.

'So what was it, do you think?' Evie asked. 'Urban fox? Or someone's cats?'

'No, not an animal. No: an animal would've left crumbs, wouldn't it? And animals don't take the pie dish as well!'

'Weird!' agreed Evie. 'Very strange.'

'And,' continued Molly, 'Some of Colin's garden tools got taken and then next morning, there they were: back again!'

It didn't sound likely that it was Colin who had been her good Samaritan in the garden, then. But who was it?

'There's something not right!' said Molly, ominously.

That evening Evie checked out the local news on her laptop. There was nothing further on Danny beyond the original report on his disappearance. Where could he be? When her distress had got too much for her she had hurried off to Nice School. Where might Danny have gone in order to find solace? She wandered around the house unable to settle, finally making some rather watery scrambled eggs and toasting a stale hot cross bun, most of which she was unable to eat.

It was Tuesday morning. Evie had walked up the hill to the vicarage, her pace slowing more and more as she did so. When she reached her destination she carried on walking, unsure whether she could face Barbie after all. After a few paces she told herself not to be such a coward, and turned back, but it was almost more than she could do to make herself stop at the gate. Even after she had walked the short distance to the front door she stood hesitating. Because of her accusing words, her anger, Barbie's son was missing; it was now in the hands of the police. What did that mean? Did they 'fear the worst'? How could she ever live with herself if…

The front door opened suddenly, making her jump.

'I thought it was you. Come in.' Barbie was wearing a pair of black leggings and a ridiculously baggy jumper. Her hair was - or had been - in a pony tail, but most of it had escaped and was now flying in several different directions.

'Are you…are you sure you want me to come in?'

'Yes, quickly, before anyone sees me. I'm pretending not to be at home.' She ushered Evie in through the front door and made to lead the way into the kitchen as usual, but Evie stopped where she was in the hall.

'Barbie, I'm so sorry. How can you ever forgive me?' Evie was trying not to sound self-pitying.

Barbie turned round, clearly taken aback. 'Why? What have you done?'

Now it was Evie's turn to be surprised. 'Well…Danny. If it hadn't been for me, screaming at him the way I did…' She couldn't go on.

'You're blaming yourself for his disappearance?

'I am so, so sorry. I know I can't expect you to forgive me…' Evie got no further because Barbie closed the gap between them and smothered her in a great hug. Both women were now crying, and after a few moments Barbie extricated herself and reached for the ever-present tissue box, which seemed to have found its way on to the hall table. Standing back the vicar looked at Evie solemnly.

'Well, I suppose I can't forgive you -' Evie started to turn away to hide the fresh tears. ' - because there's nothing to forgive.'

'But…but…'

'But nothing. Come on, let's put the kettle on.'

Over a cup of extra strong coffee, Barbie said, 'You weren't responsible for Danny taking off like that, you know. He's done it before when things get too much for him. I just wish the Citizen hadn't got hold of it and turned it into a story.'

'But the police?'

'Well, I had to report it… and obviously I want him found, but I know Danny. I know what he's like.'

There was a short silence. Evie noticed a clock ticking that she'd not registered before.

'It was the anniversary.'

It took Evie a few moments to understand. 'Oh no… the anniversary of your husband's death? And it was Easter and you had to… Oh I'm so sorry…'

After more tears and another hug Barbie put the kettle on again, despite Evie's protestations. Then suddenly both women froze as the doorbell rang loudly, and then again. Barbie whispered, 'I told you: I'm not officially at home.' After a safe interval she went to the door and opened it cautiously. There on the doorstep lay a casserole dish, and a note that read: *To keep your strength up.*

'People have been so good,' she said. For a moment she hesitated, as if unsure whether to say anything, but then went on. 'I found something else on my doorstep on Easter Day, when I got home from church.' She led the way into a room Evie had not been in before. It must have been her study, with comfortable armchairs grouped together in front of the wall-to-ceiling bookcases overflowing with books. The chairs looked as though they were having a private conversation. Near the window stood a desk piled high with books and papers, and it was here that Barbie headed. Reaching across to the windowsill she lifted up a vase containing what looked like apple blossom. As she did so, Petals scattered, confetti-like.

'It was a family thing,' she said. 'We had a big old apple tree in the garden in my last parish. We used to bring a branch into the house on Easter Day. When Andrew became so ill, he used to lie on the sofa, gazing at that blossom for hours.'

'Is this from your garden here?' Evie asked.

'No, there are no fruit trees here.'

'Then where…?'

Barbie shook her head. 'As I said: I found this on the doorstep on Easter Day.'

The journey back down the hill was much easier than the walk there. Evie's mind darted about. Partly she was so deeply touched to hear something more about Danny and Barbie's home life that she wanted to cry, and another part of her mind was occupied with the thought of Danny creeping up to the vicarage when he knew his mother would be out in order to leave his message of reassurance. That surely meant he couldn't be far away. And she knew where.

By the time she rounded the corner of Paradise Row she had made up her mind. She rapped loudly on the door of No.1, bruising her knuckles as she did so.

'OK Danny. Game's up. Out you come!'

The long silence that followed made her wonder whether she'd got it completely wrong, but she held her ground. Eventually the battered front door opened a crack.

'It's all right, I'm on my own,' she whispered.

The slight hesitation from the other side of the door gave her hope; it also gave her time to get her foot in the doorway before the door was pushed hard, making her cry out in pain.

'Come on, Danny, I'm on your side. Let me in, please.'

She pushed against the door, but it was being pushed with equal resistance from within. This was hopeless!

A sudden sound of whistling made her look round. The postman, who almost never delivered mail to Paradise Row, had inconveniently chosen this moment to appear. Not wanting to draw attention to what was happening, with reluctance she withdrew her foot, and then sauntered off around the corner trying to hide her frustration.

What was the boy up to? He couldn't hide out there indefinitely, scavenging food from Molly's backyard. And how dare he distress his mother like this? Barbie must be out of her mind with worry, no matter how carefully she hid it. Evie found she was stamping as she walked. She was furious with him. Why then was she crying? Barbie's account of the apple blossom had touched her deeply. There was good in the boy, surely, as well as all the anger and hurt. Yet how could he have done what he did to her garden when she thought she was getting through to him? And he had said that it wasn't him: could that be true? Conflicting thoughts chased themselves round and round in her head until she almost screamed at them to stop.

After a very long walk around some of the more depressing parts of the town, Evie was calm enough to make her way back home. She was still undecided on the most appropriate course of action: should she make another attempt to winkle Danny out of no. 1, or leave him to stew for a while? On balance she thought it better to leave him, and with a sigh seated herself at the kitchen table, where a mountain of schoolwork was waiting.

She could no longer put off marking her Year 13 essays on *Paradise Lost*, and as she settled to the task she found her angry feelings finally melting away. Reading the students' responses to the poetry of Milton, she thrilled once again to the ways in which literature opened up new worlds for some of them. True, they found the language difficult, and they were still struggling to understand the ideas behind the words; what did sin mean to Milton's original readers? What did it mean to them? And the garden: what did they make of that? She tried to imagine being told she must leave her garden as Adam and Eve were told to leave theirs; being told that she could go anywhere she liked, except back into her own Eden. And which of two very different places *was* her own Eden now? Tears sprang to her eyes, and she chided herself for being sentimental.

Out in the garden she wandered around, saying hello again to all her plants. It still looked like someone who'd had a really bad haircut, but she loved it anyway, and she felt - crazy as it sounded - that it loved her back. Was this how it was for Barbie and Danny? The boy was far from perfect, and Barbie's love for him was not *despite* that; not *because* of it, either, but just because: because he was her son.

Evie gave herself a good mental shake and decided that she needed a break from both work and contemplation, and hurried indoors to make a shopping list. She would go into town for a few things she needed from the stationer's, maybe have a browse in the bookshop, and then do a supermarket shop.

She was gone for much longer than she'd intended, and on her return thought she heard voices coming from the garden. Dropping her bags on the table, she peered cautiously through the kitchen window. Faint shadows seemed to be moving beneath the trees at the far end, but by the time she had flung open the back door they had disappeared, and she began to doubt herself.

Whoever or whatever it was that she had seen or heard at the edge of her consciousness, it seemed benign. The air was caressing as she stepped outside, and the garden seemed to be offering her reassurance. Nature was healing herself. It would never be the same, of course. She would always know it had been spoilt. Yet, as she looked, she saw that the muddy surface of the pond was clear, and that there was so much new growth in the borders that the damage was largely hidden. She would be able once again to enjoy walking around her little domain at the end of the school day.

At the far end stood the apple tree; there were gaps where branches should have been, and it was decidedly lopsided, yet it still exuded strength and seemed to offer a peaceful refuge as it always had. Sometimes it seemed to her that she had known the tree all her life, and then she told herself to stop being fanciful. The blossom was already starting to fade, but she couldn't be truly sad about that because already she could see where the embryonic apples were beginning to form.

One evening, as the days were getting longer and there was a new warmth in the sun, Evie flung aside her books and wandered out into the garden. She was feeling restless, and she wandered around for a while, not really seeing what she was looking at. Suddenly she noticed something in the pond, lit by the last long rays of the sun. It had the appearance of a cloud of bubbles. As she drew nearer, she noticed that there were others too. Inside each round clear bubble was a tiny black dot. Frog spawn! She called out to Colin, who happened to be in his garden admiring the dahlias.

'Guess what? There's frog spawn!'

'There you are, see? Those frogs have left you something to remember them by!' he called back

She was busy all week, but on the Saturday morning she went out to have another look. The jelly bags still hung there, orphaned just below the level of the pond water. Suddenly, one of them began to twitch, and looking closer Evie saw that the round full stops had become commas. They were wriggling into life.

The news from the pond might be encouraging, but there was still no news of Danny, and as term began she found herself looking wistfully at his empty place at the back of the classroom. She had tried the door to No 1 a few more times, but there seemed to be no sign of life. Remembering how the emergency services had rescued Rose, she wondered if she should talk to Colin about calling them, but the circumstances were completely different this time. Supposing she called them and then the house was after all empty? And she had no real proof that it was Danny in there, but supposing it *was*? Questions would be asked about why she hadn't alerted the authorities sooner, and she had no idea how she might answer them.

More disturbingly, she had passed Olly Stark on the street one evening as she walked home from a long staff meeting. She was unsure how to interpret the look he gave her, but it made her shudder. She had assumed that he would be keeping a low profile since the knife incident, if, that was, he hadn't been locked up. Danny's friend Matt had failed to return to school after being discharged from the hospital, and she understood from Rob that he was also in trouble with the police for carrying a knife.

At break the next morning, she asked Benji about it. He seemed to be the colleague most clued in to what went on at street level.

'Olly Stark? He's only the tip of the iceberg. You really don't want to mess with any of his gang.'

She remembered the damage to Danny's face just after her father's first heart attack, and the hint that drugs were involved.

'I gather he's pleading self-defence. Can't imagine who's paying his bail - most people would be glad to pay to keep him *in*side.'

'What about… I mean isn't he involved with drugs?'

Benji laughed mirthlessly. 'Up to his ears! Usual trick: runs juveniles, gives them a few freebies, gets them hooked and then they have to sell the stuff to pay him for their supplies.'

'But he's only sixteen!'

'Started young, I reckon. Plus some of the gang are a lot older.'

Evie took this in. Benji continued: 'Your little blue-eyed boy Danny made a big mistake in getting mixed up with that lot.'

'I assure you, he is not my blue-eyed boy.' Although she spoke emphatically, she knew as she did so that her anger with Danny had faded. 'I'm a friend of his mother, though, and she's desperate for news.'

'Well, don't hold your breath… Shit, is it that time already? I've got to go. Those feral Year 8s will tear the classroom apart if I'm not there before them!'

The days began to fly by as exam pressure mounted. It was keeping Evie on her toes, and she was finding it a constant challenge to convince some of her students that exams were important. In the face of everything else that was going on she felt inclined to agree with them. How different from Nice School, where exam grades were the be-all and the end-all, and so many parents seemed to think that paying fees would guarantee success. What might count as success here at Other School? Learning to enjoy learning for its own sake? Treating each other with kindness and consideration?

Report-writing season came around and Evie began to imagine the report that might be written about her: *The Genevieve Symmonds is a tender perennial that requires especial care if transplanted. However, given the right conditions, this plant is capable of blooming…*

Oh, for goodness sake! She was becoming obsessed. But the sentiment was right: she had been transplanted, very much against her inclination, and was only now beginning to feel that she was becoming established in her new soil conditions. How would it feel to be transplanted back again? In the long run could she take root in either place? How would it feel - abandoning the gardening metaphor - to walk away from Other Place, back to Nice School; from one place she wasn't sure she fitted to another? Could she bear to leave Other Place? Could she bear not to?

Reaching home one evening after a dispiriting day when she felt she had got nowhere with any of her classes, Evie walked past her own door and on impulse knocked again at no. 1. There were scuffling sounds from within, and she thought she heard someone say 'It's that bloody teacher again.'

Then a gruff voice snarled at her through the letterbox, 'Fuck off if you know what's good for you!'

It was not Danny's voice.

The pressure of schoolwork had largely turned her in on herself, although she had managed to visit Barbie a few times. She was glad she had decided not to raise her friend's hopes by telling her that she thought Danny was squatting at the end of Paradise Row, but after the letterbox encounter the other evening she wondered whether she should have at least told someone something.

The vicar was coping stoically, responding to the needs of her parishioners, and still managing to derive comfort from the apple blossom that had appeared on her doorstep. There had also been an unsigned birthday card that came through the post, with just his name and three kisses, and a few mysterious silent telephone calls. Evie could see how hard it was for her, despite her optimism, and sometimes found herself weeping on her way home from those visits.

Paradise Row was situated not far from the police station and so Evie was accustomed to the sound of sirens, but when her frenzied marking of Year 11 exam practice papers was interrupted one evening by the wailing of sirens right outside her window, accompanied by flashing blue lights, she was immediately worried. This must surely be connected with number.1. Since her attempt to coax Danny - who might not have been Danny - out of the house a few weeks earlier, no further pies had disappeared mysteriously from Molly's backyard and after her unpleasant letterbox experience she had been too nervous to attempt any further contact with whoever might be inside the house.

As the unearthly blue light continued to sweep across the walls of her little living room she found it impossible to resist the urge to go out and see what was happening. Two police vehicles were parked at the far end of the Row, and several officers were approaching number 1. She could hear them discussing their plan of action over the crackling of their radios, and then one of them began banging on the front door. One of his colleagues approached with something that looked like a mini battering ram, and the others stood ready at either side. Ready for what? Evie felt a chill up her spine. Who did they think was in there?

She stepped out from her doorway, noting that Molly's and Colin's doors were also wide open.

They nodded to her, and Colin murmured, 'Best not to get in the way. Just let them do their job.'

Evie ignored his advice. She wanted to be there so Danny would see her when they brought him out, *if* they brought him out, so that - what? So that he would see a friendly face; see that anxiety over his disappearance had overtaken her anger; see that he was forgiven?

There was a sudden flurry of movement and a sound of broken glass. The door was thrown open; dark shadows leapt across the pavement in the headlights' beams; shards of glass and confusion were hurled into the night.

How many? She couldn't be sure; it was hard to see clearly in the swirling blue light. Were any of them tall enough to be Danny? She thought not, and then wasn't sure whether to be relieved or sorry. There was rushing about and swearing, more sounds of breaking glass and raised voices. One of them made a run for it. An officer gave chase. There was a scuffle, figures scattering in all directions. Someone barged heavily into Evie, bruising her shoulder as they did so.

'Keep back, Miss,' she was warned. 'This is a crime scene. You could get hurt.'

The police officers moved swiftly to round up the youths who had emerged from the house and propelled them, none too gently, towards the first police car. She caught snatches of talk.

'How many? three? four?'

'I thought there were four.'

'Nah, Bill, you're seeing things.'

'Where's Smyth? Not got hold of the Stark boy yet?

'Losing his touch!'

Then there was the sound of footsteps skidding on the loose stones of the unmade road behind the houses, and the officer appeared from round the corner, with Olly Stark stumbling along, his arms pinioned behind him by the burly-looking PO Smyth.

Another officer emerged from the house, an official-looking plastic bag in one hand. He was wearing protective gloves.

'Pooh! It stinks in there,' she heard.

'Evidence,' he said, handing the bag over to one of the others. 'Bags of it.'

Then it became like a scene from a TV show, with handcuffs and a lot of yelling and shoving.

'All right, let's get this shower booked.'

'Right, hands on the roof of the car,' one of the POs yelled.

'Oliver Stark, I'm arresting you for the possession of Class A drugs...'

'Jason Gould, I am arresting you on suspicion of possession of Class A drugs...'

Evie was shaken. She had taught Jason on a few occasions, although he had hardly been in school since the previous autumn. She turned and headed back to her own house, past Molly and Colin, who were still standing on their front steps, murmuring quietly as the drama continued. Over by the police car a third youth was being charged.

Once inside her house, Evie sank on to the stained sofa and realised that she was shaking. She had so much hoped that it had been Danny hiding in that house. To think that the odious Olly Stark had been there all this time, just a few doors away from her…

She was shivering, despite the early summer warmth; shock, perhaps. She walked slowly into the kitchen to fill the kettle. Making tea would have been her mum's response to a crisis. It reminded her that she hadn't phoned her for a while.

As she waited for the water to boil she realised that she wasn't feeling as relieved as she might have been to know that Olly Stark was now in custody; that was only half the problem, for she still didn't know where Danny was, or if he was all right.

Then she heard footsteps above her head. She was not alone in the house.

15

Evie forgot to breathe. The footsteps moved again, slowly. They were right above her now, in the little back bedroom: the room she had designated as her study, although it had been largely abandoned in favour of the kitchen table. Her shoulder was still throbbing. She had left her front door carelessly wide open.

As she stood paralysed, her mind blank, a sort of shuffling sound came from above, suggesting that the intruder was sitting on the floor. What she heard next took her completely by surprise: the sound of sobbing. Whoever was up there was weeping, oblivious to her presence in the house.

Slowly, and as silently as she could, she moved from the kitchen, through the living room - the sound of sobbing was louder here - and step by step began to climb the stairs. It was dark up here, the only light filtering up from the living room below. She could see that the study door was ajar. One side of her brain told her to go downstairs and get help: one of the police cars was still parked outside. The other part of her brain urged her to open the door and see who was there and what they intended.

The sobbing had now become a pitiful whimpering; surely no-one in this state could do her harm? With a sudden movement she stepped forward, jerking her hand towards the light switch as she pushed the door wide open.

He was huddled, half under the little table, his long legs drawn up to his chin. His face was turned away from the light, one arm shielded his eyes. She noticed a tear in the sleeve, just above the elbow, and there was blood coming from somewhere.

Heavy footsteps approached the front door. A firm knock made her jump.

'Stay there,' she hissed. 'Don't move - and don't make a sound.'

She could feel her heart thumping as she descended the stairs.

'Sorry to disturb you, madam, but I think you are aware we have been carrying out a police operation on your road this evening?'

She nodded.

'We have apprehended a number of criminals involved in a very nasty drugs ring. They were squatting in the house at the end of the row there.'

Evie nodded again.

'It's all right, nothing to worry about, Madam. We have the people we were after, and they are safely in custody.'

'So?' She looked at him enquiringly.

'Just a few questions. There may have been another person or persons present, who fled the scene. Have you seen anyone?'

Too afraid to speak, Evie shook her head.

'And have you seen any suspicious comings or goings in your road in the past few days?'

Again she shook her head.

'Right. Thank you madam. Let us know if you see anything suspicious, won't you?' and with that he climbed into the waiting car and was gone before Evie fully recognised what she had done.

Back in the little room upstairs, Evie was trying to coax Danny to speak to her, and getting nowhere. He looked terrible.

'Danny, I've just lied to the police for you. At least tell me what is going on.' Frustrated by his continued silence, she blurted out her worst fear.

'Were you part of Olly Stark's drugs gang?'

He looked straight at her, clearly shocked. 'No! No, not since ... you know ... not since that night... then they beat me up when I wouldn't...you know.' His voice dropped to a whisper. 'Sell stuff...'

So much had happened since the night of the parents' evening, when he had rescued her from the other boys' harassment. She was still trying to come to terms with the fact that youths of that age could be serious criminals, arrested virtually on her doorstep. And she still had no idea what Barbie's missing son was doing here in her spare bedroom.

'Right, you need a bath and some food, and then I'll phone your mother and let her know you're safe -- '

He was up on his feet, frantic. 'No, please, please don't do that. They'll target her. Please don't do that, Miss. Not yet.'

'They're in custody, Danny. They can't target anyone.'

'Only for tonight. They'll be out on bail... They'll let them go once they've been charged.' He looked ready to drop.

To calm him she said ‘OK, look: you have a bath and I’ll slip out and get us some fish and chips. How does that sound?’

He nodded, wearily.

‘And, whatever you do, don’t let anyone know you’re here. Understand?’

Thankfully the chip shop was open, and not busy. Evie remembered her first day in Other Place, when she had had recourse to the same chip shop because the kitchen at No. 5 was too filthy to cook in. It felt like another life.

On her return she could hear sounds of splashing from upstairs, and called up to Danny in a loud whisper to let him know that the food had arrived. This gets better and better, she thought. If the police come back for any reason now they’ll find a naked teenager in the house. I’ll probably be arrested for kidnapping, to boot.

She took a deep breath and went into the kitchen, where she got out a couple of plates and opened the bottle of Coke she’d bought at the chip shop. Before daring to switch on the light she pulled the blind tight across the window Danny had smashed on their first meeting. Danny slipped quietly into the kitchen, his wet hair slicked back and his school jumper all twisted where he had pulled it on in a hurry. It made him look very young and very vulnerable. The jumper was inside out.

‘Have you been wearing your school uniform all this time, ever since you left?’

He nodded, with the faintest hint of a wry smile. Then he held out his wrist. He had wrapped one of her flannels around it, but the blood had seeped through.

'Sorry.'

'How bad is it?'

'Not bad enough for the hospital.'

'Then let's eat first and talk about it afterwards.'

They both ate in silence for a while, and then Evie said, 'I was wrong, wasn't I? It wasn't you that vandalised my garden.'

He shook his head solemnly. 'I can see why you thought it was, though.'

'Do you know who did?'

He nodded, but said nothing. Evie decided to leave it at that for now. The immediate priority was to unite mother and son.

'Come on,' she said, gathering up the papers from the fish and chips and dumping them on the kitchen table. 'I think we'd better go by car.'

'Go?'

'Home. To your mum. She needs to know you're safe.'

'But I'm not.' He was clearly agitated. 'And she won't be safe either.'

Too exhausted herself to argue further, and aware that he was in no fit state either, Evie made up a bed in the study, consisting of cushions from downstairs and her spare bedding, of which there wasn't much. She ripped up a clean tea towel for a makeshift bandage on Danny's wrist, after satisfying herself that the bleeding had almost stopped. *This is how it all started*, she thought. *But where will it end?*

It was a cool night, but fortunately the house had retained the warmth of the day, and in any case, the way Danny looked just now, it was clear that no power on earth could have kept him awake. She, by contrast, lay awake making a mental list of all the outrageous and illegal misdemeanours she had committed the previous evening, to say nothing of the morals of the case. The last thing she remembered was hearing the church clock as it struck four, its chimes echoing clearly in the stillness. It sounded so much louder at night.

She was awakened what felt like seconds later by a gentle tap at the door.

'Miss? Miss, are you awake? You should get up now if you're going to be on time for school.'

At least he'd had the sense not to open the door. A fugitive teenager who was somehow mixed up with a criminal gang, in her bedroom, was really something she didn't need.

He tapped again, and this time she answered.

'It's OK Danny, I'm awake.' As an afterthought she added 'Thank you.' Then she began to laugh, somewhere on the edge of hysterics. She was being woken up for school by one of her own students, in her own home, while keeping secret the fact that the boy who had disappeared had now been found...

'Are you all right, Miss?' he asked anxiously from the other side of the door.

When she assured him she was, he told her that he had put the kettle on, and she heard his footsteps padding down the stairs. The mention of the kettle almost had her in hysterics again. Now she was being mothered. For a brief moment the laughter slipped into tears as she realised just how much she longed for her mother's reassuring presence, and then she found she was longing desperately to do the one thing she could never do again: ask her father's advice. He would never have acted as weakly as she had done last night; he would have known exactly what must be done, and he would have done it, whatever the cost.

Danny looked away when she entered the kitchen in her dressing gown. It was of the old-fashioned variety, all-enveloping, but nonetheless, if she hadn't been so desperate for a coffee she would have finished getting dressed first. She took the mug back upstairs with her while she got ready, and then went into the study to rummage about in the book pile. Having found what she was looking for she placed a copy of *Macbeth: Schools Edition* and *The Strange Case of Dr. Jekyll and Mr. Hyde* on top of Danny's makeshift bed. As an afterthought she added a favourite poetry anthology of her own.

'Right,' she said, sweeping into the kitchen with her schoolbag and trying to look like a grownup professional. 'You've missed a lot of school. I've left some reading matter upstairs in your room.' *In your room?* It was as if he'd moved in with her. That was definitely not happening. 'Now listen: you stay upstairs all day; you don't come down at all, you don't go near any windows: *and you read those books*!' This last was said with mock severity.

He smiled, a little awkwardly. 'Can I take my breakfast up with me?'

'Yes - but no crumbs!'

It was tough going that day, with the tiredness and the difficulty Evie had in concentrating. She really didn't want to talk to anyone for fear she might blurt something out, or burst into tears or even hysterical laughter. More than one of her colleagues asked her if she was all right. She managed to avoid most of the adults, hiding away in her room at break and lunchtime under the pretext of work she needed to catch up on.

She could not, however, avoid her classes, but they seemed to sense that something was amiss and kept a low profile throughout the lessons. The Year 11s were the most unsettled, apart from Kelly, who had taken to sitting at the back, next to Danny's empty place. Evie watched her out of the corner of her eye: she looked sad, no, more than that: she looked forlorn. Or lovelorn? Evie felt a familiar angry frustration creeping over her again: Danny had people who cared about him, yet he kept on hurting them.

When the final bell went she headed next door instead of down the hill towards home. Nothing odd about that; she had been popping in to see how Barbie was on a frequent basis over the past few weeks. Today, though, she felt self-conscious, as though everyone she passed knew she had an uncomfortable secret.

Barbie was meeting with her churchwardens in the study, and asked her apologetically if she would mind waiting in the kitchen.

'Put the kettle on,' she said, as she breezed back out to her waiting churchwardens.

The interruption to the meeting appeared to have made them realise the time, and within minutes Barbie was back.

'Perhaps you could do that more often!' she joked. Then she stopped and frowned. 'Are you all right, Evie? You look a bit...*fraught.'*

Evie took a deep breath. 'I need to tell you something under the seal of the confessional.'

Barbie smiled. 'I'm not sure that's quite appropriate, but if you are asking me to keep a secret I can do that. Now come and sit down and I'll put the kettle on...'

'No coffee, thank you.' Evie was wondering how she was going to find the words to explain the inexplicable.

'OK. No coffee.' Barbie sat beside her at the table. 'Now tell me.'

Somehow Evie found the words to explain what had happened. Barbie's eyes gleamed with unshed tears at the news that Danny was found. She knew no more than Evie why he should be afraid for her welfare, but suggested that she visit Evie at home later that evening.

As an afterthought she said: 'You might like to bring him some clean clothes. Shoes as well - the ones he's wearing are falling apart.'

The meeting between mother and son was every bit as emotional as Evie had expected. She led Barbie up to her study, where, true to his promise, Danny had remained the whole day. Barbie had brought a casserole with her - it made a change from receiving them, she said, and with curtains and blinds tightly drawn downstairs the three of them sat around the kitchen table once the initial storm of the reunion had subsided.

'So it wasn't you in the house?' Evie asked between mouthfuls.

'That's where I was heading, when I saw the police. I didn't know Olly and his gang were there. They think I led the police to them. Perhaps I did. They must have been looking for me - I was a missing person.'

'Then where...?'

Danny looked directly at Evie, now. There was an unspoken appeal in his eyes.

'I understand why you thought it was me - your garden. When I saw them in there, trashing it...' I tried to stop them, honestly. I even tried to put it right, a bit...'

'Saw who?'

'Olly and Jason.'

'Why did they do it?'

'To get at me. And because...'

'Because?'

'Because they were angry, Miss. I know how that feels.'

'Who were they angry with?'

Danny shrugged. 'No-one? Everyone?'

None of them spoke for a few moments.

'I tried to stop them, honestly. I even tried to put it right, a bit...'

Evie's heart contracted. 'I'm so sorry for blaming you. It was wrong of me. My father had died, and when I saw what had happened to the garden it all became part of the other loss. I know that sounds weird...'

'No, it's not weird; I lost my father too, remember?'

Evie glanced at Barbie. There were silent tears running down her face. She spoke now.

'And I lost my husband, and for these past few weeks I thought I'd lost you.'

Danny reached out to hug her.

'I'm so sorry. That's why I left the blossom…'

'And the birthday card? That came in the post. You had gone away somewhere…'

He was silent for a while. Without looking at either of them, he said, 'I went back to the place where we'd been happy, all three of us.' Tears were briefly visible in his eyes before he brushed them away.

'Of course.' Barbie's smile was both relieved and sad. 'Oakton.' She turned to Evie to explain. 'My last parish.'

Evie made a pot of tea and led them into the living room to drink it, while she took herself off discreetly into the kitchen, where she lingered over the washing up. She had done exactly the same as Danny at Easter, running away to the place where she had been happy; except she hadn't been, not really. She had tried to persuade herself for three long years that it was the place where she belonged, where she could be a different sort of teacher than either of her parents. She hadn't done all that well in Other Place, but she recognised now just how much it had got under her skin. This was where she wanted to be; it was home.

Returning to the living room she caught the end of the conversation. Danny was explaining how Olly and Jason had wanted to get at him because of his defence of Evie on the night of the parents' evening. That all seemed a very long time ago now, and Evie was ashamed as she remembered the assumptions she had made about Danny and his family.

Barbie cut him short.

'Danny, I'm proud of you for standing up for what was right... and I can't tell you how sorry I am that I wasn't there for you when you needed me most. I didn't even make it to the parents' evening because I had an important meeting that night. At least...' She grimaced,' I thought it was important at the time.'

He shook his head. 'None of this is your fault, Mum.'

Now Evie interrupted. 'Danny, what did you mean when you said your mum wasn't safe if you went home?'

He looked suddenly so much younger than his sixteen years.

'They threatened to break in to the vicarage and hurt her, if I didn't give them the money I owed them.'

Barbie clearly hadn't known about Danny's drug debt. By the standards of much of the talk Evie had heard amongst her colleagues, Danny's dabblings had been minor, compared to some of his peers. Nonetheless, Barbie now had to hear that part of the story. Her only response was to sigh.

'Come on, I'm taking you home. Whatever happens, we'll deal with it.'

For the second day that week Evie went straight to Barbie's from school, leaving the moment the bell rang, surprising her colleagues, who were used to seeing her still at her desk when they left for home.

Barbie and Danny were in the study at the back of the house. They had clearly been deep in conversation, and Evie felt that she shouldn't have come.

'Nonsense. Sit down. I'll get you a mug of coffee.'

Left alone with Danny, Evie was unsure what to say. Eventually she apologised for interrupting his time with his mum.

'It's OK. We've been talking all day.' He smiled apologetically.

Over strong, hot coffee Danny filled in a few more gaps. Yes, he had got mixed up with Olly and his gang when they first arrived. He had passed the initiation test by breaking into Evie's house. Barbie showed no surprise, so he must have told her about that already. That was when they first threatened to hurt his mum. He had believed them.

'Was that why you agreed to sell the drugs?' Evie hoped she wasn't letting any cats out of bags there, but Barbie's expression remained unchanged.

'I just couldn't bring myself to sell the stuff.' He paused again. 'I was so miserable that I smoked it all instead. Then, of course, I was in trouble because I didn't have the money - so they told me I could steal money from the church.'

He looked quickly at Barbie.

'I didn't - didn't even think about it. But when I refused they...' his lip trembled. 'They threatened to break into the vicarage again, to hurt you. I was scared.'

He had asked them to give him more time to pay up. They said a week, but in his distress and confusion he ran away, back to Oakton where he thought he might find someone to lend him the money, where he might find the self he had been before... before his dad died.

'Oh Danny!' Barbie's cry came from somewhere deep inside her, and mother and son clung together for a good few minutes, while Evie felt she really shouldn't be there at all.

'So then I realised that I'd done what I'd done and I'd have to pay the price.'

He gave one of his little smiles. 'Not that I had any real idea how I was going to do that, but I couldn't go home and risk anything happening to Mum.'

'So you came to Paradise Row?'

'Yes, to ask Olly to give me more time to pay.'

'How did you know he was there?'

'Oh, I reckoned that's where he'd be. It wouldn't be the first time.'

Evie shuddered. 'So what happened?'

'The usual threats. Plus they said they'd tell the police I was part of the gang.'

Inspired by Barbie's calm resilience, Evie somehow managed to drag herself to school the next day. Her lessons went better than she had any right to expect, given her total lack of preparation, and she was immensely cheered by a brief text message from Barbie at lunchtime telling her that Danny was recovering well from his ordeal - for he had been sleeping rough over quite a few nights - and the police had been informed that he was no longer missing.

When she got home the following evening she found the local paper behind the door, with the same picture of Danny as before, under a different headline.

THE LOST SHEEP HAS BEEN FOUND.

Sixteen-year-old Danny Desmond, son of the local vicar, rejoins the flock…

Evie pulled a face. Someone at the newspaper office must have thought they were very witty. On an inside page was an account of the arrest of Olly Stark and two others, for drugs-related and other crimes. Olly Stark was already out on bail following a charge of affray and violent disorder. It was the journalist's view that he was likely to be detained in youth custody and given a stiff sentence. Suddenly, Evie was breathing more easily. Just as her hellebores, bowed down by the weight of the winter frost, had nonetheless shrugged it off as the sun warmed them, so Evie found the weight of the past weeks slipping away. She walked into school with a smiling hellebore face.

16

The first part of the summer term was flying by. Exam preparation kept Evie on her toes, even if some of the students needed constant pressure to remember why they were in school. Danny was keeping as low a profile as possible, and Evie strove to regain some professional distance. He had shyly handed her one or two more of his poems. She always responded by telling him what she liked about them, but privately they made her weep, with their raw, adolescent emotion. At least he had an outlet in writing, she thought, unlike some of his angry and alienated peers.

It gave her an idea. The Year 11s were studying poetry for one of their exam units, and so she took the opportunity to set up a lunchtime poetry club, after persuading Rob to set up a competition as an incentive.

On the first Monday lunchtime she sat for 15 minutes in an empty classroom, feeling foolish. The weather had turned warm, and the sunshine streaming in from the concrete yard filled the room with dancing clouds of dust motes, making her long for the coolness of her garden under the fruit trees. This sort of thing would have gone down so well back at Nice School, she thought. What on earth had made her think she could do it here? She had imagined that at least some of the girls would come. On the other hand, she didn't expect Danny, not after the beating he'd had last time his writing had been seen by the other boys.

She was just thinking that she would give it five more minutes and then head back to the staffroom when the classroom door opened a crack and Gary and Matt and a handful of Danny's other friends crept in self-consciously, followed by Danny, who was apparently there to prevent their escape, and a whole gaggle of Year 10 girls. Kelly was the last to arrive, and she seated herself next to Danny.

In between times Evie found herself phoning her mum more frequently. Since the holiday with Sheila she seemed much more like her old self - insofar as she could ever be, thought Evie, with her partner of thirty years gone. Talking to her on the evening after the poetry club's first session, Evie became suddenly aware that she was talking about Other School with enthusiasm.

'Four boys and five girls - not at all bad for a first session,' she was saying. 'I had some more of the boys asking about the Poetry Club in my lesson this afternoon, too.'

'Do you remember the poetry you wrote at that age?' her mum asked.

'Oh, Mum, don't embarrass me!'

'It really helped you when you were struggling to fit in at school.'

'Perhaps I should have taken it up again while I was teaching at Nice School,' she laughed.

'Never mind, Love, you'll be back there soon.'

'Yes, I suppose I will.'

Evie's mum wondered why her daughter's voice suddenly sounded so flat.

Out in the garden next morning, making her usual round, Evie marvelled at the way Nature seemed capable of renewing herself. Now that the fruit trees were fully in leaf, the uneven shape of the broken branches was barely noticeable. The pond was alive with thousands of froglets, their tadpole tails getting shorter by the day. She spent long minutes watching them exercising their new legs as they swam, reminding her of her own feeble efforts at breaststroke; she had never been a strong swimmer. Tiny white roses smothered part of the fence along one side, and Colin had long stopped trimming back the buddleia that overhung his garden. She had even seen him watching the butterflies that alighted there with a look of fascination on his face.

The news from the Forrester Centre continued to be positive, and Evie hoped she would be allowed to visit Rose before too long. Molly was busy preparing for the summer fair at St. Mary's, in between visits to Seth's nursing home and invitations to Evie to stop by for a cup of tea. The poetry club had given way to extra revision sessions, and Evie found herself singing as she strode up the hill to work. It would all be so much easier doing this for a second year: she knew the school now, liked its ethos, understood more about the lives of the students. She had a much better idea of how to handle them, knew that their apparent hostility wasn't personal, had even won a few of them round to giving up their free time to read poetry and express themselves through writing their own.

The grey buildings loomed before her; she remembered her feelings the first time she saw them. How strange: looking at them now she saw a friendly welcome, a place where she was known and even valued

It was on Saturday, as she at last sat out in the garden sipping a glass of chilled wine, something she had long ago imagined herself doing, that the irony struck her. It had taken her some time, but at last she seemed to have found her place. Pity then that she would be leaving it soon.

She went into the house to phone Rosalind.

'Hi Ros.'

'Hi Evie.'

Evie was no longer sure what she had wanted so urgently to say to Ros.

'Evie? Are you all right?'

'Yes. Yes, I'm all right. I really am.'

'Are you sure? You sound a bit strange.'

'Sorry, Ros. I've been sitting in the garden drinking wine and thinking...'

'And would you like to share your thoughts with me?'

'Well...I was just thinking that I'm all right here...'

'You're all right?'

'Yes...well more than that, really. I've realised how much I love this place - it's the people, and my house and the garden and...just everything.'

'You love the house?'

'Yes, it's...'

'Would that be the house with the filthy kitchen in the middle of a post-industrial wasteland that you were telling me about?'

'Well, maybe I wasn't all that keen on it at first, but it, well, it's sort of grown on me...'

'So what are you going to do about it?'

'What do you mean?'

'Well, are you going to stay?'

'Stay?'

'Stay there and not come back here.'

'Oh!'

'Evie, how much wine have you drunk?'

'It's not the wine, Ros. I've only had one glass. But you see, I can't stay. I have to come back. The arrangement is for one year, an exchange.'

Evie's dejection was tangible in the silence that Ros was struggling to break. She said gently, 'Speak to your boss, Evie. See what he says.'

Evie returned to her seat in the garden. The sun had disappeared behind a cloud, and a cool breeze had risen from nowhere. She let her mind range over the thought of never, ever, having to see Mr. HOD of Nice School again; never being humiliated by him, never having to sit, squirming in the visitors' chair in his office, never even having to talk to him again. It was a nice daydream.

Evie slept badly that night. Perhaps she would check with the estate agent next time she was in town to see if the lease on no. 5 could be renewed? No harm in just finding out, surely? Perhaps her counterpart at Nice School was feeling the same? Perhaps she would like to stay on? But hadn't Ros said she could hardly wait to leave? And hadn't she, Evie, signed a contract?

As she took her place in the staff room before Briefing on Monday morning, Pat Robinson sat next to her, giving her a friendly smile.

'Well, Evie, your year of exile is nearly over. You'll soon be back home.' She placed a gentle hand on Evie's arm. 'I'll tell you this: you'll be really missed by your colleagues here.'

'And I'll miss them… Actually, Pat, I'd really like to stay if there is any way I can.' She felt her eyes moistening as she spoke. Had she even known she was going to say that? 'I've learned so much since I've been here. I know I've made lots of mistakes too, and everyone's been so kind and helpful. Now I understand the pupils so much better, and the ethos, and everything…' She knew that she was burbling, and was relieved when the bell rang.

'Well, you need to speak to Rob as soon as possible.' Pat's voice was kind. 'Let me know if I can do anything to help.'

'Thanks, Pat. I really do appreciate all the support you've given me.'

As she rushed off to first lesson she wondered when she could manage to talk to Rob; it wasn't easy at this stage in the term, with everyone so busy.

In the meantime there was teaching to be done. Danny was reacclimatising nicely to being back in school, and the others had stopped pestering him about his time away. He was clearly making a real effort now with his schoolwork, and for the first time since September she could be sure he would be in class every lesson. There was no getting away, though, from the fact that he had missed a lot, and being bright was not going to be enough to get him the grades he was capable of. It seemed that the boy who had avoided school for so much of the term was now keen to stay on for a couple more years, and even, he hinted shyly to Evie, to take A Level English. He had also had a bit of a haircut.

She was seriously worried about what would happen if he found himself disappointed, come results day in August. What could she do to help? And then it struck her: if she offered him extra tuition after school, working one to one without the usual classroom disruptions, she could soon make up for the time he had lost. She put the idea to him as he was leaving the classroom after the Friday afternoon lesson.

'So, what do you think?' She wasn't entirely sure how he would react.

'You'd do that for me, Miss? After all the trouble I've caused you?'

'You'd be giving up some of your free time, Danny, and I'd be expecting you to work hard.'

He looked at her for a moment before speaking. 'You'd be giving up your free time too, Miss. And you'd be having to do extra work as well.'

'I happen to think it's worth the effort, if you want to go on to do A Levels.'

She looked away discreetly as he rubbed a sleeve across his eyes. Did he really have so little sense of his own worth?

Rob was happy to sanction Evie's suggestion of the extra lessons as they spoke briefly when passing in the corridor next day. It was a hurried conversation. The bell rang as they were speaking and they both headed off in opposite directions. Her life was ruled by bells and rushing about at present. Next term it would all be different. If only she could still be there.

As Rob moved on along the bustling corridor, she could hear his calm tones casually enquiring how some of the boys had got on in their match the previous evening.

'We beat them to a pulp, Sir.'

'I'm not quite sure that's the purpose of football, is it?'

She loved this place.

Evie smiled and headed off to her lesson with Year 13. They had been practising exam topics on Paradise Lost, and it had been impossible to get through a single lesson without some humorous reference to Adam and Eve's birthday suits. Somewhere along the line they had wangled her name out of her, and that gave rise to more amusement.

'Genevieve? What sort of name's that?' asked one of the more outspoken girls.

'It's the sort of name my parents gave me,' she'd replied. Some teachers kept their names a closely guarded secret; indeed, at Nice School it was almost a capital offence to tell a pupil, although Evie had never quite understood why. She added: 'Most people call me Evie, though,' and then wished she hadn't as she was then subjected to some more good-humoured ragging about Adam and Evie in the garden of Eden.

Walking home she reflected on this. How strange that she'd had to travel so far, from a place of unspoilt beauty and calm, to find her own Eden in this hectic place of noise and dirt. She laughed to herself as she turned the corner into Paradise Row, and for the first time the name of the place, so seemingly incongruous, registered with her.

There was something different about Number 5. She stopped so suddenly in front of the house that her bag slipped off her shoulder, cascading books and pens onto the paving flags. It seemed minutes before she could fully take it in. The big, ugly wooden sign fixed to the front window frame bore the logo of her estate agent, the agent who had blithely arranged the let ten months ago. The words ‘For Sale’ in red lettering leapt out and hurt her eyesight.

She hammered on Colin’s door.

‘Steady on! Steady…whoa there,’ he said, opening it with a look of alarm on his face. ‘Whatever’s the matter, Lass?’ Then he noticed her things lying on the pavement and went to gather them up.

‘Never mind that!’ she screeched. ‘Did you see who did this?’ and she flung her hand dramatically at the sale board.

‘Aye, the usual. Two men in a van - from that estate agent up the hill. You know…’

‘But it says ‘For Sale.’ When he didn’t respond, presumably because he could very well read what it said, Evie repeated, ‘It says ‘For Sale.’ Not ‘To Let’!’

‘Ah,’ said Colin. He stooped, a little stiffly, to retrieve her things from the pavement. ‘Come on in with me, Lass,’ he said, handing over the crumpled pile of books. ‘I’ll make you a cup of tea.’

Back in her own house Evie tried to ring the estate agents, but they were closed. She would have to wait until the following day to go round and ask them what on earth they thought they were doing. If she was going to stay, she would need to extend her lease. What would happen if someone else bought the house? It was so unfair that this obstacle had been placed in her way, just when she finally knew where she wanted to be. She stumped around the garden for a while, refusing for once to allow it to soothe her, and sensed Colin watching from an upstairs window like a guardian angel. By contrast, Seth, who so often seemed to hover at the edge of her vision as a reminder that it had been his garden long before it was hers, was entirely absent.

She found herself muttering under her breath about the unfairness of it all and failed to notice the rockery looming up until she had stubbed her toe on it. She gave it an angry kick, and that made it hurt twice as much. Then she laughed out loud. She was behaving just like Danny. *Remember*, she told herself, *you're the grownup!*

Once more inside the house she tried to calm down by doing the ironing but singed her best white tee shirt and flung it down in disgust. She needed to think rationally. The owner had every right to sell the house. Was Seth still the owner? She'd never been quite clear about that, having dealt only with the agency. So, they were selling it on behalf of the owner, whoever that was. That meant that someone could buy it - and what if that someone were Evie? The sudden clarity of the idea had her laughing aloud again; the next instant she was groaning at its stupidity: she had no savings for a deposit, no certainty about her future, and even if she did, would she get a mortgage on such a run-down property?

Evie decided to go and see Molly; she could always be counted on to provide a different perspective. However, there was no response when she knocked, several times, on the bright red door, and she had to give up. She was just turning away when Molly herself appeared around the corner of the terrace, moving at a surprising speed that made the poppies on her hat nod up and down like angry birds.

'Molly? Are you all right?'

'No. No, I'm not. Come in, come in,' she said, opening her front door and bustling inside as she motioned Evie to follow her. She didn't even put the kettle on before collapsing onto a kitchen chair. Evie perched on the one opposite.

'Molly, what's wrong?'

'I've just come from the WI. Mrs. Gordon - she's the one whose husband's on the council - says there's an exhibition going up next week. Something about redevelopment. *Redevelopment*!'

Evie waited for more, but Molly appeared to think she'd said all that was necessary. Eventually she asked, 'What redevelopment? Where?'

'Here...' Her friend waved her hands around vaguely. 'Here... all round here...' For the first time Evie realised that Molly was older than she looked, and felt a wave of sadness, like when she had first seen the damage to her garden. Why did these things have to happen? Why couldn't things just stay the same?

'I don't think it can be affecting us, though,' she said aloud. 'Have you seen the For Sale sign outside my house? It wouldn't be up for sale if they were going to, you know, clear us out of here.'

A tiny brave smile lifted the corner of Molly's mouth. 'Is that right? D'you think so?' She moved to the sink. 'Shall I put the kettle on?'

When Evie stormed round to the estate agent's the next day after school there was no-one there apart from the temp, who was busy typing up letters and looked annoyed at the interruption.

'But what right have they to put up a For Sale sign without consulting me?' Evie asked for the third time.

'Well, you're not the owner, are you? I expect it was the owner who asked for the house to go on the market.'

'Don't you know?'

'It's Mr. Benson who deals with that side of town. Why don't you come and see him when he's back in the office?'

'When will that be?'

The young woman shrugged her shoulders. 'They don't tell me their comings and goings.' She sighed and turned back to her keyboard. 'They just leave me with all the boring stuff. It's no fun being a temp.'

As Evie stepped back out into the street, closing the door harder than she'd intended and making the glass in the windows rattle, she repeated the phrase under her breath. *It's no fun being a temp!* Didn't she know it! She'd always felt temporary, even as a schoolgirl, changing schools every few years, out of place at Nice School, and all year she'd been temporary at Other School. But no more! As Rob had pointed out to her at the start of the year, what the students most needed was consistency. And that was what she needed too, if only she could make the estate agent see sense.

There had been caution in Ros' voice when she'd told her she was staying, hadn't there? For the first time she wondered if there would be a battle to make that happen. She gritted her teeth and growled a bit, walking with her head down so that she failed to see Barbie coming in the opposite direction. She had almost knocked the vicar off her feet before she was even aware that she was there. Brushing aside her apologies, the other woman said, 'Heavens! You look as though you could do with a coffee. Come on; there's a really nice coffee shop just down the road.'

Seated in front of a cappuccino in a cup the diameter of a soup plate, Evie inhaled the smell of roasting beans. She could hear the grinding of the machine and the clashing of cups and saucers as she exhaled, sighing.

'I probably need a tranquiliser more than this,' she said.

'So, tell me.'

It all poured out: the job, the For Sale sign, the rumours Molly had heard, the feelings.

'OK, probably best to look at things one at a time. Which is the most pressing?'

'The house, I guess. I just can't believe they can do that.'

'I assume you have a lease. When does it end?'

'End of July.'

'So you have a roof over your head for the next three months.'

'I suppose so.'

'Do you think three months is long enough to sort out the job issue?'

'I hope so.' Evie took a long sip of her coffee, wiping off the frothy moustache that came with it. 'But what about this redevelopment plan? Molly's really worried.'

'I'm not sure how long it's realistic for Molly to stay there anyway,' said Barbie carefully. 'She's older than she looks, you know, and she finds the walk up the hill a struggle on Sundays now. Between you and me...' She lowered her voice and leaned forward a little. 'Please don't let her know I've told you, but she is waiting for some tests.'

Evie felt her eyes fill with tears, for no reason she could account for. Another change. Pulling herself together, she said, 'I'm glad you've told me. I'll keep an eye on her. She's been so good to me.'

Barbie smiled reassuringly. 'I know you will. She speaks very warmly of you, you know. Now, it is true that there is a redevelopment plan for this part of the town, but I think we'll have to wait for the exhibition to find out exactly what's happening. It will be in the Town Hall, starting next week, I think.'

'I'll make sure I go. Then I'll be able to reassure Molly, and Colin.'

'You may not be able to reassure them of course.' Barbie gave a rueful smile. 'Just think about it, Evie. There is all that land, and in the middle of it a little row of houses, semi-derelict, two of them unoccupied - '

'And Rose...'

'No, I don't think Rose will be coming back to live there.'

This time the tears overflowed. Evie wiped her eyes with the back of her hand and apologised.

'So what's really troubling you, Evie?'

'So much is changing, and I don't know who I am or where I belong any more - if I ever did.'

Barbie smiled.

'What?' Evie asked.

'Sorry, it's not really funny, but you do sound exactly like Danny.'

'Must be because I spend my days with adolescents, then. I'm turning into one!' Evie produced a watery smile. 'How is that particular adolescent, anyway?'

Barbie looked alarmed. 'Don't you see him at school?'

'Oh yes! Don't worry: the truanting is a thing of the past. I was only wondering how he is, you know, at home, and with you…'

'We've been a bit worried, to tell you the truth. The police came to interview him, in connection with the Olly Stark business.'

Of course! The gang had threatened to implicate him in their activities. 'What did they say?'

'Well, they asked where he was when the stolen drugs were being handed over, but of course Danny was at Oakton then.'

'Won't the police need proof?'

'Well, as it happens, he has witnesses. He tried to borrow the cash he owed the Stark gang from his godfather in Oakton. We're just waiting for them to interview him. There were other old friends who saw him too.'

Evie realised she'd been holding her breath, and released it slowly.

'What about the threats to you?'

'Well, the only witnesses were other members of the gang. And they never actually harmed me.'

'Did he tell the police about that?'

'Yes. It meant admitting he'd been in possession of a small amount of cannabis, but to be honest, I got the impression that the police felt they had bigger fish to fry. He may not even get a caution.'

'Oh, Barbie, you've had such a terrible time! I'm sorry for bothering you with my worries.'

'Don't be silly. They're real enough, aren't they? And you've done so much for Danny; you've really made a difference.'

Evie swallowed hard. There was no greater gift her friend could have given her.

'And now I'm sorry, Evie.' Barbie glanced at her watch. 'I'm afraid I've got a meeting shortly, but if you want to come up to the Vicarage for a chat, you know you're always welcome. Any time.'

'You've been so good to me, and I'm not even really one of your flock...'

Barbie laughed. 'Well, technically you are, because you live in the parish, but actually I'm not offering you professional services, just a shoulder to cry on and a listening ear, if that helps.'

Evie gulped. 'It does help - just to know that. I'd better let you go,' she said, rising, and the two women parted.

On the way back Evie passed the fish and chip shop. It felt like a lifetime since her very first meal in Other Place; she didn't want even to think about her more recent visit on the night of Olly Stark's arrest. The smell was overwhelmingly tempting, and suddenly feeling hungry, she went in and bought a large haddock and chips. She hurried round the corner, anxious to reach home before they cooled. The sign board was still there, with its big bold lettering, but now it proclaimed: Sold. Evie almost dropped the package of fish and chips, just managing to hold onto them as she wiggled the key and put her shoulder to the door. With so much uncertainty one thing more didn't seem to make much difference, somehow.

17

The days rolled on. Most of the Year 11s were at last remembering to bring writing equipment with them, and some even brought back with them the revision handouts she gave them. This was a relief, as the school had to watch its photocopying bill.

The extra lessons with Danny were going well too. Along with analysing the set texts for his GCSE exams and guiding his essay writing technique, she had begun to whet his appetite a little by describing her A Level classes and the works they were studying. Setting aside any lingering uncertainty about next year she allowed herself tentatively to look forward to teaching him as a Sixth Former, and her heart warmed.

She was tired when they met for the lessons after school, but the tiredness tended to drop away once they started: she was nurturing a tender plant that would one day burst into bloom and bear fruit; of that she was sure.

There was an awkward moment when she first began talking about Paradise Lost, about how sin had entered the world, about the significance of the garden.

He was hesitant at first. 'You know that I…'

'It's all right, Danny. You don't have to say anything about that.'

'But I've been thinking, Miss. I'd really like to do something to help, to make amends. If it hadn't been for me, they wouldn't have had it in for you.'

Evie took a deep breath: things were so interconnected, weren't they? If she hadn't been walking home that night, if she hadn't met with Olly Stark's gang, if Danny hadn't happened to be there... She was so long in her thoughts that Danny prompted her.

'Miss?'

If her father had rested more after his first heart attack, if she hadn't cared so much about the garden in the first place, if she hadn't been a failure at Nice School, if she'd been more supportive of her mother... The list went on and on.

'Sorry, Danny. I was just thinking.' She straightened her shoulders. The ifs were a waste of time and energy; you just had to live in the world as it was. She wanted to make amends, to feel less of a failure, and so did Danny. She smiled encouragingly at him.

'What was it you had in mind?'

'Could I, maybe, come and help you, sometimes, you know, if you needed things carrying, or lifting, or anything? I could learn a bit about gardening by watching you.'

Danny proved useful in the garden. She had not yet had the heart to do anything with the broken branches lying around the base of the trees, and Danny was able to make a pile in a corner in far less time than it would have taken her. He was disappointed when she absolutely refused a bonfire, but he warmed to the idea of providing a home for sleepy ladybirds and other tiny creatures.

'Maybe even a hedgehog,' said Evie, more relaxed than she'd been for a long time, and oblivious of the smears of dirt across her cheeks.

He was happy to take on the task of mowing too, leaving Evie free to deal with the weeds that popped up the moment her back was turned. In her mind she could already see the garden with its autumn display. This year she would definitely do something with the fruit, and meanwhile she would plant rudbeckias and asters and enjoy a blaze of late-flowering colour. She would still be here to see it; somehow she would make that happen.

Conscious that she should really have been spending her Saturdays doing schoolwork, she solved that difficulty by combining Danny's now regular Saturday mornings at her house by transferring his extra coaching to that time too, thus freeing up the after school time she had previously given him.

.

Rob invited her into his office one lunchtime, and she reflected that his manner of doing so could hardly have been more different from Mr. HOD's. As it turned out, that was the very subject he had in mind.

'I've been trying to get in touch with The Cedars.'

'Oh?' Evie held her breath.

'There's something in the agreement about feedback.'

'Oh?' She seemed incapable of saying anything else.

'Don't look so worried, Evie. We've loved having you. You've contributed a lot.' Past tense, she noted. He wasn't about to beg her to stay. He didn't even know that was what she wanted. Why hadn't she talked to him sooner?

She pulled a rueful face. 'After all the things I've got wrong?'

'Yes, but look at the things you've got right; and you've made significant relationships with the students, and that's the key to good teaching. Above all you've learned by the mistakes you've made. Some teachers are so inflexible they stop learning, and then they lose touch with what learning is like for the kids. We've always encouraged the staff to take advantage of evening classes here: learn something new and identify with the young people they teach.'

Evie considered this. She hadn't taken an evening class, but she *had* learned about gardens. Would that count?

'Anyway,' Rob continued. 'As I understand it, the feedback is really meant to be in terms of how the exchange itself has worked, as an arrangement. It's not an end of year report on an individual.'

'So, what now?'

Well, I'm not entirely clear about the format and so on - that was all handled from the Cedars' end. When I spoke to your Head of Department he wasn't particularly helpful.' He pulled a face. 'He's a bit of a charmer, isn't he? Or thinks he is, anyway.'

Rob pushed his shirtsleeves up his arms. It was a hot day. Evie recalled Mr. HOD's immaculate grooming and realised now for the first time that it was part of his intimidation technique. Rob was genuine, she thought. He didn't need to pose and posture with his students, or his staff.

'And?'

'Well, that's just it. I wasn't asking for fine details, just what the process was, really, but he was completely vague, almost as though he really couldn't be bothered, and when I tried to pin him down to a time when it would be convenient, he wasn't sure when he would be available in the near future.'

'Oh?'

'All wrapped up in the most florid language, of course, and politeness itself, but making it clear that his time was far too important...'

'That sounds like him.'

'So, when I do know something of the format for the feedback I will of course share it with you.' He caught her expression. 'Don't look so worried, Evie Even if I was being asked to write a report on you there would be a great deal to say that is positive. And anyway…'

He stood up as the bell sounded.

'The most important feedback is really yours: what you have learned from being here, how that could be applied to The Cedars and so on…'

Evie gave a sigh. How could she ever express all that she had learned here? And how could any of it be made relevant to The Cedars?'

'OK.'

She stood and picked up the pile of handouts she'd been clutching when Rob stopped her in the corridor.

'Well, thanks for trying to find out. I really appreciate it.'

'By the way,' said Rob as they both headed back to their teaching rooms, 'What's happened to your extra lessons with Danny?'

She explained.

'At your house? Is anyone else there when he's with you?'

'Well, no; I live alone.'

'Hmm.'

‘Oh come, on: you’re not suggesting there’s a safeguarding issue here are you?’

‘What you do outside of school isn’t really my business, Evie. All I’m saying is: be careful.’

She should have taken his warning.

Evie had barely closed her front door that evening when she heard agitated knocking, and opening it found both Colin and Molly on the doorstep. They were waving identical pieces of paper, folded A4 letters bearing the council logo.

‘Compulsory purchase,’ said Colin, slapping his down on the kitchen table as soon as Evie had ushered them through. ‘Our houses. Compulsory purchase.’

Skimming the letter, Evie read aloud:

...Compulsory purchase orders (CPOs) ...property in this instance obstructs a regeneration project ...therefore, for the “greater public good”...

Molly began wailing and Colin tried to calm her.

‘Wait a minute,’ said Evie. ‘There’s more: you’d also be entitled to

...reasonable costs for appointing a Chartered Surveyor specialising in Compulsory Purchase to negotiate for you... and for a solicitor to transfer ownership to the buyer if agreement is reached.

'What - go to court?' Molly started wailing again. Colin patted her shoulder until she quietened.

'So...' Evie took a deep breath as she tried to think how best to proceed. 'You both own your own homes?' They nodded in unison.

'So: the letter says that the public body concerned - the council, in this case - are required to pay what the Market Value would be in the absence of the regeneration scheme. Have you any idea what that would be?'

Colin looked at her. 'These houses? Here?' He shook his head slowly and let out a mirthless laugh. 'Next to nothing, I should say.'

'But how much did you pay? I mean you've been here a long time, haven't you? That must mean you've...' She hesitated: 'made a profit' didn't seem quite like the right phrase.

'They might be worth more than we paid for them,' said Colin, as though reading her mind. 'But how much will a new house cost?'

Molly had sat, silent, slumped on one of Evie's kitchen chairs like a deflated cushion. Now she raised her head. 'It's not just that, though, is it? I mean, these are our *homes.* This is where we *live.* I'm used to it here.'

Evie turned her attention back to the letter. 'It says the exhibition will open next Monday,' she said. 'We should go and see what it is they're proposing to build. After all, you might be able to find somewhere really nice - with a modern bathroom and closer to the shops...' She tailed off. Molly's expression showed that she was far from convinced.

'Even a one-bedroom flat would be too dear,' said Colin, quietly. Have you looked in the paper recently?'

Evie pulled a sympathetic face. How could she find a way of giving them some hope?

'And a one-bedroom flat...' Colin shook his head slowly again. 'I mean ...no garden.'

Evie tried not to show her surprise. Until recently Colin's gardening had seemed to her to be more a matter of duty than anything else.

'Would you mind that?' she asked, and was startled to see tears in his eyes. He turned away slightly.

'Life wouldn't be the same, would it?' he said, simply.

To her own surprise Evie found herself giving him a hug. 'Come on: there must be a way to fight this. After all, someone wants to buy my house, so they must be worth something.' She added, as an afterthought, 'And what about Rose's house?'

'Oh, she rented. Landlord used to come round sometimes,' said Molly from the depths of the kitchen chair.

Evie took a breath and spoke in as bright a voice as she could manage. 'Look, I'll go round to the estate agent tomorrow and see if I can find out who's buying my house, and then we should all go and see the development plans at the town hall next week. I'll ask around: there must be someone round here who knows what we should do. The letter says something about paying for professional advice, and…' She peered closely at the letter again. 'And there's this thing called "disturbance compensation".'

After her neighbours had left, Evie sat for a long time, brooding over a mug of coffee that was quickly going cold. Deciding that she could think better if she went for a walk, she slipped on a jacket and picked up her bag. As she stepped out into the street she stood for a moment trying to decide whether to head right or left. Turning her head to the left she saw what she had failed to notice earlier: Rose's house now sported an identical sign to the one on her own.

She approached the house. It had always looked a little uncared for, but now it looked sad and dejected. *Pull yourself together,* she thought: *a house doesn't have feelings*. Still, she couldn't find any other way to describe it, and it somehow fused in her mind with Rose herself: Rose who always stood as though trying to occupy as little space as possible, all folded in on herself, her voice quiet as a whisper. Evie recalled how she had given her the name Shrinking Violet, and how hopeful it had seemed when she learned her real name. The front door still showed the marks left by the emergency services when they had broken in to rescue her earlier in the year, and there were slates missing from the roof. A ridge tile had slipped, hanging dangerously from the guttering, and much of the mortar was missing from between the crumbling red bricks.

Evie had a sudden glimpse of the little terrace as she had first seen it, and she opened her eyes now as she strolled round to the back of the houses. It was like looking at an old black and white photograph of urban deprivation: the stinking abandoned mattresses, the plastic bags and empty beer bottles, the gullies formed by rainwater and other unpleasant liquids. Her feeling of outrage towards the council for their neglect of the place gave way to understanding. Of course they had done nothing: they were already planning sweeping change to the whole area, possibly for years. *Change and decay, in all around I see* she thought. Where had those words come from?

The temp was still in the office next day when Evie called in after school, tapping sulkily away at her keyboard, but Mr. Benson was also there, and had obviously been warned to expect her.

'Do take a seat, Miss Symmonds,' he said unctuously. 'Now how can I help you?'

As she opened her mouth to speak, he added, 'Coffee?'

Evie shook her head impatiently. 'Tea then?' he added as she again tried to speak. 'That's probably more appropriate for this time of day. I expect Kim here could rustle up a plate of biscuits.'

'Mr. Benson,' said Evie between gritted teeth. 'Can you please tell me what is going on?'

He shuffled some papers, then gave her his estate agent's look of utter sincerity, which she instantly distrusted. 'Miss Symmonds, the owner of your rented property has asked us to sell, and we have done so. It doesn't affect you in any way as a sitting tenant, and in any case your lease has only a very short time left to run.'

'And who is the purchaser?'

'Well, of course you are not the owner, and so strictly speaking…'

'Is it the same as the purchaser of Number 4?'

He hesitated. 'Well…'

'Has it any connection with this local authority redevelopment scheme?'

'Well, now, since you've guessed, yes, the local authority is indeed the purchaser.'

'And the price?'

'That I am not at liberty to tell you.

It was raining again when Evie left school the following afternoon, much earlier than usual. She normally waited for the chaos of pent-up teenage energy to be well clear of the concrete yard before she left, but today she was in a hurry. She was jostled by students trying to avoid puddles, while some of the boys were deliberately making a splash. The girls shrieked and the boys retaliated. In the general press Evie was unable to open her umbrella, and her legs were wet from the splashings, deliberate or otherwise, so that she arrived at the town hall, only a short distance from Other School, looking utterly bedraggled. Standing on the steps leading up to the ornate Victorian building, she shook herself like a cat before pushing hard at the heavy revolving door.

A bored-looking woman on the reception desk directed her to the first floor, where the council offices were located, and with a feeling of apprehension Evie climbed the majestic marble staircase, which had clearly seen better days. She had seen nothing of Molly over the weekend, and even though she had spent some time on Sunday mowing her lawn, there had been no sign of Colin in his garden. She thought sadly that he must have felt too disheartened. Who would have thought that the garden was so important to him?

A white notice on a metal stand met her at the top of the stairs, informing her by way of an arrow which way to go if she wanted to see the 'exciting new plans' the council had for the redevelopment.

Inside the room a number of free-standing display boards offered a history of the town, from small settlement to prosperous centre of industry. There were photographs from the town's heyday, contrasted with a number taken in the present. Paradise Row featured amongst these, with an unflattering, although not unjust, comment on the state of the houses. Evie moved on to look at the architect's impressions of the proposed redevelopment, with its modern housing and apartment blocks, its cafes and shops, its tree-lined avenues. The houses were grouped around small cul-de-sacs - 'Bringing Back Community' the caption called it. 'More like 'destroying community' Evie muttered to herself.

A young couple were animatedly imagining themselves living there. Where would she be living a few months from now? Guiltily she set that thought aside: she was here for Molly and Colin, and must extract as much information from the exhibition as she could.

She moved over to the model on the table for a bird's eye view, complete with tiny trees and cars and contented people strolling its streets. It was totally unrecognisable as the town she knew. After quite a few moments' squinting she was able to identify a few remaining landmarks, the spire of the church among them, and thus to establish where Paradise Row was - or rather wasn't any longer - right at the heart of the scheme. It was by no means the only street earmarked for demolition, but she could see that its position made it crucial to the council's plans. That, she thought, meant two things. One: it was essential for them to get hold of the houses - and they already had hers and Rose's - and two: perhaps it gave Molly and Mr. Plod some bargaining power when it came to compensation.

A man in a suit had been hovering for some time. He wore a name badge with the council logo on it. Once or twice he tried to offer his assistance to the visitors, but mostly they waved him away and carried on talking with their companions. He must have been extremely bored at the end of a long day, and so when Evie caught his eye he came over to her with almost indecent haste.

'Is there anything you'd like to know?' he asked, perhaps seeing in the young woman an interested purchaser of one of the town centre apartments.

'I understand the council is issuing compulsory purchase orders on some properties as part of the plan for the redevelopment?'

'Oh, that's interesting. I wonder where you found that information?' he said, his face falling slightly as he glanced round the display boards.

'Oh it's not on public display,' Evie said. 'But it is true, isn't it?'

'Well, I believe so. But very few; only a few old houses that are falling down anyway. The owners will be much better off when we've cleared that whole slum area – '

'I live in one of those houses.'

His eyes nearly popped out of his head. Although bedraggled from the rain, Evie was clearly a professional woman, and after an afternoon spent in front of obstreperous Year 10s her tone was peremptory.

'Well, I don't personally deal with the CPOs,' he said, recovering slightly and retreating into what Evie thought of as passing-the-buck mode, 'But if you've received a letter from the council you should have details there of who to contact. Anything else I can help you with?'

Just then another be-suited council employee came into the room. 'Closing in five minutes, Ladies and gentlemen,' he said, and people began to drift away.

'Thank you,' Evie said grimly, and headed for the stairs.

Somehow Evie's feet took her to the vicarage. Barbie answered the door with a mobile phone clamped to her ear, her shoulder hunched to keep it in place, while her hands were occupied with a pile of papers and a pencil. She nodded to Evie to come in and concluded her phone conversation.

'…Yes, yes I understand. Well, thank you very much for telling me. Yes… I'll let you know. Thank you. Goodbye.' She scribbled a note on one of the papers, dumped the pile on the kitchen table, and slipped the phone into a bag that was lying open on a chair. 'Well, that's good, news of a sort. The person I was going to see is indisposed - between you and me I think he's got the runs - and so I suddenly have a couple of hours free.'

'And I turn up and spoil it. I'm so sorry.'

'Don't be silly. I'd sooner see you any day of the week! That man is a born complainer. He's a believer, not so much in God as in *They*.'

Evie looked puzzled.

'You know: 'They' should do this and 'They' should do that - and sometimes 'You' should… But does he ever volunteer to do anything himself? Or recognise what other people actually do?'

'A bit like: "It wasn't me, it was the snake,"' said Evie, remembering her discussions with the Year 13s.

Barbie raised her eyebrows. 'Been reading Genesis, have we?'

'Well, next best thing: Paradise Lost.'

Barbie threw her head back and laughed. 'I heard all about your trip to the theatre. You gained a lot of street cred amongst some of the students.'

'How did you…? Oh, did Danny…?'

'Oh yes. Word spreads.' Barbie laughed again. She moved across to the worktop where a bottle of wine stood open, and lifted it in invitation.

'That would be lovely,' said Evie, sinking into the only chair without piles of papers on it. Barbie carried the two glasses across.

'Who'd have thought being a vicar would be so paper-intensive?' she asked, removing a pile from her own chair and looking around for somewhere to put it. A sudden thought struck her. 'You're not here about Danny, are you? If you are we'd better talk first and drink later.'

'No, Danny's not in trouble. He's doing fine.' She bit her lip and then plunged into what had really brought her.

'Molly and Colin have received letters from the council issuing Compulsory Purchase Orders. I've just been to the town hall to see the plans. Their houses are right in the middle of the development.'

They batted the topic back and forth for some time. Barbie had seen this sort of thing before, and thought that her friends needed professional advice. She was also sure that they should be entitled to some compensation for the upheaval and need for new furnishings and so on. What she was less sure of was whether it was worth lodging an appeal, given the location of the houses and the state they were in.

'And what about you?' she asked, as Evie began preparing to leave. 'Where are you in all this?'

Evie sighed deeply. In turning her energy to Molly and Colin and their situation, she had been able to forget her own for a while.

'That bad, huh?' said Barbie, sympathetically.

'You know, I walked round there, the night they told me about the CPOs. I looked, really looked at the place. It's awful. I can see why the council want to tear the houses down and build something new and fresh.' She hesitated, struggling to put into words her understanding of where Molly and Colin were coming from. 'But for them - it's their *home*, it's where they feel they belong. And,' she added quietly, 'For a while I thought it was my home too.'

'Here we have no abiding city,' murmured Barbie.

'What?'

'Well, someone a lot wiser than me once said that, basically, home isn't so much a place as something we carry inside us, an ideal.'

Evie absorbed this for a few moments. Could it be true for her? Then she remembered something. 'Where does this come from: *change and decay in all around I see*?'

'Oh thou who changest not, abide with me.'

'Don't tell me: it's a hymn.'

'Yes. Very popular at funerals. Or used to be. Nowadays people want to celebrate the life of the dead person rather than let in the pain of loss. But I'm not sure that helps. I think you have to do both. Everyone needs to grieve in their own way, but they do need to grieve. You and I both know that. Grief takes its own time: there are no short cuts. The cheerful songs, the bright colours and celebration, yes, they have their place, but so often it feels too soon, an avoidance of the fact that someone they loved has died.

'The man who wrote the words of that hymn knew he was dying, you know - that's what makes it so powerful for me. It says that death doesn't have the last word. Maybe that's what they are trying to do with their cheerful songs, but it still feels more like whistling in the dark to me.'

There was a slight pause. Evie wondered what she was thinking.

'It's a bit like *All Things Bright and Beautiful* or *Morning has Broken* at weddings,' Barbie continued. 'They remember singing them at school and don't know anything else - although at least they are better in tone.' She gave a short laugh. 'I did try to draw the line at a cowboy wedding once, though. In the end we compromised: they could dress up as Annie Get your Gun or whatever, but absolutely no guns. And I refused to wear a sheriff's star during the ceremony.'

Evie smiled, unsure whether she was being teased, but it dispersed the gloom and allowed her to leave without feeling she had dumped too much on Barbie.

As she walked back down the hill - the rain had at last stopped - Evie found herself thinking back to what Barbie had said. As a vicar she lived in tied accommodation, just as Evie herself did back at Nice School. Barbie's life was temporary in many ways, but she seemed able to cope with that. Perhaps she did carry in her heart the ideal, the other home that made earthly permanence unnecessary. What would it be like to have such a faith?

18

The rest of the week allowed very little time for such metaphysical pondering as the pace of things was heating up at school, and she was also seeing more of her neighbours than usual as they met to discuss how they should proceed in the face of the CPOs. Evie found out who to contact at the council in the small print of Molly's letter, but Molly was far too flustered to do anything about it herself, and so Evie had to find time to phone during her lunchbreak, which she did several times. It seemed the contact person was also on their lunchbreak. Eventually she stormed up the hill after school on the one evening she wasn't running a revision class, to find that the mysterious council officer had taken the day off.

The answer seemed to be to take legal advice. Both Mr. Plod and Molly were adamant that they wanted to fight the council, and so Evie said she would try to find out about the appeal process. In her heart she felt it would be a waste of time, but thought that might be better coming from a solicitor. She also needed to explore the financial implications of hiring a legal expert, and made some enquiries about compensation on the part of the council. They were unwilling to discuss specifics with her, as her house hadn't been CPO'd, and in any case, she wasn't the owner, but she picked up enough general information to be hopeful that costs could be met.

And then it was the weekend again, and Danny was due for another gardening and English literature session. It rained, a slow, miserable, relentless rain that showed no promise of stopping. They sat indoors and talked, and he showed her the poems he had brought with him.

As she showed him out a group of lads passed the end of the Row. She recognised them as students from St. Mary's.

'Oi Danny!' shouted one.

'A bit of the old extracurricular, eh?' another of them called, making lewd gestures as he did so.

Danny blushed scarlet. ‘I’m so sorry, Miss.’

‘Don’t worry, Danny. It’s not your fault. Now don’t you forget what I said about planning your essays, will you?’

He grinned with relief and waved a cheery goodbye as he set off in the rain.

Evie went slowly indoors and sat and did the worrying for both of them.

Barbie rang out of the blue, quite late one evening.

‘I’m sorry to ask, Evie, but I’m wondering if you can help. Are you going to be at home over half term?’

‘Yes, I should think so. Why?’

‘So you might be free on the Tuesday?’

‘Yes,’ Evie replied cautiously. ‘What is it?’

‘I promised to take Molly to the hospital for her tests that day, but I’m going to have to take a funeral on the Tuesday morning. The family live some distance away, and that’s the only time they can all be here, apparently.’

Evie said that of course, she’d be happy to take her place with Molly. Did Barbie have any idea what was wrong with her?

‘Well, I don’t know for certain, but I think they suspect angina. To be honest, I don’t think all this stress over the CPO is doing her any good.’

After Barbie had rung off Evie sat for a long time trying to decide what to do. Should she suggest giving up the fight and accepting whatever compensation was on offer, or would that too have a negative impact on Molly's health? And if they went on fighting the council it wouldn't only be Molly whose stress levels would rise. She herself was struggling to keep up with work and manage her confusion and uncertainty over her own future.

She rang Ros that evening.

'Hi stranger! How's it going?'

Evie gave her a brief resume of recent events.

'You've certainly become part of the community up there.'

She could sense Ros' indulgent smile, and then heard her tone turn serious.

'So what's happening next year? It's pretty clear Sandy doesn't want to stay here a minute longer than she has to - where does that leave you?'

'What's she like?'

'Stop dodging the question.'

'No but… just tell me: what's she like?'

Ros chuckled. 'She doesn't get on with your Head of Department, that's for sure!'

'She must be OK then.'

'So?'

'I really don't know, Ros. You could say that the situation's all a bit fluid at the moment.'

'You mean you haven't spoken to your boss yet.'

'Well, no. Rob tried to speak to Whyttingham-Smythe about the official feedback but didn't get a straight answer.'

'Yes, that figures. He's been very elusive recently. I really think you need to speak to your boss. You never know: it might be good news.'

'I suppose so.'

Evie made a reluctant mental note to arrange to see Rob the next day, or soon, anyway. Yes, it would all be sorted out, soon… soon.

She put her phone down and realised that what she needed was some time in the garden. The air was still and warm, even at that time of night, and the sky was the deep navy blue of a dusk that follows a cloudless day. It looked like velvet and for an instant she imagined herself reaching out to touch it. Somewhere a late blackbird was singing. She had heard the sound of Colin's lawnmower earlier, just after she came in from work, and now she could smell the cut grass, mingling with the other scents of green and growing things. A police siren sounded in the distance, and she could hear the crunch of someone's trainers as they took a short cut across the land behind the house. Up the hill, towards the town centre, a car engine revved, music blaring from an open window. She loved this garden, she realised, not because it shielded her from the realities of the ugly, painful life around her, but because it made it possible for her to live in and amongst that life.

She went in and made some cocoa, then came out again to drink it in the garden. For the first time in weeks she felt calm, as though there were answers to some of her dilemmas, even though she didn't yet know what they were. A few of the brighter stars were visible now, despite the sodium glare from the town. She gazed up, dizzy with the knowledge that their light was reaching her from the distant past, across unimaginable distances. People say that the stars are coming out, she thought, but that's not true: they were there all along; we just couldn't see them.

Evie's newly calm state of mind persisted all the next day, even when Wayne spilled a full can of coke over Savannah's homework book and Savannah retaliated by splitting his lip with a lucky punch. She remained calm when she glanced at the calendar and realised how little time was left before the exams to finish Year 13's Paradise Lost revision, and even when she caught her sleeve on a nail and ripped it, she accepted it philosophically. As she approached the house after school, pulling faces at the offending 'Sold' sign, however, sshe did begin to wonder whether her calm would survive any more grappling with the ins and outs of Compulsory Purchase Orders and intransigent council officials.

'It's all your fault!' she said to the 'Sold' sign, as she struggled to get her key out without dropping everything else she was carrying. Her calm had vanished.

'Sorry?'

She hadn't seen the young woman standing uncertainly a few doors away.

'Oh, take no notice of me,' said Evie in embarrassment. 'The houses are being compulsorily purchased and it's causing a lot of distress to the residents.' The young woman nodded, but her mind was clearly elsewhere.

'Can I help you?' Evie asked. 'Are you lost?'

'I don't know. I think I'm in the right place, but I haven't been here for ages - since I was a child - and there's no one in and everywhere seems deserted.' She moved closer to Evie, shielding her eyes from the sun as she spoke to her directly. 'I don't suppose you know if Colin Preston still lives here do you?'

Evie apologised for the chaos in the kitchen as she swept her papers aside to give her visitor a seat. *Goodness,* she thought, *I'm turning into Barbie!* During the light evenings she had taken to working at the kitchen table so that she could keep the back door open and feel closer to the garden.

'No, I'm the one who should be apologising for disturbing *you*. It looks as though you have a lot of work to do.'

Evie assured her that it was fine, thinking that one more late night wouldn't make much difference.

'So,' she ventured. 'Are you a friend of Colin's?' She had worried initially in case this pleasant-seeming woman turned out to be from the council, come to wreak more havoc on their little community. As she hesitated, Evie said: 'I'm Evie, by the way.' Her visitor held out her hand.

'Lily,' she said, as they shook.

'Oh... you're Colin's daughter!' Evie called to mind the photographs neatly lined up in Colin's chintzy sitting room. There was still some resemblance to the child she had been, and Evie could see a softer shadow of her father around her eyes and mouth.

'So he's told you about me?'

'Yes, and I've seen your pictures - including the one where your front teeth are missing!'

Lily laughed. 'How embarrassing!' Then she stopped laughing. 'Did he tell you about us - Mum and me - leaving?' Evie nodded. 'And did he tell you why?' Evie nodded again.

'He said you were OK with all that, once you were old enough.'

'Oh yes: he's still my dad. But my mum never forgave him. And I met Tom, my husband, and we had three children very quickly and life got so busy...'

'It can be hard, fitting everything in,' said Evie.

'And then when Mum got so ill she had to come and live with us. It turned the house upside down. She needed her bed downstairs, you see, and with the children and everything...' All Evie could do was nod sympathetically. 'And then, last week... Well, I don't know if he'll want to go to the funeral, but he has a right to know. They never got divorced ...'

Evie thought she heard sounds from next door.

'I think that's him coming in now,' she said. 'But before you go, I need to tell you about what's been happening here.'

At school she seemed to be getting funny looks from some quarters. The PE teacher was doing a lot of nudging and winking. He had never quite let her forget her failure to handle the fight between Kelly and the other girl that lunchtime early in her time at the school.

'How's it going with the toy boy, then?'

She was sitting at a desk in the staff room doing some marking, and he was reading the Daily Mail and distracting her by slurping his tea.

'What?'

'I've been hearing things about you!' He gave her a knowing look.

'I've no idea what you mean.'

'So you don't have any young boys visiting you at home at the weekends, then?' He gave a lascivious wink.

She swung round in her chair to confront him. 'Who told you that?'

'You've been seen,' was all he said, before folding his newspaper and walking out, still sniggering. She noted with irritation that he had left his half-full mug where it was.

It must have been those boys the other Saturday. She had been right to worry. She felt even more worried the next morning when she found the letter in her pigeonhole, handwritten and badly spelt. She tried to arrange a meeting with Rob at break, but he was unavailable for the next couple of days. Here was yet another thing hanging over her.

The Year 13s were doing a practice exam essay. Evie sat watching them through glazed eyes. As they scribbled away she had time to brood. She had messed up. Again! Had Rob also received a letter, accusing her? She had been trying to do the right thing and it had put her in a position where Rob would surely have to discipline her.

The Boy: a year on, almost, and he was still causing her trouble! But no, that was unfair: she was the grownup, and the extra lessons had been at her suggestion. A series of images flashed across her mind: Danny surly and resentful, his arm in a sling; Danny taking charge when Olly Stark and his mates were harassing her; Danny in the garden, shocked by her accusation; tearful as he explained his poem; defeated and afraid after his disappearance. No, she had done the right thing, she was certain.

'Miss? Miss Symmonds?'

How long had Hannah been trying to get her attention?

'Yes, Hannah?'

Hannah had long finished her work, and yes, she had read it through and checked it over. Luke was still feverishly scribbling, and the others were drooping over their papers. Evie had a sudden visceral flashback to her own time as a Sixth-Former and the sheer exhaustion of preparing for A Levels. She smiled encouragingly at them.

The bell rang and as the little group trooped out she realised just how fond of them she had become.

Sitting in Rob's goldfish bowl of an office two days later at break time Evie realised her hands were shaking as she took the proffered cup of coffee.

'So, what is it, Evie? You're looking a bit tense.' It was the stage in the term when even someone as unflappable as Rob was starting to look a bit ragged, and she realised he probably didn't need her coming to him with problems of her own making.

He took a sip of his coffee. Evie was too afraid of spilling hers to risk raising the mug to her lips.

'I should have listened when you warned me about seeing Danny on his own, in my house.' She handed him the letter.

He read carefully. 'Is there any truth in this?'

'Rob! No!'

'Sorry, Evie, but I have to ask.'

She explained about the boys who had seen Danny there, and about the PE teacher.

'Yes, Jake and Noah are the core of the football team. Quite good, too, I believe, but hopelessly immature. Judging by the spelling it's come from one of them.'

'What are you going to do?' she asked tremulously.

'Are you continuing with the lessons?'

She shook her head. 'I phoned his mum last night, to explain… to apologise.'

'Would you like me to take over, give him some extra help? In school, with the classroom door open, naturally?

'Oh, please don't rub it in, Rob. I know you warned me. It's not a mistake I'll ever make again. But, yes, please do give him the help he needs.'

She finally plucked up the courage to ask him about it again, a few days later, over coffee in a quiet corner of the staff room.

'No, Evie. You've done wonders for that boy, and that letter was just a bit of mischief. No formal complaint, no harm done, and certainly no need for action on my part.'

She took a very deep breath, 'There's something I've been wanting to tell you…to ask you. I really want to stay here, and you said you'd, you know, valued me as a member of staff…'

'Well, yes, I'd love you to stay on, but that's not part of the arrangement, is it?'

'Well, no, but… well, you know how much I love being part of this school…and I would love to be able to teach Danny next year.'

Rob sighed. 'Evie, I know how much you would like to do that. I'm sure we'd all like it too, but it's not up to me because it's a formal arrangement between two schools, and it involves two teachers. You are here in place of Sandy, and we are expecting her back next year…'

Ros had said that, hadn't she? Why had she failed to take it on board? Evie had been so caught up in her own struggles and longings… yet surely it was still true that Mr. HOD wouldn't want her back?

'But couldn't I stay?' She realised she was sounding childish.

'Evie, if I had a vacancy and you applied for the job, I've no doubt you'd get it. But the fact is...' The bell rang, and Evie jumped, slopping some of the coffee onto the pile of exercise books on her lap.

'Is there nothing you can do?' she pleaded. 'Do you know if Sandy *wants* to come back?'

'I'm not sure that's even the point...' he began. 'Look, I've got to go. If I don't get to the classroom before Year 9 they'll tear it apart. They're high as kites today for some reason.'

Evie found it almost impossible to settle to anything constructive during half-term week. She was almost glad of the distraction of taking Molly for her hospital appointment on the Tuesday, although both of them found the waiting around between the various tests frustrating, and Molly was clearly tired by the end of it. She was given an appointment to see the consultant for the test results a couple of weeks later.

By the end of the week Evie realised what was wrong. She had not been out in the garden once. How had that happened? As soon as the thought struck her she rushed out without even getting changed into her dirty-jobs clothes. It had been bright and sunny at the front, but the sky above the garden was a sickly yellowish grey. That was all wrong: usually it was brighter out here in the garden than in the town, as though the garden had a special micro-climate of its own. She wandered round restlessly, looking for the calm she usually found here and not finding it. Nothing seemed right today. A strange feeling of dread swept over her as the sky darkened and a wind whipped up out of nowhere sending the branches clashing and the pond water rippling. She went back indoors to make some coffee and cursed because she had no milk. She set off to the shops in a bad mood. It was sunny again.

'Lovely day!' said the lady in the corner shop.

Evie paid for her milk wordlessly and left.

After her cup of coffee - drunk with the kitchen light on because it was now so overcast - she went out into the garden again. As she stepped through the door she caught her breath: surely there was someone there, someone standing very still under the apple tree. The light was poor and she couldn't make out who it was, but she knew that she didn't feel afraid. Indeed, as she approached she felt a strange calm. The man - she could see him now - had long grey hair and an untidy beard. He smiled benignly at her, raised a hand... and then he was no longer there. She stood watching. There was clearly no-one there, and yet there had been, hadn't there?

She became aware of a knocking at her front door, and reluctantly tore herself away to answer it. Colin stood there, blinking a little in the bright sunshine.

'I've got some news!' he said.

'Have you heard from the council?'

'Oh, better than that!' He was beaming from ear to ear. 'I'm going to go and live with Lily and her family. What do you think of that? They can do what they like to my old house now!'

Evie said that she was very pleased for him.

'I'm sorry we've put you to so much trouble,' he added. 'You've been so kind, trying to find out what was going on and looking into the compensation and everything, but now it won't be necessary.' He was trying very hard to look apologetic, but the smiles kept bursting out. 'And do you know what? She's got a big garden at the back; too big for her to manage. Says she wants me to sort it out.'

'That's really wonderful, Colin. I'm so pleased for you.'

After Colin had gone, Evie returned to the garden. It was warm and sunny again there, and her heart lifted to see the line of hollyhocks along the side fence. She knew she would have to leave this place soon; even if she stayed at the school it would never be the same. Paradise Row had been a special, a unique experience, but its days were numbered. She wondered how she would break the news to Molly.

Once more there was knocking at the front door. She wondered what Colin had forgotten, but when she opened the door with a smile on her face, it was Molly who stood there, hatless and with tears in her eyes.

19

Evie was sitting with Molly in Barbie's kitchen. There was something comforting about the chaos, as though it was saying: life is a mess and a muddle, but it goes on.

'You know he didn't suffer, don't you Molly?' the vicar said softly. Molly nodded, and a few more tears slid down her nose.

'But I should have been there,' she said. 'All those times I went to see him, and today…today of all days I didn't.' She scrubbed at her nose with a crumpled tissue.

'I think you made Seth's final years very happy with your visits, Molly. He loved talking about the old days, and about his garden. He died contented.'

'And he never knew about the council,' Molly sniffed. 'Never knew they're going to destroy it. I'm almost glad he didn't live to see that. He put so much of himself into that garden.'

'He was a very special person,' said Evie, feeling close to tears herself.

'You only met him the a few times though, didn't you?'

'Well, yes and no. Every time I went into the garden he seemed to be there, just beyond my field of vision. His presence in that place was very strong.'

There was a kind of respectful pause.

'And what about your own health, Molly? How did you and Evie get on when you went to the hospital on Tuesday?' Barbie asked.

Molly groaned. 'I've got to see the consultant again next week. Bloomin' nuisance.'

She seemed to sink into herself, and without a hat she looked small and vulnerable. 'If it clashes with the funeral I'm not going and that's flat.'

'We'll make sure that doesn't happen. You just tell me when your appointment is and I'll get on to the undertaker.'

The kettle boiled and Barbie busied herself making and pouring the tea.

'Did Seth have no family?' Evie asked Molly.

'No, he never married.' She looked mournful. 'He wanted a wife who would go travelling with him. Wouldn't suit me: I'm a home bird.'

There was a heavy silence, until Evie asked gently, 'What about, you know, brothers and sisters, cousins…?'

'He never mentioned no-one.'

Barbie placed the mugs of tea in front of Molly and Evie and went back for her own.

'He wasn't on his own, though, was he?' she called over her shoulder.

'Oh no,' said Molly quickly. 'Everyone round here knew Seth, and he knew everyone. And everyone loved him.' As Molly's tears threatened to start up again Evie threw in another question to divert her.

'Colin said he travelled a lot?'

'Oh aye, he went everywhere.'

'Do you know why he travelled so much? Was that in the way of business?'

'Dunno, really. He was a bit of a nomad at heart, I s'pose. Wanted to see the world, he said. And so he did!' There was another, slightly awkward silence. 'But his heart was always here.'

She fumbled at the neck of her dress, pulling out a length of gold chain and at the end of it a locket bearing some exotic engraving. 'Brought me this back from India.'

Evie examined it, entranced.

'I wonder what language that is,' she murmured.

'Said it was Sans-something.'

'Sanskrit?'

'Summat like that. One of them dead languages.'

'Do you have any idea what it says?' asked Barbie.

'He said it meant "love".'

The A Level exams started immediately after the half term break, and Evie found herself with a few gaps in her timetable. She was unable to use the time to prepare for the new school year after the summer because she still had no idea where she would be: negotiations with Nice School had stalled. She asked Rob, a little tentatively, if she could use the time to take her friend for a medical appointment, and he had no objection.

'Molly?' he said. 'Oh, I know: the knitting and baking lady with the hats!'

'That's the one,' Evie agreed. 'But she hasn't done much knitting or baking recently, I'm afraid.' In explaining about Molly's illness and her sadness at Seth's death, Evie must have mentioned Colin as well.

'Oh, I know - the policeman? Keeps himself to himself?'

'My next-door-neighbour!' Evie replied, smiling. Is there anyone in the town you don't know?

Rob laughed. 'Not many! So, what time do you need to get away on Wednesday?'

Evie told him, adding, 'It's such a funny time of year, isn't it? For the Year 13s it's all over - well, apart from the exams, obviously - but it won't be really over until they get their results in August and know where they'll be next year, will it?' *And I won't be here to see the looks on their faces when they open those envelopes.*

Rob nodded in agreement. 'Yes, it's hard to know when to say goodbye to them. They tend to just fade away once they've done their last exam.'

This gave her an idea. 'I had wondered whether I could invite them for a picnic at my house,' she told Rob. 'Although, given what's happening with Paradise Row and everything, there are quite a few more people I'd like to say goodbye to as well. Do you think it would be all right to invite them all to a party in my back garden?'

Sounds like a great idea!' her boss said. 'Do I get an invite?'

And so it was arranged, and a date pencilled in: something to look forward to, and to stave off thoughts of the great unknowable gap on the other side of the summer holiday.

Arriving at the hospital again with Molly, Evie was reminded not so much of the previous time, but of her first visit, now nearly a year ago, with an as then unknown Danny. Perhaps it was the young clerk on Reception that made her think of that, the same one that had been there that night, unsure of how to deal with a patient who had no name. Perhaps it was just that her thoughts had recently been turning back to those awful last weeks at Nice School. She sighed deeply, and Molly instantly misinterpreted it.

'I'm sorry to drag you away from school, Chuck. It's so good of you to bring me, but I could have got the bus.'

'No you couldn't, Molly. And I don't mind at all, not in the least. I was just thinking about the fact that I'll be leaving soon. I'll miss you.'

Now it was Molly's turn to sigh. 'Everything's changing. I'm going to be the only one left in the Row. Did you know Colin's going to live with his daughter?'

Evie nodded.

'Don't know how I'll manage.'

Just then a nurse called Molly's name and indicated the room where she was to be seen.

'Will you come in with me?' asked Molly. 'I get all flummoxed and then I don't remember what these doctors have said to me.'

The news was not good, from Molly's point of view. She would need to change her lifestyle, take medication, possibly even have an operation at some time in the future. The consultant was kindly, in an old school, three-piece suit kind of way. He mostly addressed Evie, as though she were Molly's keeper, and Evie kept trying to deflect his remarks back to Molly. As they waited in the pharmacy for what seemed for ever, Molly said, 'By-pass! Makes me sound like this bloomin' whatjamacallit - regeneration thingy.'

Evie laughed. 'He only said *possibly.* It depends on how you take care of yourself, and if you remember to take your medication.' Had there been mention of a by-pass in the plans she'd seen at the town hall? She couldn't remember: the road system certainly needed some improvement. The drive to the hospital had taken them far longer than she'd expected, and it had worked in their favour that the consultant was running late.

'I mean,' Molly was saying, 'If they change all the roads round, it'll mess up the bus routes, and then how will I get to the nursing home? Oh...' For a moment she had forgotten that Seth was no longer there. They lapsed into silence as Evie navigated the intricacies of the pay station and then shepherded Molly gently back to the car. She was aware that Molly was wheezing as she walked, and felt desperately sad for her.

Barbie came round to see Evie that evening, on her way to number 3 to talk funeral arrangements with Molly. In the absence of relatives or a significant other, Molly was the nearest to a next of kin. The nursing home had no record of anyone. Barbie had checked.

'What will you do about the objections to the CPO?' she asked Evie.

'I really don't know. I can't think that a whole lot of stress is going to be good for Molly right now. On the other hand, we ought to see if we can get the maximum amount of compensation; I mean, she'll need it to set up her new home, wherever that is going to be.' She ran her fingers distractedly though her hair. It was getting ridiculously long; she really should have found a hairdresser by now, but she always seemed to have so many other things on her mind. 'I've been looking online. The prices round here are sky high, and the new development won't be any cheaper. It's not fair, is it?' She looked glumly at Barbie.

'I had a word with the manager at the nursing home while I was there,' said Barbie. 'They have a vacancy, now that Seth's...'

'Dead man's shoes? I don't think Molly would go for that.' Evie was shocked. 'Besides, Molly may have angina, but she's not ready to sit around staring into space with a whole lot of old people.'

'Well, she is getting older... But anyway,' Barbie gave herself a shake. 'Firstly, they don't just sit around. That's not how it is any more. I go in there to take a service every month, and I've got to know quite a few of the residents. Some of them are very lively and there are lots of activities. Besides, there is another option. They have a few one-bed apartments on site. I've looked: they are really very nice.' Seeing Evie's doubtful look, she added, 'Honestly, they are! The residents are independent, but if they need help they have instant access, including professional nursing, and as they become increasingly infirm, they can move into the main building.'

'Do these apartments have a kitchen?'

'Oh yes, Molly would still be able to bake.'

Evie wondered whether Molly would be able to afford one, and Barbie suggested that the only way to answer that question was to find out how much they cost and how much Molly could realistically expect from the compulsory sale of her house.

'Anyway,' said Barbie, glancing at her watch, 'I'd better get next door and talk about the funeral. Do you want to come?'

Molly had gone overboard with the baking for their little meeting and in amongst the clatter of mugs and plates and the murmurs of appreciation it was difficult to talk seriously about anything until they had all declined, at least twice, to eat another crumb. Colin was there too, and the manager of the nursing home, a pleasant and surprisingly young woman.

'I don't know how easy it will be to arrange,' she was saying as the others subsided into chocolate cake-induced stupor. 'But quite a few of the residents would like to be there. He was quite a favourite.'

'Are you worried about getting them there physically?' asked Barbie.

'We have a specially adapted bus,' said the manager. 'But we still have to get them out of it and into the church.'

'There's an entrance round the side with a ramp.'

'Well that will be a help, but we will still need people to push the wheelchairs, and I can't bring too many staff with me or we'll be under ratio back at base.'

'Surely some of them can walk?' asked Evie.

'Oh yes, but even they might need help.'

There was a thought-filled pause. 'I wonder…'said Evie. 'Look, this might be crazy, but if I can find enough students who aren't doing exams, and if I can get permission…What do you think?'

They moved on then to discussing hymns.

'Abide with me,' said Colin. 'Has to be.'

'Do you know if he had any special favourites, Molly?' asked Barbie.

'Dunno. Are there any hymns about gardens?'

'Even if there aren't, said Evie, 'we should include the garden in some way.'

'We can do that in the readings,' said Barbie.

'And we can bring things in from the garden.'

'My hellebores!' said Evie.

'Not really,' said Colin, apologetically. 'They're not exactly at their best at this time of year, are they?'

There was a glum silence. Finally Evie said 'And anyway, how will we pay for all this, if we have to go to a florist, that is? Come to that, who's paying for the funeral itself?'

Barbie and the nursing home manager began to speak at once. The vicar indicated that the other should go first.

'As far as I know, Seth still had a considerable amount of cash in the bank. But of course, we won't have access to it until after his will has been read.'

'He made a will?'

'Oh yes, we encourage all our residents to think about doing that if they haven't already.'

'In any case,' said Barbie, 'The church has a discretionary fund for cases like this where someone has no known living relatives.' She smiled at the others. 'It might even stretch as far as some greenery,' she said.

Molly gave a watery smile. 'Greenery. Yes, Seth's got to have greenery. We'll give him the send-off he deserves.

On the day itself the students were magnificent. Evie had never seen most of them out of uniform before, and she found it touching to see how hard they had tried to dress appropriately, within their means. Wayne was there, specially wearing a pair of black trainers that looked as though they belonged to someone else. Kelly had made an effort at decency by wearing a black cardigan slightly longer than her mini-skirt, and the Sixth Formers, some of them with memories of dressing for University open days or job interview, had all managed to look smart with well-brushed hair and no outlandish make-up.

She mentally compared their appearance to that of the Nice School students; fashionable, tasteful and expensive was the order of the day there. She knew that she was being unfair, because some of those parents worked hard and did without things in order to pay the fees, and presumably to enable their offspring to compete in the fashion stakes with their better off peers. However, she was certain that not one of them would ever have had recourse to the clothing equivalent of a foodbank, which she had seen several of the St Mary's students leaving, with carrier bags they were trying hard not to acknowledge as theirs. But maybe that was unfair on the Nice School students too: how were they to know what it was like if they'd never experienced it?

Not all the care home residents were in wheelchairs, while a good few were leaning on sticks and walked slowly from the bus, where the care-workers were helping them down before turning to the hydraulic lift at the back and freeing the wheelchairs from their safety restraints. Evie was amazed - and proud - at the patience shown by the students. Wayne was positively charming the frail looking lady with wispy grey hair that he accompanied to her seat near the back of the church, and some of the other elderly residents were clearly enjoying their outing and looked more as though they were on their way to a party than a funeral. She couldn't blame them, she supposed, and anyway she overheard all sorts of snippets of conversation that told of how much Seth had been loved. Surely he would not have begrudged them a bit of fun as they remembered him?

Evie herself had brought Molly and Colin in her car, and they were waiting patiently, still done up in their seatbelts while she checked on the guests. Molly was looking shell-shocked, and Colin was desperately attempting conversation of the traditional kind at funerals. Coming back to the car to let them out, Evie caught the tail-end.

'Well, it's a good turnout.'

Molly sniffed.

'You can see they're determined to give him a good send-off.'

Molly sniffed again.

'It's nothing less than he deserves.'

At that point Evie saw the hearse approaching up the hill. Molly and Colin were to walk behind the coffin as chief mourners, and she knew she would be required to support Molly. Although she had not really known Seth, not as these others had, she felt it was right for her to be there: she had known Seth through his garden.

As the undertakers slid the long wooden box from the hearse and moved into their well-practised routine for raising it to their shoulders Evie gently ushered the others into position behind them, noting as she did so the bright colours of the flowers cascading over the coffin. Barbie patted Molly's shoulder reassuringly, and took her place at the head of the little procession as it moved in through the west door.

'I am the Resurrection and the life…'

Evie could hear Molly sniffing, and quietly slipped her one of her own tissues. Although the whole atmosphere of this funeral was so different from her father's, the familiar words suddenly transported her back to that same moment of following the coffin, and she wondered if she would also need some of the tissues herself. At her father's funeral her mother had stumbled as they walked to their seats at the front, and Auntie Sheila had taken charge of her, rather as though she had been a difficult child. It was almost as though crying were not allowed. This time, it was different.

20

Back at school the next day the atmosphere was strange. Classrooms stood empty while the hall and the gym filled up with white-faced students clutching their plastic bags of writing tools and shuffling nervously from foot to foot. The day of reckoning had come, and in the minds of some it had become absorbed into the previous day's experience: they realised now that they were not immortal. They had seen the frailties of old age up close, and it served as a *memento mori.* Silently they filed into their allotted places; no arguments, no pushing and shoving. Even the students in the younger classes were affected by the sombre atmosphere, and Evie struggled to summon up the energy to teach them.

Two days later she found that Rob had left a note in her pigeon-hole: *can you come and see me at break? I may have some news for you. Rob.* Now everything was changed. Her students must have wondered at her ebullient mood, as she rattled through lessons and bounced along corridors. So her exchange partner had decided to stay at Nice School, or at least she wasn't planning to return to Other School? Evie could get on with her life: she had a future in this place; she no longer had to face saying goodbye to the friends she had made here.

The moment the bell rang she left her classroom, where she'd been enthusiastically trying to impress on her Year Nines the importance of punctuation, and managed to get up the stairs to Rob's classroom before the main student rush for the canteen. Rob was still gathering up books and papers from his desk when she entered.

'Hi. I got your note.'

Too excited to sit down, she began pacing about the classroom, half-glancing at Rob's display boards, and exulting to herself that now she could start planning for next year.

Her boss smiled.

'Ah, Evie; thanks for coming. I'll be with you in half a sec.' He shuffled the papers a bit and took them into his office.

Evie forced herself to take a seat at one of the student's desks.

Rob re-emerged, looking thoughtful.

'So - Sandy has decided to stay after all? At The Cedars? I can stay here?'

The expression on Rob's face told her that this was not the news he had for her. She felt her face fall, and bit her lip to hold back the tears.

'Ah, no, Evie. that's really not on. We did talk about this before, didn't we? The whole point of the experiment, as I understand it, anyway, was that you should both return to your original schools and complete it by spending a year *cascading* ' - he made quotation marks in the air - 'cascading what you have learned on your year's secondment to your colleagues back at base.'

'Oh, but...' Evie was struggling. Her shoulders sagged. 'Well, fair enough. I haven't exactly covered myself with glory while I've been here, have I?'

'Two things, Evie: firstly, teachers don't do *glory*.' He gave a wry smile. 'We are here to enable our students to learn: about themselves, about the world, and about a number of academic subjects. Secondly,' he went on, quickly, as he saw her about to protest, or possibly cry. 'Secondly: we have valued having you here; you've made some important relationships among our young people. You've even got them interested in poetry, for goodness sake! I personally would love to keep you in the department.'

'So...?'

'So the news is this. Pat Robinson has just told me - entirely informally at the moment - that she would like to take early retirement in a year's time.'

Evie sat, wondering how this affected her.

'So there'll be a job vacancy next year. It will be advertised after Easter.'

'Oh.'

'Is that all you've got to say? I thought you'd be pleased.'

'Well, of course I am. Thank you for telling me,' she said, aware that she must seem ungracious. 'But that's a whole year away, and there's no saying I'll get the job, is there?'

'And there's no saying you won't, either. Really, Evie, you have a very good chance.' He smiled a little ruefully. 'We don't usually have candidates queuing at the door for jobs here, let alone someone like you who actively *wants* to work here.'

'Thank you, Rob. I really do appreciate your telling me.' She was still feeling deflated.

'I have some other news as well,' said Rob. 'Olly Stark and his pals have been sentenced for their drugs activities. Olly will be away for some time, because of the charge of violent affray following the knife incident outside school. Danny won't be having any more trouble from that quarter.'

Evie did her best to look sympathetic. 'I'm sorry, Rob. I know you had a soft spot for Olly when he was younger.'

Rob sighed. 'Sometimes it's too late, or there are just too many obstacles to overcome.' Then he brightened.

'But you were able to help Danny, at just the moment he needed it.'

Evie smiled. 'Yes, as you say: right place, right time.'

After a brief pause, Rob said, 'And the other positive news is that Kelly Wilson's grandmother is moving in with the family. She's a sensible woman and she'll look after Kelly and give her the attention she needs.'

It didn't quite take away Evie's sadness at the thought of leaving, but it did soften the blow a little. And who knew? Perhaps there would be another miracle.

The following day there was an official-looking envelope on Evie's doormat. Even after she opened it the letter heading made no sense: The Department for Education. Why on earth were they writing to her? She forced herself to read it. *Dear Ms. Symmonds* blah blah blah *Congratulations on completing* blad blah blah... *Guidance... standard format for feedback... within six weeks of the start of term...thank you for taking part...*

So that was it. No eleventh hour reprieve. She was contractually obliged to return to Nice School. Not-so-nice school.

She dropped the letter on the kitchen table and headed out into the garden. She had mown the grass too short and now, in the July heat it was wilting and turning brown. She should water it, but what was the point? A painful parting lay ahead. It was like breaking up with a lover: they were being parted by forces stronger than either of them, and the garden and its little house would soon be gone.

The end of term came at last, and Evie's garden party didn't happen. She had to be out of the house, with no possibility of extending her lease, and the students had already begun to disperse as soon as each of them finished their final exam. In some ways she was glad to be spared the painful necessity of saying lots of goodbyes. In the end she herself slipped away quietly, after a brief word of farewell and thanks to Rob.

'You really have been patient with me this year. I've learned such a lot,' she said, during a quiet moment in the staffroom on the last morning. 'I'm going to miss St. Mary's so much…'

'And we'll miss you. Really, Evie. I mean it.'

'I'd like to come back for the exam results, if that's OK?'

'It certainly is! We need all the help we can get on results day. And not just setting up the tables and putting out the envelopes either.' Rob smiled at her. 'We'll need you to lend a sympathetic ear. There may be tears to mop up.'

So Evie once again packed up and drove to her parents' house, remembering the previous year when she and her father had argued and her mother had been driven to distraction by his irritability. She had been mourning her sudden banishment from Nice School, and had left in haste to begin her exile in Paradise Row. Now she had returned from exile, and was beginning a new one.

There were positives, though: her mother was no longer on edge, her grief tempered with the good memories finally returning to remind her of a long marriage. She and Evie talked, sitting up late into the night, and Evie heard stories of her parents' early married life that were completely new to her, as well as some of the old, familiar ones. At times they shed tears together too, and Evie recalled what Barbie had said about the need to face your feelings in order even to begin to deal with them. Her mother's need to depend on Auntie Sheila had lessened, and Evie began to understand how much the need was mutual: Auntie Sheila had needed to be needed, had needed to take control. Like Colin and his need to be in control of the garden, Evie thought, and her feelings towards her aunt mellowed.

Then it was mid-August and Evie travelled back up north to be there when her students opened the dreaded envelopes; she intended to be there a fortnight later for the GCSE results as well. Barbie had insisted she stay with her on both occasions, and it gave her a chance to catch up with Molly in the retirement home. She received a warm welcome.

'Come in, come in. Sit yourself down. What do you think of my new home?'

'Molly it's lovely! It all looks very comfortable - and you seem very settled here.'

'Oh, I am that, Luvvie, I am that. Now you rest your legs while I put the kettle on.' Molly disappeared into what Evie supposed was the kitchen. It seemed odd to be in Molly's sitting room instead of seated in her friendly kitchen at number 3.

She looked around her at the tastefully decorated walls, the matching curtains and the feature wall papered with large peony-like flowers. She recognised from her Paradise Row days the china dogs and shepherdesses Molly had arranged along the window-sill, and the glass knick-knacks on a shelf on the opposite wall. The window looked out onto a sloping lawn, framed by shrubs, and Evie felt a sharp pain of longing for her own garden. *Although it was never my own,* she thought. *I was just looking after it for others.* She sighed, thinking of all the generations who had lived and worked on that spot, long before the building of Paradise Row. It had not always been a garden, but it had always been a part of the earth, a living thing, even when ploughed up to grow food. All of them, all the generations, had held it in trust for the next. *But it ends with me*, she thought, and sighed again at the thought of the bulldozers and the heavy lorries, the bricks and mortar and concrete that would replace the green space, the flowers, the trees. They had survived the winter snows, even the depredations of teenage boys, but they could not survive a Compulsory Purchase Order.

'Here we are, m'Luv!' Molly breezed in, bearing a tray with cups, saucers and, of course, a chocolate cake.

'Took me a while to get the hang of the new oven,' she said, putting the tray down on the coffee table. 'But I reckon this cake's as good as any I've baked before, so I must be getting it right.'

Talk was suspended for a while as they got down to the serious business of pouring tea and eating slices of Molly's ever moist and extra-chocolatey chocolate cake. Eventually, Evie sat back and asked her,

So, how are you Molly? Really?'

'Well, m'Luv, better than I expected. Better than I ever expected. There are some nice folk here, and we have get-togethers some afternoons.' She sat back in her chair. 'Yes, I like it here well enough.'

'What about your health?'

'It's OK. I keep taking the medicine. And praying. The vicar comes and takes a service here some Sundays and we have coffee afterwards. I generally make cakes or gingerbread or summat to have with it. Some of the other ladies have offered, but...' She shook her head and pulled her mouth downwards to indicate that, although she was too modest to say, their cakes really weren't as good as hers.

Evie suddenly realised that Molly wasn't wearing a hat. Molly must have seen her looking in the direction of her head, because she answered the question Evie hadn't asked.

'So warm in here! Have to take me layers off. And me head gets so hot!'

There was silence for a while, and Evie heard Molly's clock ticking on the mantelpiece. She noticed too that Molly's breathing sounded a little uneven.

'I do miss him, though, Seth,' she said simply, and Evie moved across to give her a hug. She missed him too.

A level results day was such a contrast with her experience at Nice School, where anything but the top grade was deemed failure, so that students who had worked hard all year and done their best still often left in tears. At St. Mary's, Evie was surrounded by a cheerful group of Sixth formers, none of whom had gained top grades, but all of whom were proud of what they had achieved. Evie congratulated all of them warmly. She was quietly thrilled that Hannah and Milly had both gained the grades across all their subjects that they needed to take up university places - not the most prestigious universities, but places where Evie believed they would be happy. She was utterly delighted that they had both chosen to study English.

At last all the envelopes were gone, all the students sent on their way with heartening words wherever possible, and the staff gathered to drink coffee and exchange news. There was a lot of talk about the new term, and Evie did her best to hide her disappointment that she would not be there with them. Strange to think how much she hadn't wanted to be here a year ago.

'Come on, cheer up Evie.' Rob broke into her thoughts. 'We're meeting up for a drink later on. Come with us.'

The pub was noisy and crowded, and after a quick glass of orange juice Evie scuttled off back to Barbie's, where she knew her friend would understand how hard it was to be there, with the old crowd and yet no longer part of it all.

A fortnight later Evie was back again for the GCSE results, and on the day itself she was at the school so early that the caretaker was only just unlocking the doors. She went straight to the hall and began to help with setting up the tables where the envelopes would be laid out in alphabetical order.

Rob came in. He had a list of the English results, and they pored over them together, exclaiming every so often when a student had done better than expected, tutting when the result was a disappointment. The students Evie had taught didn't seem to have done any worse than any of the others, which was a great relief. She realised that she had unconsciously brought with her the dread of results day that pertained at Nice School, where any failure by any student under any circumstances was laid squarely at the door of the person who had taught them. The unfortunate teacher would later be the subject of a dispiriting post-mortem.

To her utter delight Danny Desmond had passed both English and English Literature with creditable grades.

'Will he be able to go on to A Level?' Evie asked Rob anxiously.

'Do you think he wants to?' her boss asked.

'Well, I did talk to him about it.' Evie smiled with satisfaction.

That evening, at the vicarage, they had a celebratory take-away - Danny's choice of reward.

'Thanks, Miss,' he said, giving her a serious look.

'Well it was you who passed the exam, Danny,' she said.

'But I couldn't have done it without you.'

When he had gone out to celebrate with his friends, although in some cases it was commiseration that was in order, Barbie and Evie opened a bottle of wine and took their glasses out into the vicarage garden, a wild and tangled affair, rather like Danny himself as she had first known him. Evie wondered if she should say that to Barbie and describe in detail her first encounter with him, but then decided that some things were better left unsaid.

'Danny's right,' Barbie said. 'He couldn't have done it without you.'

Evie waved the words away, but was glad to hear them, anyway. Her year of exile had not been wasted.

They sat, enjoying the warm evening sunshine, sipping at their wine and listening to the blackbirds calling above the noise of the traffic.

'So,' Barbie said at last. 'How are you feeling? About going back to Nice School?' She had caught Evie's habit of giving names to people and places one day when Evie had inadvertently let something slip.

Evie groaned. 'I've thought about it so much I don't actually know any more how I feel,' she said.

'Then just let it gestate,' her friend advised.

21

When Evie had parked her car in the usual spot outside the flat, she headed up the familiar staircase, noting the way it leaned to the left where the wood had warped over the centuries. The third stair from the top squeaked. She had forgotten these things, even since Easter.

Ros was there to greet her with a hug and chocolate biscuits.

'Come on, I've got the kettle on. Tea or coffee?'

They settled into Ros' living room - smaller than Evie had remembered. It was strange what absence did to the memory. Ros had lots of light-hearted stories and gossip to share and Evie was glad to listen; she wasn't ready to talk yet. Eventually, when Ros had run out of things to say, Evie asked:

'Have you been in my flat? What state is it in?' This was easier than asking what Sandy had been like.

'Oh, the flat's all ready for you. And if you're wondering, we all got on fine with your temporary replacement, but she wasn't you.'

Evie said nothing. It was good to know that she'd been missed.

'Actually,' Ros continued. 'I don't think she was particularly happy during her year here.'

'Well, having seen where she came from, I'm not surprised.'

'Oh?'

'There's something I must do,' Evie said suddenly, jumping up. 'I've left something important in the car.' Ros walked down with her and watched with bemusement as Evie hauled out from where it had been wedged between the front and back seats a large earthenware pot containing the remains of a half-dead plant.

'Evie - what on earth…?'

'It's from my garden.'

'It's not in very good shape, is it?'

'It will be; it'll flower around Christmas time. You'll see.'

Ros decided to give her friend the benefit of the doubt, but ventured to ask where she planned to put it. Evie's face fell.

'I don't know,' she wailed. 'But it had to come back with me: it was a special gift, and it's seen me through some tough times'

Ros decided not to question her any further, and suggested there might be room for it on the landing between the two flats while they considered a more permanent home for it out of doors.

After that Evie suddenly found she had the energy after all to recount some of her experiences at St. Mary's, and enjoyed watching her friend's expression as she described fights and school uniforms purchased on market stalls, students with multiple piercings and young people who were carers. She told her about Danny and all her hopes for his future, and she knew she was starting to sound wistful.

'Doesn't sound as though you're all that happy to be back,' said Ros.

'Hmm,' said Evie.

After she had lugged her cases up the stairs and put some of her books back on the shelves in her tiny living room, Evie decided to go for a walk about the grounds. It was still two weeks before the start of Nice School term and it seemed strange to think of her colleagues - former colleagues - at St. Mary's already hard at work in front of their new classes.

Deep in thought, she let her feet find their own way, and came to herself at the far perimeter of the grounds. From here she had a view right across the lawns and flowerbeds to the main building. It was a beautiful garden, right enough, and it would be churlish to compare it unfavourably with the rough patch behind Paradise Row, but it failed to lift her spirits in the way they had always been lifted the moment she stepped out of the back door. Her thoughts floated back to her Year Thirteens, struggling to make sense of Adam and Eve expelled from their garden, and she thought how ironic it was that she had left this place a year ago feeling exiled, and yet now her return felt like another exile.

A stranger caught her attention, a man doing much what she was doing it seemed, a stranger who didn't seem like a stranger, somehow, for she could easily imagine him in her garden at Paradise Row. He was wandering around the grounds enjoying the air. Smiling he came across to her and then paused a few feet away.

'Hello,' she said.

'Hello,' he replied. 'I don't think we've met. I'm Alex Fairfield. I'm new to the English department.'

'Oh, then we'll be colleagues. I'm Genevieve Symmonds. I've been away for a year on an exchange scheme.' She smiled at him, noting the jeans and open necked shirt and wondering how he would fit in.

'Oh good,' he said. 'I've heard about you.'

There was a slightly awkward pause as Evie wondered what he'd heard.

'I'm looking forward to being your line manager.'

Evie frowned. This made no sense.

The stranger added: 'I, er, actually, I'm going to be head of department.'

Evie stared for a moment, trying to take this in. 'So…? What…? I don't understand… What's happened to…?'

Her companion looked around as though checking whether there was anyone to overhear. 'I never actually met my, er, predecessor; it was the Principle who interviewed me. I gather Mr. Whyttingham-Smythe left under a bit of a cloud.'

Evie's eyes widened, and then she laughed. 'Would you like some tea? I was just thinking of going back to my flat to put the kettle on.'

After Alex had left, Ros appeared on the threshold.

'Yes, I thought you two would get on,' she grinned. 'Any tea left in the pot?'

Evie boiled the kettle again; she felt she was turning into her mother, but since it was too early in all conscience to start drinking wine, tea it would have to be.

'Why didn't you tell me?' she asked, as soon as they had a mug each. 'About old Whyttingham-Smythe?'

'I thought you'd enjoy finding out for yourself.'

'Alex said he left under a cloud. Do you know what happened?'

Ros settled down to tell the story. Mr HOD's general attitude and high-handedness, to say nothing of his squirrelling away of departmental funds for his own use, had finally reached the attention of the Principle, who tended to have his mind on other things, such as wooing new parents and publicising the excellence of Nice School. At another time Mr. Whyttingham-Smythe's misdemeanours might have occasioned merely a slap on the wrist, but even before that could be administered, something worse had happened.

'It wasn't something you'd have wanted to hear the moment you got back anyway, Evie. It was, well, it was pretty horrible…'

'Oh come on, Ros. What happened?'

Her friend hesitated.

'Did Whyttingham-Smythe ever strike you as a bit of a bully?'

'A *bit* of a bully? You're not joking! He bullied me right enough.'

'Yes, that's what I thought.' Ros took another slurp of tea. 'Well, I don't know if you remember a Sixth Former name of James Langley-Jones? Bit of a poser but all right really?'

'Yes, I taught him. Not that he did much learning, I have to say. And his mother…' Evie stopped as she caught her friend's expression. 'What?'

'Well, when his mother's cancer came back -'

'Cancer? Mrs. Langley-Jones?'

'You probably didn't know. James used to come to the sick bay sometimes. He'd complain of a headache or a non-specific pain. What he really wanted was to talk. Whyttingham-Smythe gave him a really hard time: told him to stop whinging, man up, that sort of thing.'

'And all done with that insincere smile on his face, no doubt.'

The friends were quiet for a while, and then Evie asked, 'So what happened?'

'Mrs. Langley-Jones died just after Easter. Your friendly Head of English told James to pull himself together, and the lad took an overdose of some pills he'd managed to get hold of somehow. He spent an unpleasant night in hospital having his stomach pumped. I went with him. It was grim, I can tell you.'

Evie felt her stomach muscles tightening. How could she have been so wrong about the Langley-Joneses?

'What about his father? Where was he when all this was going on?'

'He lives in America. The school couldn't get through to him until the next day. Poor little rich kids, eh?'

'Oh Ros, don't. You can't imagine how bad I feel.'

She remained still for so long, staring unseeingly into her teacup, that Ros finally came across and placed a gentle hand on her arm to bring her back.

'You weren't to know...'

'Do you think he meant to do it? James, I mean? Was he trying to... you know?'

'Kill himself? Oh yes. He left a note. He named Whyttingham-Smythe as a contributory factor. There may have been more going on there than we know about.'

'How is he now?' Evie asked, shaken.

'He's going to repeat the year. He'll probably be in your class again for English.'

'I didn't even know the parents were separated. I really didn't know anything about him at all.' Evie shook her head slowly. 'Oh Ros, that's terrible.'

'Well, money and private education are no protection against the harsh realities of life. I know...' Ros continued quickly as Evie opened her mouth to protest, 'I know you have felt very protective towards your students up north over this last year, but that doesn't mean our students don't have needs too.'

'But he'll never have to face Whyttingham-Smythe again?'

'No, and neither will you. He slunk away in the dead of night. A coward as well as a bully.'

Evie went to find Alex the next morning. It was the first time she had been to the English Department since her visit to Ros at Easter. Now from the outside she could see that the extension had been completed, creating a pleasing section of garden enclosed by the curve of the boundary fence. To her utter surprise, however, she saw that the lawn, damaged by the building work, had not yet been restored, and that the border along the fence was wildly overgrown. That would not have been allowed to happen in Mr. HOD's day; no doubt it would have been his first priority. Appearances mattered to Mr. Whyttingham-Smythe. She felt pleased that it had not been Alex's first thought.

Entering the building, she headed for what was now, she supposed, Alex's office, but found her approach along the forbidding corridor blocked by dust sheets and stepladders. The door of the office was open, and a cheerful man in overalls was singing along to the radio as it blasted out the sort of music her old boss would never have countenanced. Peering inside she could hardly believe the transformation. The heavy furniture was gone; the room was painted in light colours; the dark oak door had been replaced with a new one, its upper half all glass.

'What do you think?'

She hadn't heard Alex approaching.

'Wonderful!' she said. 'A breath of fresh air.'

Not many of the staff had yet returned from their long summer break, and after a quick coffee in the almost deserted staffroom Evie and Alex both naturally gravitated back to the English Department. Alex went in to work in one of the classrooms, but Evie wandered around outside for a while, thinking, before heading back indoors to find Alex.

He was sitting at a student desk in one of the empty classrooms, scrunched up over a pile of papers.

'Sorry to disturb you,' she said tentatively.

'Oh, please do! My head's going to explode if I have to look at any more of this stuff.'

She crossed to where he was. Excel spreadsheets fluttered to the floor and she bent to pick them up, but he put out a hand to stop her.

'No, honestly, leave them. Budgets and statistics are not my forte, I'm afraid. I'm going to have to delegate this stuff!' He smiled ruefully, and Evie gave him an answering smile.

'OK, well if I'm not disturbing you, can you tell me which room I'll be in this term?'

Alex was clearly serious about being happy to be disturbed, because after walking with her to her room - a different one from before, with no memories - he perched on a desk and they talked. They talked for quite some time: about books, about their young people, about Alex's aspirations for the department. Evie somehow found herself telling him about Danny Desmond, and he listened, nodding gravely. It was impossible to imagine his predecessor engaging in this way. The thought of the former Mr. HOD led her back to thoughts of James Langley-Jones.

'I just find it awful to think that the boy was so terribly unhappy and I never knew,' she said. 'With Danny it was obvious that there were problems, even if it took some time to find out the cause. But to think of James, knowing his mother was terminally ill, separated from both his parents, suffering in silence...'

'I wouldn't beat yourself up about it,' said Alex. 'No-one knew, except perhaps your friend Ros. I think she suspected something. When I went to see him...'

'You've been to see him?'

'Yes. He's living with an aunt when he's not at school. She seems a sensible woman; and if I'm going to be effective in my role as head of department I need to start getting into it before the start of term. There didn't seem to be anyone else taking the trouble to get involved. Ros came with me. It was all above board and professional. James seems really keen on English.'

Evie laughed. ‘Really? How can you tell?’

‘We talked about books. He must have had a good teacher!’

‘Stop teasing,’

‘Seriously, though, I do think school was the one constant in his life, his safe place; or it would have been if it hadn’t been for… what happened.’

They both fell silent for a little while.

‘Was it awkward? I mean, you’d never met him…’

‘True, although that might have been an advantage. And anyway none of his other teachers was around…’

‘What did the head of Sixth Form say?’

Alex laughed. ‘Who?’

‘Yes, he does have a reputation for being a bit inconspicuous. You’ve picked that up already?’

He laughed, and Evie felt that here was someone who had already got the measure of the place.

It felt to Evie as though she had known Alex for ages, and for the first time she had a real ally at The Cedars. Over a pint in the Green Man that evening, they continued talking.

'So do you think you'll stay with us?' Alex asked as he carried their glasses to the table, setting them down carefully. It was still warm, with the low sunlight streaking golden across the fields beyond the pub garden. Somewhere a blackbird was singing its heart out.

'Oh, you heard?'

'I heard you didn't want to come back.'

'Yes, I got very fond of the kids at St. Mary's. And the place. And the people.'

She paused for a moment, trying to frame her thoughts into words.

'I think I lost sight of the fact that our young people here also have needs: they just learn to hide them more.'

'Did you find yourself questioning the system? I mean, wondering why parents send their children to boarding school?'

'Yes, I suppose I always have, but perhaps I was too judgemental.' She sighed. Since knowing Barbie she had learned a great deal more about what it meant to be a parent. 'What about you: do you sometimes wonder why they do it?'

'Oh yes.' He was silent for a moment. 'I asked myself that question at the start of every term as my parents packed me off.'

'Oh, I'm sorry. I had no idea...'

'No reason why you should. I only found out later that when they split up the most contentious part of the divorce settlement was over who I was going to live with.'

'They both wanted custody?'

Alex gave a short laugh. 'No. The argument was over which of them didn't have to have me. Boarding school was the perfect answer. It's OK,' he said, seeing her expression. 'I coped. Perhaps that's why I wanted to work here. I hope I can make a difference.'

'What helped you to cope?' Evie asked tentatively, and Alex described a childhood spent in the library as much as possible, books read by torchlight under the covers after lights out. It so much mirrored her own experience that she laughed aloud with delight.

He told her about his teen years. 'When I told my dad I was going to read English Literature at University he was horrified. Thought it was a cissy subject.'

'Do you still see your parents?'

'Not much. What about you?'

Evie found herself telling him about her father's death, and then somehow Molly and Colin and Seth's garden all came tumbling out.

'Oh, dear. We'll have to work hard to keep hold of you,' Alex replied.

They returned to the safer ground of books, and it was late when they returned to the school, creeping in through the gate like naughty children.

Within a few days other members of staff began to drift back, and then it was the time for departmental meetings in preparation for the new term. The English Department, one of the largest in the school, met in a friendly atmosphere of mugs of coffee and chocolate biscuits that was completely new. As they left, Evie caught up with Alex.

'I've been thinking,' she said and she told him about her poetry club at St. Mary's. 'Do you think I could give it a go here?'

'What would you want to do, exactly?'

'Give them a chance to explore their feelings in a safe environment, quite separate from academic pressures. And maybe enjoy poetry?'

'What would you need?'

'Nothing, except a room to meet in.'

22

Once term began, Evie found she had almost no time for thinking. For the second year in a row she had a new timetable and a new syllabus to grapple with. Some of the students before her were familiar from before, but others were new, and she needed to get to know them. She was also getting used again to the fact that the students didn't disappear from the premises at the end of the afternoon, and for the first time began to be curious about their lives beyond the classroom.

Even though she had taught James Langley-Jones before, she realised she didn't know him at all. He was quiet in class, as she had expected. She invited him, along with the others, to join the poetry club, but he didn't seem to want to join in. Perhaps it was too soon for him.

As she looked out of her window one day during the lunch hour, she spotted him crossing the grass and heading towards the unkempt border at the boundary fence. For a moment she was afraid he was going to truant, but then she saw that he was bending down, looking at something. On an impulse, she went out to join him, walking softly so as not to startle him until she was close enough for him to be aware of her presence.

'It's good to get out of doors on a day like this, isn't it?' she said.

'Yes, Miss Symmonds. Yes, it is.'

Looking down she saw that he was clutching something.

'Oh,' he said, looking a bit abashed. He opened his hand to reveal several dandelions and some couch grass. 'This border is full of weeds. I hate to see it like this. Should I have asked permission?'

'Do you like gardens?'

'Yes. My aunt has a beautiful one. A sort of real old-fashioned cottage garden. She lets me help. I like being in the garden… it gives me thinking space.'

She didn't manage to catch Alex until the next day. He was in his office, with the door wide open, a small group of students chatting and laughing with him.

'Oh, I'm sorry. I'll come back later.' Evie felt stalled in her purpose, even while noting approvingly the warmth of Alex's response to the students. She wasn't sure what to do.

'No, that's fine,' he said, standing up. 'It's time this lot got on with their prep.' He turned to the little group. 'Go on now. And remember: I want something that will surprise me tomorrow when you hand it in.'

'That sounds dangerous!' Evie remarked as they left.

'We'll see. I'm trying to persuade them that it's all right to experiment with their writing. Now, what can I do for you?'

'Do you fancy a stroll in the grounds?' She led him out to the place where she had found James, explaining as she went.

'So, let me get this straight,' Alex said. 'You want permission to dig this bit of ground over, get youngsters planting things…'

'Yes. A gardening club.'

'Well, it's not up to me…'

'No, I know, but with a senior member of staff behind me… and if you explained about James, and the therapeutic nature of gardening and so on…'

He appeared to be thinking. Evie was suddenly nervous. It felt as though more than an extracurricular activity depended on his answer.

Finally he said, 'I'll back you on one condition.'

She waited.

'That you let me be involved too.'

'So you think it's a good idea?'

'I think it's brilliant. Just what we need!' He turned and gave her a hug.

'Oops, sorry,' he said.

'Don't be,' Evie replied.

The gardening club proved surprisingly popular, once Alex had smoothed the way with senior management, and before long James was not only a stalwart member but had taken to gently coaching a group of younger pupils. He was often out in the little garden, even on days when the club was not meeting. One mild evening in early October Evie watched from her classroom window as he carefully dug a hole and sprinkled something in the bottom, before upending a plant pot and tapping it to dislodge the plant within. Then he carefully separated out the roots and placed it tenderly in the hole, backfilling and watering before firming it down with the soles of his feet.

Evie went down to join him.

'I'm sorry, Miss Symmonds,' the boy said. 'I should have asked if it was all right to plant something here.' He looked wistfully at the plant. 'This is from my aunt's garden.'

Evie reassured him that it was fine and asked what it was.

'A Christmas Rose. It'll be one of the first things to flower after the winter. They look delicate but they're really hardy. And…' he hesitated for a moment. 'It'll remind me of home. It was something my mother loved…'

'I think that's a lovely idea, James.' She had a sudden idea. 'I wonder if you could do something for me? If you don't mind waiting a few minutes?'

James was still there, watering in his Christmas Rose, when Evie returned with her pot and its bedraggled contents.

'Oh, you have one too!' he exclaimed.

'It's a hellebore from my garden,' she replied. 'My previous garden.'

'Yes,' the boy said. 'I just think Christmas Rose is a much prettier name, don't you?' Evie found herself thinking of shy, sad Rose back in Paradise Row, and of how she almost died just after Christmas, and promised herself a long phone chat with Barbie after dinner to find out how all her old friends were faring.

In the end it was Evie's own decision. When Pat Robinson's job was advertised she did not apply. She had discovered a sense of belonging, but it had more to do with state of mind than place. She made the long journey up North the following summer, once again staying with Barbie. One of the highlights of the visit was when Danny appeared with Kelly in tow and they launched into a discussion of the poets they had studied in Year 12, once or twice asking Evie's opinion and offering their own. Kelly had changed a lot: she was much quieter and calmer, holding herself differently somehow, as though she had discovered her place in the world.

Evie felt a real pang then. It would have been so satisfying to be teaching Danny and some of the other students from her Year Eleven in this new phase of their lives. She could feel the past drawing her back; not just her own past of the previous year, but the past that was all around her in the town. She walked through the streets, barely recognising her surroundings. Paradise Row was gone, as she had known it would be, and the empty land with its detritus of discarded objects was full of sound and activity. The house building was coming on apace and you could see roughly where the streets would be. It was a perfect summer's day, exactly two years after her arrival at a time when her world had felt completely different. The smell of fresh timber was carried on the slight breeze as the builders hauled the roof trusses into place, and her ears were filled with the sounds of hammering and pulleys squeaking and the shouts of the men high above on the roofs.

It was from Barbie that she learned of Seth's bequest. He had loved his garden, and couldn't imagine others living without such a joy, and so his surprisingly large sum of money had been left to the town on one condition. The condition had been fulfilled: now, instead of the original plan, concentric swirls replaced the straight lines. Everything radiated out from a central area where paths had already been laid between what would one day be lawns. Flower beds had been dug and filled with topsoil, and there, at the very heart of the park - it already had a nameplate: *Seth Adamson Park* - was a little group of fruit trees. Evie felt the tears spring up as she saw this. The trees that Seth had planted, that she had tended, that two boys had attempted to destroy, the trees that marked where Paradise Row had once stood: they were still there.

When she visited Molly, still contented in the care home, but noticeably less active, there had been a new addition to the windowsill: a box that turned out to contain Seth's ashes.

'Can you do that? Is it allowed?' Evie asked.

'Yes. He named me next of kin,' Molly smiled. 'And…' She beckoned for Evie to come closer. 'I want you to do something for me. Promise!'

Back at the vicarage, Evie waited until she and Barbie were on their own.

'I didn't know what to say. I didn't really promise, but I think she thought I did. I mean, we can't, can we?'

'Well, no, it's not strictly illegal, if that's what you're asking.' Barbie had a twinkle in her eye. 'The law's a bit flexible, but you do need the landowner's permission, and this council doesn't always give it, to be honest.' Barbie had a twinkle in her eye. 'But, you know, people do it anyway!'

Evie sighed deeply. 'I hate to think of her going too some day. She's always been so full of life.'

It was another three months before Evie received the call from Barbie. Molly had died peacefully in her sleep.

'Peacefully. That's what everyone says,' Evie grumbled.'

'Well in this case it's true; I was there to give her the last rites...' Barbie's voice faded a little at the end of the line and then came back. '...so if you can get away it's next Tuesday.'

'Tuesday? Well yes, it'll be half term. Oh, I'm glad. I want to be there for her.' She hesitated before speaking again. 'Barbie? Do you think it'd be all right if I brought someone with me? I mean, he didn't know Molly, but...'

'He?' Evie could hear Barbie raising her eyebrows at the other end of the phone. 'If you need someone - someone special - with you at the funeral of a friend, then of course it's all right. Colin will be there too, and his daughter. I'll see you next week.'

The ashes were ready on the Friday. Barbie had collected Molly's effects from the care home, and Seth's casket sat amongst the chaos of papers and tea towels in the vicarage kitchen when Evie and Alex arrived to collect them. On this occasion it had not seemed quite proper to stay at the vicarage, and she and Alex had taken a room in the newly completed hotel next to the theatre.

'There you are,' said Barbie as she handed over the casket. 'You do understand that I have no idea what you're planning to do with them, don't you?' They nodded in unison.

'So,' she said turning to Alex. 'Evie tells me you've revolutionised the English Department at Nice School.'

Alex raised an eyebrow and turned to look at Evie.

'Nice School?'

'Sorry. That's how I used to think of it.'

'What's it actually called?' Barbie asked. 'You never told me.

Evie and Alex spoke simultaneously. 'The Cedars. An Education that adds polish....'

'Well, you've obviously changed things for the better. Last we knew Evie really didn't want to go back there. Something must have happened to change her mind. Or someone.'

Evie was blushing furiously. 'It's not just that I want to be with Alex,' she said. 'But he agrees with me about a lot of the things that are wrong. He's also made me see that people are people, and that many of our students have needs - different needs from the ones here, to be sure, but needs all the same.'

'Well, I hope you succeed in making a difference, because I know Evie is missed here. Danny wouldn't be studying for his A Levels without her, that's for certain. Rob was devastated that you didn't come back and apply for the job.'

Evie turned to the casket on the table. 'What about Molly's?' she asked, a little tremulously.

'Oh, I, er, happened to spill them, and they ended up in there,' Barbie said.

Alex said, 'Aha. I see. Ready mixed. Don't worry, Vicar: your secret is safe with me.'

In the park the trees were starting to put on their autumn display. Over the years this place had sometimes been open land, sometimes farmland, sometimes gardens large and small; loved at times and at others neglected, but there stood the apple tree, older now than when she had last stood so close, but the same tree, and the same feelings of being beyond the ordinary business of life. They waited until they were quite sure no-one else was about, and then Alex handed her the bag he had been carrying. It was an ordinary plastic bag. He took a small pair of scissors from his pocket and snipped a corner.

'It's all right, Evie. I know it's hard to let go.' He waited, and then said, 'If this feels right for you, then do it.'

She looked up at him mournfully and took the bag.

Alex continued: 'I didn't know them, but I feel I know them in you. I can see how important they were to you - how important all of this was.' He stooped to kiss the top of her head with infinite gentleness. 'I'll be over there.'

She approached the tree. The garden had given her so much, at a time when she needed its protection, its inspiration, its blessing. Slowly she let the corner of the bag fall, and as the gritty grey powder began to run she circled the tree with careful steps. She walked round it several times, and as she did so faint shadows joined her: a woman in a ridiculous hat, a man dressed as a woman, a crowd of teenagers, all were somehow there with her, and yet she was alone. Fainter still were the shadows of a farmer's boy, a young squire who never made it to the crusades, a white-bearded old man raising his hand in farewell.

When she had done, she stuffed the bag into her coat pocket and looked round for Alex, who stepped forward with a gentle smile and held her in a wordless embrace for several minutes.

Now, for the last time, she left the garden. No angel with a flaming sword forced her out, although she went with sadness. She would make her own garden, one that cannot be seen with the naked eye. As a teacher she would continue to try to shape the world around her. A gardener encourages growth, but not by leaving the plants to themselves. There is a difference between a garden and a wilderness.

ABOUT THE AUTHOR

Carolyn Sanderson has dipped her toes into the world of academia, and worked in a number of fields including counselling, training and working for the Church of England. She has also had a number of years of being at the sharp end in front of a classroom full of adolescents!

She has written articles, reviews and a number of hymns, and lives in Milton Keynes, a surprisingly green city. When not writing, she loves tending her garden.

Also by this author:

Times and Seasons (in the Weidenfeld &Nicolson series Hometown Tales)

Women don't kill animals (in The Word for Freedom, Short Stories of Women's Suffrage, Retreat West Books)

Printed in Great Britain
by Amazon

23556062R00205